Sara Rose

Betty

Let your memories in your heart, for they will never fade!

Bob

1

Sara Rose

A fictional novel by Robert R. Sytnick

In memory of a friend

Sara Rose

Chapter 1

Summer is in full retreat, and signs of fall are evident in the midday air. The passengers have boarded, and the cargo holds restocked with supplies and freight.

The last of the luggage is delivered to the deck of the ship. A scruffy little mouse pokes its nose from a crack in a luggage trunk. Within seconds, the little stowaway scampers from its hiding place, and across the wooden planking, terrifying the female passengers.

The Sara Rose is in the process of leaving the docks of St- Nazaire, France. She has a crew of twenty-two, along with their seasoned Captain, Captain Mcbaine.

The fifty-six-year-old Captain is of Scottish descent. Being of medium build, he supports a full, brisk, greying beard, and his confident eyes are the colour of the sea. He is a handsome, rugged looking man in the uniform that he wears. His cap partially hides his wavy grey hair. The brass buttons that line the front of his uniform and the cuffs of the sleeves, glitter in the day's sun. The stripes and bars on his jacket, sewn from golden thread, command respect.

Captain Mcbaine stands on the deck of the Sara Rose and salutes the Port Major of St-Nazaire. The Port Major presented Captain Mcbaine with a gift, a bottle of champagne. The Captain and the Port Major have been friends for some twenty plus years. Theirs is a friendship that deepens with every visit to the Port of St-Nazaire.

The large anchor of the ship is pulled aboard, displaying years of rust and coral from the ocean bottoms of its hundreds of homes. The anchor, like the sea, holds the secrets of the Sara Rose.

As night slowly creeps its way onto the deck, the crew works at a fast pace to get the ship on course. The night horn stretches its sounds as darkness comes to the sea, and the night crew begins lighting the lanterns. For the passengers of the Sara Rose, their first night aboard the ship must feel like a haunting, unfolding in a timely manner. The night holds them in their sleep, while the vessel finds her course this night.

As if on cue, the moon guides the ship through the night, and reflects its beauty on the inviting sea. The stars play their part and act as a map to point the way for the Sara Rose.

The constant rocking and the soothing sound of the sea settles the ship's little stowaway, as the mouse finds sleep on the deck.

* * *

Dawn eases its way from the horizon and gently lifts the darkness. The first signs of the new day send the crew extinguishing the lanterns. A weary night crew is anxious for their share of sleep, as the day crew begins their shift on the vessel's decks. The cooks can be heard calling for more food from the storage holds, which are deep within the ship's hull. The aroma of the morning's breakfast cooking on the hot coal stove escapes into the morning air, waking all, even the mouse.

The Captain makes his rounds with his young Lieutenant, Timothy Rodgers. They both examine the ropes and the condition of the sails. Lieutenant Rodgers stops at the entrance to the lower stairwell, checking off the inspected area from his clipboard. He quickly rejoins the Captain who is looking over the prisoners in the lower deck that were brought aboard the ship before the passengers boarded.

"Lieutenant, we have a fine bunch of scallywags with us on this journey as we sail back to England. The French government was kind enough to give England's scum back to her, so these prisoners can hang in the Crowns gallows. My, my, Lieutenant what a collection of riff-raff we have here."

"Yes, Captain. I agree with you, a fine bunch."

The mouse is intrigued, and scurries along the deck, through a hole in the deck floor. It has found the perfect perch in the lower deck while it listens to the Captain speak.

Captain Mcbaine reaches into the right pocket of his jacket and takes out the documentation given to him by the Port Major of St-Nazaire. He shakes his head in disgust as he reads, stepping toward a black man sitting on the wooden floor. The man has his hands and feet shackled together and sits in a very uncomfortable position with his back to the divider in the poorly lit room. Crusty dried blood scabs have formed on the man's wrists from the constant rubbing of the shackles. The black man's toes and heels appear to have been chewed by the rats that roam freely in the French jails, and now infection has set in. The stomach-turning smell clings to the helpless stale air. His worn-out, dirty clothes are almost non-existent and blend in with the colour of his skin.

"You, Sir, are accused of high treason against England. This document states that you were a crew member on the 'Serpent', which terrorized Her Majesty's southern seas, looting and killing at will."

The shackled man keeps his head down, refraining from comment, spitting on the floor, disrespecting the Captain. The Captain turns to his other prisoner, chained in the same manner. He's dressed in a full-length evening coat and white shirt. The man's crinkled top hat lies next to him. The prisoner's boots have retained their partial shine, even with the cladding of the rusty chains around his footwear. The accused man looks up at the Captain with a grin. His piercing eyes burn into whoever stares at him, revealing a dark empty soul. The Devil himself would refrain from eye contact with this man.

"Lieutenant, we may be in the presence of Liverpool's, River Butcher."

"Is it possible, Captain? I heard his trail had gone cold. That would explain his capture in France."

5

"If I had my way Lieutenant, this man would be walking the plank as we speak," says the Captain.

A scream from a female comes from the other side of the partition. Her loud searing voice causes the Lieutenant to step back, dropping his clipboard.

"River Butcher. Get that son of the Devil off the ship, Captain. Make him walk the plank, for he will have a knife to my throat and will dissect me like he has done to all the women he fancies."

Frantically, the mouse backs into the darkness. Its pulse treks to new heights to what it has heard, and now fears it may be a victim of the River Butcher.

"Madam, you're a common streetwalker. No better than these two accused men I stand before. It says on this document that you are Katie, a streetwalker that prostitutes herself for shillings. It may be a simple crime, except you prefer men with thick wallets, giving them simple satisfaction, then a knife to the belly."

"A fine bunch, Lieutenant. You best keep an eye on our Katie. She attracts trouble and will have a few of our crew dancing to her tongue. Let's get back to the top deck; the stench of our prisoners is getting to me."

Captain Mcbaine gives command of the vessel to Lieutenant Rodgers, and leaves for his breakfast in his cabin. During his morning meal the Captain plots and maps a course for the ship to maintain. He opens the ship's logbook and begins to write:

'September 2, Eighteen Hundred and Fifty-Three. The Sara Rose is on route to Brighton, England.'

Lieutenant Rodgers takes command of the Sara Rose for the first time. He now sports a smile that lights up his face, but the proud Lieutenant walks the deck of the ship somewhat unsure of his ability to command. Lieutenant Rodgers is a commissioned officer and carries a sabre at his side at all times. With his hand resting on the hilt of his weapon, he walks among the crew and passengers gaining confidence in his new duties. The Lieutenant begins to walk with a swagger.

All the sails are open, trying to capture a breeze. Even the Union Jack barely displays any motion this day. The sailors claim that a windless day at sea is an omen, and that there will come a time to pay.

The stale breeze has slowed the ship's pace. Seagulls surround the vessel in search of discarded waste. Some of the passengers have found their sea legs and stroll on the decks before darkness descends once again. Small clouds of cigar smoke join the evening air as passengers gather in the lounge area. A few enjoy a cup of tea, and some prefer stronger spirits. Men participate in a game of chance, while others simply enjoy conversation. The ladies gather in circles, talk of their children and their hopes for the future that the new world may bring. Friendships are made easily aboard a ship, and soon most become close as family. Onboard, the word 'secret' does not exist for gossip spreads quickly and is often true.

The lights of the small towns on the French coast are seen in the distance as night descends on the Sara Rose. The passengers shake hands and bid each other a good night.

The moon is quickly shrouded over as clouds rush in, forcing the moon to hold its blush for another time. It seems God himself gathered up the stars this night, leaving the skies in total darkness. The only light to be seen comes from the lanterns on deck. Occasionally the crew wave the lanterns outward to the sea, warning approaching vessels of their presence. The stillness and the eclipse of the night add new fears aboard the ship. The crew members stand their posts calling with voice and the sounding of horns — every creak of the ship echoes along the decks adding a ghostly effect to the still bound vessel. The ripples of the water against the vessel become silenced, and the massive sea calms as if a covering of glass has sealed this body of saltwater in time.

Even the rodent that stowed away prays for daylight to return. The terrified mouse quivers in a dark corner alone with its eyes wide open this long night.

Chapter 2

The passengers awake to a new day, unaware of the fears of the 'Omen.' The morning sun appears, finding its place in the sky. Captain Mcbaine writes *The Night of the Witches* in his log. This term is used on the high seas and translates to 'Ghost ship.' Captain Mcbaine knows the tales of the sea and must be firm when commanding his crew to stay the course. He hopes the new day will send a northern wind, breaking the Omen.

The crew know too well the stories and rumours of 'The Night of the Witches.' The tale goes; that a ship gets caught like a spider in a sea of invisible webs and is held there for days and nights that never seem to end. The sea is glazed over with a layer of glass. The stillness of the ship portrays the look as if the ship were painted into a picture. Jaws from the depths of the seabed lock onto the ship's hull, like the tentacles of an octopus.

The Witches of the Night, with their magic brooms, sweep the winds and stars back beyond the horizons. The moon loses its liberty and is forced into an eclipse, while the sun is permitted to display its full powers.

The crew and passengers have been known to go completely mad. Some have jumped overboard to relieve the crushing pain in their minds. Others drop the jolly boats to the sea of glass and try to paddle to freedom. The ship no longer hears man's heartbeat, thus becoming a 'Ghost Ship.'

The silent sun takes control of the day once again, and the Sara Rose is held prisoner on the sea. The Captain and his young Lieutenant inspect the ship while mingling with passengers. Captain Mcbaine holds his silence regarding last night and the Omen that follows a ship on her voyage.

The waters of the English Channel are silenced, perhaps locked in prayer. The vessel is displaying all of her sails, yet the ship barely moves. Other ships can be seen in the distance, while a motionless sea holds them on the same enduring spot for hours. The warm sun makes the crew's work extremely repetitive and tiring. The hands of time force the minutes into hours. The hours eventually retreat and vanish slowly.

* * *

Loud cheers of "Hoorah" suddenly come from the sailors. They excitedly point to their flag; the Union Jack has found a breeze, and now proudly displays its colours. Captain Mcbaine hurries from his cabin to investigate the cause of all the excitement onboard. He displays a rare smile while approaching Lieutenant Rodgers.

"Lieutenant Rodgers, Sir. An extra ration of rum this evening for the crew." Knowing this will bond the crew together, the attentive Lieutenant pays close attention to the Captain's logic.

Evening has found the ship and crew in good spirits, as they eagerly wet their lips with the extra ration of rum. The men raise their tin cups, toasting the Captain and the newly delivered wind. It is an unwritten law of the seas that commanders shall not share a drink of spirits with their crew that do not warrant a title or marked uniform.

At the stern of the ship, off-duty crew members gather. Jackal, one of the high riggers, begins to play his violin. His mates encourage him to play **'Just a Closer Walk with Thee,'** a tune everyone knows. The sound of the instrument reminds the crew of home, as Jackal's violin weeps into the night air. A fog is woken and begins to settle onto the deck of the ship, as if waiting for another tune from the violinist.

The sweet smell of cigar smoke lingers along the ship's deck in the night air. Some male passengers play a game of chance. The ladies sip tea or knit to occupy their time. Others add the day's adventure to their diaries or write letters to loved ones.

Darkness retains its grip on the evening as the lanterns are lit. The fog that slowly crawled onto the deck of the Sara Rose to listen to the violinist remains, but now has woven together and melted into puddles.

The lingering smells and cigar smoke continue to dance in the night air, taking on a life of their own.

Morning breaks the rhythm of the night, and the sea prepares for a storm. Clouds turn into a twisted tapestry of greys and chilling ebony.

The mouse wakes from under a bench with a constant pounding in its head. The rodent stands and begins throwing up, recalling the droplets of rum it consumed off the planked deck last night.

Realizing the morning sun has exposed him to the crew, the panic-stricken mouse runs across the deck in a flurry, to the hole in the wall. The little stowaway is thankful that it never met a big boot from a crew member.

Chapter 3

Captain Mcbaine approaches the helmsman, First Mate Roddy Downing, who only retains fingers on his right hand. A story exists aboard the Rose that First Mate Downing lost his fingers in a game of chance many years ago, but no crew member dares to ask. The Captain and Helmsman Downing use the ship's sextant and charts as they begin to plot a course for the Brighton harbour.

It will be another night at sea before the anchor of the Sara Rose is lowered to the seabed. Tonight, Jackal and his fellow crew members will gather for games of chance, and perhaps a tune or two, while they sip on their daily ration of rum. The stern of the ship is the area set aside for the crew and steerage passengers. The helmsman on duty closely watches the area. If a fight or argument breaks out, it's regarded as an offence against the ship and the country that the sailors serve. The penalty is swift and carries the punishment of being tied over a barrel to receive lashes, and then being left in the sun for an indefinite period. If one is lucky, salt is thrown on the wounds to help the healing process. Crew members do not make fun nor tease each other for having been over the barrel. They, themselves may have been placed over the barrel, perhaps more than once.

Again, like clockwork, the call from the galley sounds and the passengers begin to seat themselves for dinner. A new excitement radiates from the tables. Anxious passengers are aware they will soon be docking in Brighton. Some will disembark, for this will be their port of call. Others will leave the ship and stroll the streets and visit the shops until the ship's bell calls for them to board. Many friendships have been made in these short few days with promises to write letters to each other, once they settle. Tonight, there will be talk and stories amongst the passengers on a more personal level, for bonds between the travellers have been created.

Captain Mcbaine enters the dining room and seats himself with the passengers for the first time. They dine together, and the passengers enjoy the company of the Captain. After the meal, stories of home are told by the passengers, who mingle from table to table. The children giggle, staring and pointing their fingers at the Captain's uniform decorated with ribbons and medals that shine in the lantern's light.

A young girl, perhaps five or six years of age, comes quietly to the Captain's table and tugs at his sleeve. The Captain turns and looks down. The child has hair as dark as night. Her two front teeth are missing, and she holds her hands crossed behind her back while she sways back and forth. Her smile overwhelms the Captain, as she says in a shy voice, "Captain, Sir. If everyone calls you Captain, what does everyone call your wife?"

The room becomes silent momentarily. Even the mouse that roams the deck of the ship stops and listens. Then the passengers suddenly roar in laughter while the red-faced mother runs, picking up her child.

Captain Mcbaine smiles and slowly massages his greying beard. He stands to leave, and the passengers rise to acknowledge this humble man. They quickly arrange themselves in single file, taking turns shaking the hand of their Captain.

Jackal and crew gather this evening at the stern of the ship, for yet another game of chance. The men light their pipes during their time of relaxation. Jackal clutches his violin in his hand, as one would hold a cherished gift. Arthur, an ageing seaman who tends to lighter duties on the ship, begins to play his accordion. Jackal quickly joins him.

The sweet smell of tobacco mixes with the melodies to create a gentle hush across the sea. The crew grows pensive, thoughts of home touch all. The sea waves dance in the distance, reflecting soothing images to the Sara Rose.

The lights of Brighton can be seen on the horizon when the Captain is woken by a knock on his door from Samuel, an apprentice aboard the Sara Rose. This is Samuel's first voyage, and he works with the high riggers when needed. The Captain proceeds to the helm, motioning to the apprentice to bring tea for himself and First Mate Downing. The two men study the charts and harbour entrance, before deciding where to drop the anchor.

* * *

Hours pass and dawn starts its magical countdown. It gives light to the sea and bids the moon a good evening. Squawking gulls circle the Rose in search of a free meal, as the sun begins to wake and slowly smiles on a new day. The stars, which shone on the ship during the night, are now covered with God's hand. Smells of fresh tea boiling in the galley romances the morning air.

A shout from Mr. Downing, the helmsman. "All Stop." The duty crew rush to the deck. High riggers spring into action and climb the great masts. Their work cannot be explained for it is an unconducted symphony, swinging from rope to rope without fear. They call out the order of the next sail to come down, while the deck crew help with the ropes and pulleys. The work is a continuous flow of perfection, performed by these masters of the sea.

The great anchor of the Sara Rose drops to its new home at the bottom of Brighton Harbour. Lieutenant Rodgers counts the links of the chain that sink to the seabed. He then calls out to the Captain, "Fourteen Fathoms! Sir."

"Thank you, Mr. Rodgers," the Captain replies, entering the depth in the ship's logbook.

The daily routine continues on the ship, and the men await a signal from the dock for the ship to proceed. Several ships pass her on the port and starboard sides as they jockey for position. A red flag is hoisted below the Union Jack to show the ship is in a holding position. There are flags on ships from every part of the world, sailing to, and from the port of Brighton. The crew wave to passing vessels as if they were old friends.

The Sara Rose is behind a freighter from Norway, and behind the Rose is a cargo ship from the Americas.

A signal from the port allows the Sara Rose to proceed after several hours of waiting in the harbour. The great anchor is pulled up onto the deck. The anxious vessel slowly makes her way to the wharf. Her thick mooring lines are thrown down to the dock workers who swiftly tie the ship to the massive bollards. The large hatches open for the first time since leaving France. Clouds of dust rise from the vessel's large holds and disappear into the warmth of the September sun.

The gangway lowers to the dock and passengers are allowed to disembark. The Captain and his Lieutenant thank the passengers for choosing the Sara Rose for their transport, shaking their hands as they leave the ship. Noticing the young girl who questioned him at dinner a few nights ago, the Captain smiles. Holding her mother's hand, the young girl approaches with her parents. The Captain nods to the girl's parents and takes the young child by the hand. They walk a short distance away from the other passengers. He kneels before her, and asks, "What is your name, young lady?"

The young girl places her hands behind her back and sways from side to side with a smile. She quietly whispers to the Captain, "My name is Faith."

"Well, Faith, I am not sure what everyone would call my wife, for no one on the ship has met her." The Captain reaches into his uniform and pulls out a picture of his wife, which he shows the young girl. Then he whispers to her, "I call my wife, Darling."

Faith looks at the picture of Mrs. Mcbaine and smiles at the Captain who is kneeling before her. He hugs the young girl and walks her back to her mother.

When all passengers have left the ship, the Lieutenant readies the crew for the unloading of the cargo. Captain Mcbaine looks over the railing and can see Faith standing on the dock waving at him. He returns the wave to the young girl who has touched his heart.

Crews from both, the dock and the ship work into the night loading and unloading the cargo. Rain begins to fall, and soon work halts when the Lieutenant orders the ship's hatches closed.

Now that the weather has control of the evening, the crew are allowed to venture into the streets of Brighton in search of taverns. It does not take long for Jackal and his mates to find a drink and begin to celebrate. They are a lively group who have worked hard and now drink hard, well into the night.

With the rain stopping, the ship's bell rings out a morning call for the crew to return to the ship. A final bell sounds for roll call. The Lieutenant is surprised that one seaman, Hardie Jenkins is not accounted for. Hardie has been trouble from the moment he set foot on the deck of the Sara Rose.

The Captain steps forward, ordering six men to go into the streets and taverns. "Bring Hardie Jenkins back to the ship. Be quick about it!" commands the Captain with urgency.

The first-class passengers begin to board, followed by the second-class. They present their boarding passes and are shown to their cabins. The steerage passengers line up on the dock, soon they will be allowed to board the ship. The local law authority patrols the docks in search of criminals who try to stowaway on ships. The dock area is the perfect place for pickpockets and local gangs. Boarding passengers have all their valuable possessions on their person and are on constant guard. It is common for fights to break out while steerage passengers jostle for position on the dock.

As evening approaches, the hung-over mouse awakes as Hardie is dragged up the gangway by his shipmates. The shaky rodent listens as the Captain orders Hardie to be tied down to the dreaded barrel, where he will be dealt with later.

The steerage passengers begin to board the ship. The Lieutenant oversees the process, and eyes up the new group. These passengers are directed to the lower decks of the vessel. The male passengers and older boys are placed in one large room. The females, along with the young children, enter into a separate area. There are few comforts, and certainly no options. Each takes a boarded bunk close to one another.

Evening descends quickly onto the ship. The Port Major of Brighton signals that the vessel is allowed to leave the dock. The large ropes are released from the bollards and drawn back on board. Two small boats escort the Sara Rose out of the harbour to safe waters. The ship lowers her anchor, waiting for the morning light.

The crew has worked hard and need rest, but the Captain has an issue with Hardie. He knows he must deal with this matter immediately. The crew remain quiet, knowing what is about to happen to their shipmate. Hardie Jenkins remains tied over the barrel calling out for a drink of water. His sobering request goes unanswered. The Captain insists all his crew witness the punishment Hardie Jenkins will receive. He orders Lieutenant Rodgers to carry out the sentence of ten lashes to Hardie's back. The young Lieutenant is terrified by the order but knows he must obey.

No passengers are allowed to witness the punishment about to be delivered to Hardie. The little mouse roams the decks in search of a meal, but stops to watch. It murmurs to itself, as if in prayer for Hardie.

The young Lieutenant's hands are shaking as he holds the whip. He looks around at the crew, who have their heads down, standing in silence. His inner strength gives him the courage to carry out the dreaded deed.

The Captain reads out a statement of crime and punishment to Hardie. He nods to the Lieutenant to carry out the sentence. The sudden silence on the deck breaks, as the whip cracks its vengeful wrath on Hardie's back. The crew shudders with every strike of the whip. Blood seeps from Hardie's back, dripping onto the planked deck. Occasional screams come from their bound shipmate. The Lieutenant hurls the lash onto Hardie's back for the tenth and final time.

A tear finds its way down the Lieutenant's cheek. He quickly wipes the tear aside, as if it were sweat from the nasty deed he has just performed.

"Hardie Jenkins will remain tied to the barrel for the duration of the night without food or drink. Lieutenant, dismiss the men," shouts the Captain.

The lonely light from the lanterns sends its curious stare out to sea. "All Clear!" echoes the voice of Jimmy Brown, positioned in the crow's nest. Not much is known about Jimmy. He is quiet, but everything he says comes out loudly. He keeps a watchful eye out for rogue ships that may have broken anchor.

There is always a threat of pirates in the night, who try to sneak aboard to rob the first-class passengers of money and jewelry. There are no games of chance or music this night for everyone needs their rest after the long day. Jimmy Brown can hear the calls from Hardie, begging for water. Jimmy ignores his requests, for he would be placed over the barrel for disobeying the Captain's orders.

Chapter 4

The stowaway that rules the deck at night roams free to gather its rations for the coming day. It stops near the dreaded barrel, staring at Hardie. Hardie spits his bloody saliva at the intrigued mouse. The little rodent runs away blindly and does not look back.

The minutes turn into hours and the hours slowly begin to bring a glimpse of a new dawn. The mouse finds its way home to the hole in the wall.

Captain Mcbaine rises early to find the crew already at work. He orders a crew member to cut the ropes holding Hardie Jenkins to the barrel. Hardie is then helped to his bunk on the lower decks by two shipmates. Hardie, the troublemaker, quietly snarls at his shipmates, "Arrr! I'll get even with every last one of you, Matey! Mark my words. I will get even."

"Pull Up!" orders the Captain. Now the great anchor slowly gets pulled onboard the ship. The high riggers are called upon to perform their graceful skills. They stay at their posted positions until all is secure and the vessel is under sail; then the riggers swing down to the deck like spiders on a web.

Captain Mcbaine raises his arm to the crew as if saying, 'Well done Mates!' and continues on the ship's inspection. He proceeds to the lower deck, checking the condition of his prisoners.

The crew gather their breakfast from the galley and proceed to the stern of the ship, where they sit and eat their meal. The cooks begin preparing meals for the first and second-class passengers. Napkins are placed on the tables next to the plates and silverware. The first-class passengers are the first to be seated and served by stewards; second-class will enter the dining area later, helping themselves. Any leftover food is added to the steerage passengers' rations.

In a large room, which days before was a cargo hold, the women and children of the steerage section eat before the men. Each passenger is given a tin bowl, a tin cup and utensils which will stay with them for the entire trip.

The steerage passengers are not allowed in the forward sections of the ship. They get their fresh air and drinking water at the stern and have few options or comforts. Their washing and bathroom facilities are best left unspoken.

Even the adventurous mouse that explores the ship by night fears to venture into the steerage class quarters.

* * *

The Sara Rose leaves the sun behind as her bow gracefully divides the new waters. The large sails create shadows, leading the ship into the unknown sea. The Union Jack proudly displays its colours to passing ships in the new-found breeze.

Captain Mcbaine confides in his young Lieutenant, "Mr. Rodgers, it's a great day to be at sea."

"Lieutenant, you're excused," continues the Captain. "I am going below to have a few words with our guest in chains. Doctor Eden informed me that our Katie fancies giving pleasures of the flesh, to certain crew members who visit her."

The Lieutenant quickly salutes his Captain and walks away red-faced. Captain Mcbaine makes his way down the steps, turns, and walks toward Katie.

"Miss Katie, it has come to my attention you are trading specific favours my men may want, for rum rations and shillings. I do not object to your profession. I disagree with what you are giving my men. Dr. Eden has insufficient medicine to treat the men that you are infecting.

"Captain, a lady such as I, enjoys pleasuring men such as yourself. Be a good mate, Captain, and invite me to your cabin for the night."

"Thank you for your offer, Katie. My cabin is mine alone. Madam, if you persist in entertaining my men, your legs will be shackled together. My metalsmith assures me that he can fashion a horse bit for your mouth."

"Aye, Captain. I will abide by your wishes."

Many of the steerage passengers leave their cramped quarters and make their way to the stern area for a breath of fresh air. Some light their pipes and converse with each other. The majority of these passengers are on their way to the new world in search of a better life, making this the usual topic of discussion between them.

The first and second-class travellers mingle on the decks. Tea is the drink of the day, to which some add a drop or two of rum. The young children cling to their mothers' skirts and peek at one another. They have cold expressions, for this is their first day aboard the ship, and all is new to them. The young men parade around the deck without fear, showing off their gallant presence. They walk with their noses slightly raised, pretending to be cultured. The young single ladies are intrigued and giggle into their hands, as these young roosters strut before them.

The sound of the dinner bell rings from the galley. The crew gather their evening meal and seat themselves at the stern.

The first-class passengers enter the dining room and are seated at tables with fine china and silverware. The second-class humbly wait in the lounge area until the first-class passengers leave the dining room, and once again, the meagre leftovers will be shared by the steerage passengers.

Chapter 5

The hands of time slowly retract the light of day into an evening setting. Softening blues and greys tantalize the endless horizon. The sinking sun in the west continues to melt its warmth into the sea. A perfect sunset tells these masters of the sea that they will have good weather until the next lunar phase.

Tonight, there is a rare golden sunset on the sea, and it's often referred to as 'A Sailor's Mistress.' This term has been used by seamen for generations and still holds true to this day.

The excitement of the magnificent sunset causes a rush of upper deck passengers to the port side of the ship. They cling to the railing on the Sara Rose as if they are witnesses to an event that only the Creator could have painted on the horizon. Some cross themselves, and kneel; they do not comprehend what this glorious event means.

The male passengers remove their top hats and hold them close to their chest, while some raise a hand and try to touch this splendour, as the event unfolds. The children held by their mothers are set down. Each of these mothers now has a free hand to place over her pulsing heart.

The Sara Rose is in true splendour, as gusts of wind find her sails giving new energy to the ship's speed which is unmatched. The Union Jack reveals a new spirit. The reflected sunset bounces from the sea, illuminating the sails. The continuing back and forth motion creates a feeling that the vessel is driven by more than the sea winds. The ship sails closer to the magic painting that is unfolding in front of the passengers and crew. A gentle hush hangs in the air, passenger's sense that they are about to meet the artist. Suddenly the sun in its true glory melts into the waters of the Atlantic. Everyone remains spellbound.

The passengers are in awe and move back from the port railing. A chill runs down to their spines. They remain amazed by what they have witnessed this evening, but yet, fearful.

Captain Mcbaine walks among the passengers to calm and explain what they have witnessed. "Yes." He states in a stern voice, "You have witnessed what we at sea call a 'Sailor's Mistress'. Nothing to be alarmed about, for it's Mother Nature performing a scene one shall never forget."

A passenger asks the Captain, "Have you ever seen this before?"

"Yes, many times, and I treasure it every time. I often wish Mrs. Mcbaine were to witness the event with me someday," says the Captain.

Most passengers relax and enter the lounging area. Others remain to stare towards the darkened sea and watch the moon deliver a glimmer across the waves. The children are taken to their respective rooms by their mothers, leaving the men to toast the day with a few glasses of spirits.

The steerage class dress in poorer fashion, but they are a lively lot. Many of the men roll a cigarette, puffing away as if this were their last breath. Some chew tobacco, but lack proper etiquette, and expel the chewed tobacco on the planked deck of the ship.

The children are a happy lot but seem to have noses that continuously drip. The sleeves of their shirts are like cardboard, for they constantly are being used as handkerchiefs.

The women appear to be very tired and tend to have a sleepy look about them most of the time. Even walking is an obvious struggle. This forlorn appearance comes from giving care to their husbands and their constantly crying children. Ladies of such low grace, not of their choosing, often conceive shortly after giving birth. It is a continuous cycle for some. Many of the men sleep with more than just their wife, a common practise for the times.

The off-duty crew, ready with their pipes and tobacco stored in the pockets of canvas-like pants, gather for a smoke. The talk soon goes to the sighting of the 'Sailor's Mistress.' The crew have seen this wonder several times. They believe; when there is a death onboard, and burial is at sea, the deceased will inherit the sea, becoming one with the 'Mistress of the Sea'.

The sweet smell of cigar smoke lingers in the lounge area as the upper-class passengers enjoy talk and laughter together. They slowly sip beverages the stewards pour for them, while they converse. The women proceed to their cabins to remove the jewelry they wore at the dining tables, and tend to the children.

A young lad from steerage is getting a breath of fresh air at the stern. He watches Jackal holding his violin firmly. Curiously, the lad walks towards Jackal, who notices him. "Ahoy, Matey! What is your name?"

"Joseph Cunningham. Sir," replies the nervous youngster, staring at the violin in Jackal's hand. "My brother and sister call me Joey. I'm thirteen years old, and can play the violin."

"Would you like to play my violin?" asks the surprised Jackal.

With a boyish grin, Joey takes the violin and fondles the revered instrument in his hands. Joey places the violin under his chin and with the bow held high, he gently strokes the strings. A crowd begins to gather as Joey's gifted hands play the instrument. The evening air fills with the tender notes of **'My Sweet Home'**.

The contented sound from the violin whispers across the deck, seeping into the hearts of the gathered steerage passengers. The crowd claps their hands in appreciation for Joey. He smiles and gratefully nods, handing the violin to Jackal.

Jackal is surprised at the youngster's talent as he takes the violin, rubbing Joey's head, "Well done lad, well done."

The talkative Joey begins to tell Jackal that his father had a small shop in Brighton where he made mandolins and violins. He goes on to say that he and his family are bound for America in search of a new start.

The lounge and dining areas are quiet, giving the mouse freedom to roam and pick and choose its meal tonight. The mouse quickly moves around the deck, always aware of the direction it must scurry in the event someone enters the room.

A fog rolls onto the deck of the ship this night. Jimmy Brown is in the crow's nest and calls out, "All Clear, Matey."

Lieutenant Rodgers is patrolling the ship tonight. He checks the pantry and taps the cupboards with his drawn sabre. The galley is quiet while the Lieutenant searches for steerage passengers who may be stealing food. This almost seems to be a game of hide-and-seek, becoming a nightly ritual.

The Lieutenant quickly grips the sabre tightly in his hand. His heart rate reaches new heights. Sounds of hurried footsteps across the planked deck are heard as two youths fearfully make their way back to their bunks. Mr. Rodgers knows it is unsafe for him to follow into the steerage area alone. The Lieutenant stops, allowing his stirred emotions to settle. The youth of the steerage are often sent by a parent to prowl on the upper decks in search of food and objects to trade for cash or kind.

* * *

Under the watchful presence of the moon, fog settles and roams the deck at will. The stars will rest this long evening for it seems blankets have been placed over them. They gracefully lose their glow to the fog.

Second mate Patrick Quinn is on duty at the helm this morning. He is a veteran of the seas and under the command of Captain Mcbaine for more than a decade. The crew refer to the second mate as Patty and hold great respect for him.

Patty is called a dry-land sailor for he lives near London and often goes home in the slower shipping season. He is thirty-nine years of age and has seven children thus far. One of his children, Thomas, is an apprentice on the Sara Rose and dreams of following in his father's footsteps. The younger Quinn is called Tom by his friends and crew.

Captain Mcbaine and Patty plot a course for Liverpool. The two men stop their work; curiously they keep watch on an oncoming ship. A shout is heard from the crow's nest, "She's a German freighter. Mates. She sails in our shipping lane."

"Lieutenant Rodgers, quickly get to the bow of the ship with the signal flags and contact the vessel. The ship is in our sea lane," shouts the Captain.

Helmsman Quinn quickly turns the ship's wheel to starboard. There is no response from the German vessel which remains in the Rose's lane. The Captain spontaneously orders the crew to fire canon flares at the German ship to gain their attention.

The Sara Rose continues on a sharp turn toward starboard. The crew and passengers are startled as the event unfolds. The Sara Rose, with the crew's swift action is out of the collision course. The sea wash and large waves caused by the freighter disrupts the entire ship. The ship maintains her starboard turn and keeps at a ninety-degree angle to the freighter until the waters calm.

The Captain takes his spot on the helm deck and shakes his fist at the freighter, shouting "Vengeance shall be mine." A rare display from the Captain.

The German ship stays on its original course and does not acknowledge that there was a situation. The crew of the Rose send offensive gestures to the passing freighter with their hands and fingers.

The mouse closes its eyes, as Arthur slips his trousers down, pointing his buttock to the German vessel.

The quick thinking of Second Mate Quinn saved the Sara Rose from a mishap at sea. Captain Mcbaine hurries back to his cabin and begins to write in his logbook of the event.

A report will be made and given to the British Navy when the Sara Rose arrives at Liverpool. An incident of this magnitude is a violation of the seas and country the ship sails under and will be dealt with swiftly by the British Admiralty.

Jimmy Brown calls from the crow's nest quietly. "May I be relieved, Lieutenant Rodgers?" The crew laugh together at Jimmy's comment. He was forgotten about during this close encounter at sea. His personal needs require attending, and his soiled pants need changing.

Chapter 6

The city of Liverpool shows off its horizon to the crew and passengers aboard the Sara Rose as the ship anchors in the harbour. Third Mate Benjamin Johnson is ordered by the Captain to report to the bow. He takes the signal flags and begins to signal to the Liverpool docks.

Johnson is no stranger to the seas. The crew call the Third Mate, Benjie, when they are off duty. Benjie has been at sea for thirty years and is a trusted veteran. There are always whispers and gossip on board a ship. A rumour circulates that Benjie served aboard pirate ships in the Caribbean. His bearded face, large stature, and mannerisms seem to suggest this. Johnson has a tattoo on his neck that moves in a frightening manner when he speaks. The skull and crossbones tattoo add to the fear factor. No man aboard the Sara Rose would dare to pick a fight or to enter into an argument with the Third Mate. His speed with a sword is unmatched, while his burly look demands respect.

Young Joey Cunningham strolls on the stern of the ship with his brother and sister. Neil is eleven and small for his age. Frances is an attractive young lady at the tender age of seventeen. Her two brothers keep a close watch on their sister, for her appearance draws attention.

Joey is in search of his new-found friend, Jackal, but he is nowhere to be found. The three Cunningham children walk back to the railing and take turns dropping spitballs to the sea while bragging that their spitball was the biggest and went the farthest.

Another evening at sea slowly edges its way into darkness. The crew and passengers know they will remain anchored for the duration of the night. The lights of Liverpool stretch across the vast horizon. Glimpses of other ships anchored around them show through the night's lights. All who are on deck tonight are amazed at the beauty the night brings to life. The night crew light the lanterns and hang them across the sides to prevent other ships from colliding with them.

The 'All Clear' sound rings down from the crow's nest as Parker keeps watch tonight. Parker has only one name and claims this is all he needs, leaving people unsure if that is his first or last name. Parker claims he never knew his father and proclaims he is a mistake of nature.

The evening air entwines with the aroma of tobacco from the men's pipes in the steerage section. A few of the ladies join their partners and roll tobacco in precut paper, then draw smoke from their handmade cigarettes.

The first and second-class male travellers enjoy a sociable drink while the ladies sip tea. Some have succumbed to their dreams in the lounge chairs. This night at sea is extremely memorable and becomes a sacred moment. The passengers are caught up in the view of the lights of Liverpool. The beauty of the lights and glow of the moon give the seaport a magical look, but the dawn will rewrite a story of poverty.

The little mouse that roams the deck at night is about to leave the safety of its hole in the wall. Circling on the planked deck, the rodent curls up its nose at the cigar ashes on the floor. The mouse searches for crumbs, preferring the first-class tables. The distant lights of Liverpool that reflect onto the deck scare the ship's little stowaway. It cuts dinner short and runs back to safety.

* * *

The sun melts the last of the darkness from the eastern horizon and a new day begins.

Lieutenant Rodgers makes his rounds. Everyone onboard with whom he chats, mentions the extreme heat. There is a slight breeze from the east causing ripples on the seawater. The crew know there is a storm collecting its nerve and soon it will unleash its hidden powers.

The Union Jack awakens as gusts of winds tease the morning air. Suddenly, there is a sea of flags proudly waving the colours of their respective countries. The easterly breeze is acting as the conductor of this colourful symphony. Ships are anchored in the harbour waiting to unload their cargo from all corners of the globe.

The quiet mouse pokes its curious nose out of its hole in the wall. The rodent senses the oncoming storm, causing it to act nervous and uncomfortable. The hair on the little mouse begins to stand up. It releases quiet squeals as if to communicate with other mice on board. This nervous rodent knows better than to make an appearance on deck during daylight hours and backs into a darkened corner.

Third Mate Johnson approaches the Captain and salutes "Sir. We have the orders to proceed from the port."

"High riggers, let's get to it!" shouts the Captain.

The riggers climb the masts to the spars, swinging from sail to sail. The deck crew pulls on the ropes to release the sails. They repeat this action with each sail.

Captain Mcbaine orders 'Half Mast', and the Rose begins to move with the strength of the wind. The vessel eases into her berth, and crewmen throw the large ropes over the sides, allowing the dock crew to tie the ship to the large bollards.

The gangway lowers and the first and second-class travellers line up to disembark. The passengers who will be returning are advised to report back to the ship within twenty-four hours, or chance missing the ship as she sets out to sea.

Second Mate Patrick Quinn prepares the steerage passengers for their departure to the Liverpool docks. Some of the travellers will stay on board while others venture out for personal supplies. For some, this is the final destination. The Captain is not present as the steerage passengers leave the ship, for his main concerns lie primarily with the upper deck guests.

Most of the first-class passengers are met by family, business representatives, or their servants.

Workers begin to open the large hatches of the vessel, and the unloading begins. No dock workers or onlookers are allowed to board the ship.

* * *

"Come, Lieutenant, let me treat you to supper on dry land tonight. I see there is an inn at the corner of the street," says Captain Mcbaine. The two men relax and enjoy their meal together, talking candidly. The Captain pays the inn-keeper two shilling and sixpence for supper. He then lights his pipe, drawing smoke before he and the Lieutenant leave the inn.

The two men arrive back at the ship where the Captain immediately goes to his cabin to retrieve the ship's logbook. With the logbook under his arm, he salutes Lieutenant Rodgers. "Sir, you're in charge of this vessel. Mr. Rodgers, we will release our prisoners to the authorities, under cover of darkness." Leaving the ship, Captain Mcbaine waves for a carriage on the dock and requests a ride to the office of the Admiral.

The friendship between the Admiral and the Captain goes back many years, to the time they served in the Royal Navy together. Captain Mcbaine describes the incident at sea with the German freighter that refused to comply with the rules of the sea, almost causing a collision. The Admiral guarantees that the Royal Navy will deal with this rogue vessel. With business completed, they sit and enjoy a cup of tea and talk of bygone days. The conversation quickly changes to their families and their children. The hours pass by quickly. The two veterans catch up on life and memories. They stand and salute one another, then shake hands, bidding each other a farewell.

Shortly after the Captain boards his ship, the weather becomes violent. The rain has begun, and the Lieutenant orders the large hatches closed as the Sara Rose begins to rub and clash against the pier. The crew retie the ship to the bollards, and all work comes to an end as the storm now commands the day.

"Captain, Captain," shouts the Lieutenant, pounding on Captain Mcbaine's door.

"What is it, Lieutenant?"

"Its Katie, the female prisoner. We found her murdered when the crew and I came to remove the prisoners and place them with the authorities.

Her clothing was ripped from her body. Sir, she was molested and strangled by a crew member of the Rose."

"Damn vultures. What are the port authorities suggesting we do?"

"They are leaving that decision to you, Sir."

"Remove the prisoners and Katie's body. We sail in the morning. Place guards to the entrance of the upper deck passengers. We will find our murderer at sea, and deal with him then."

There will not be any visits to the taverns this evening; the gangway lifts and the Rose becomes a closed vessel for the night.

* * *

Dull skies usher in the morning and allow the showers to continue. The crew open the hatches, and the loading resumes. From the crow's nest, Parker can see the devastation the night's storm has unleashed on the ships anchored in the harbour.

Passengers have begun to line up on the dock. The first-class passengers have boarding preference. They are shown to their cabins upon arrival, followed by the second-class as per protocol.

The light rain showers slowly retreat, as the steerage passengers begin to board. The sun escapes from the grey sky and warms the day. Most of the steerage travellers only have what they carry with them, unlike the first-class passengers, who travel with volumes of luggage.

Lieutenant Rodgers calls out, "All Aboard!" The ropes are released from the bollards, and the gangway is slowly pulled up.

Shouting is heard from the distance, as two young men come running toward the ship. The Captain takes notice and orders the gangway lowered for the two, who are waving their boarding tickets. They are allowed to board, and the Captain pays close attention to these two young men. The younger of the two waits, when the other begins coughing and hanging on to the rail, trying to catch his breath. "Sounds like you may be coming down with something," comments the First Mate.

The Sara Rose slowly drifts from the pier, and the winds find her sails. Captain Mcbaine salutes the Port Major. The ship's crew and passengers are shocked to see the destruction caused by the storm. A few ships that had their anchor chains broken, now are wrecked on the breakwater. A smaller vessel capsized, and its cargo is floating in the harbour.

* * *

The men get into their routine once more. Samuel, one of the apprentices aboard, who is a mere sixteen, is allowed to join the high riggers and work the sails. Jimmy Brown calls down from the crow's nest, "All Clear." The Rose is rigged and on route to Prestwick, Scotland.

The Captain rarely mingles with the steerage passengers, but now notices the two young men who boarded the ship with only a moment to spare. He enters the stern area and begins speaking to the two young men. Martin, aged twenty-six, shakes hands with the Captain and introduces his twenty-one-year-old brother, Matthew. There seems to be an instant bond between the three men chatting together.

Chapter 7

The Sara Rose calls the sea a friend, who guides her graceful sails to new speeds. The port of Liverpool becomes distant to the ship, but not to the passengers and crew, who witnessed the horizon of Liverpool romanced by the dancing lights of the previous evening. This sight will forever remain etched in their minds.

The warm waters of the Irish Sea are clear this fall day. Perfect colours of blues and greens pulse vibrantly, giving the sea life of its own. One by one sharks come to the sides of the ship in the colourful waters, almost as if they were being called to a church meeting by a sounding bell. The frenzy of the sharks seems to entice the Rose into faster speeds. They tease the ship to a point where it becomes a game of tag. The school divides equally into the port and starboard side, and all sizes of sharks join together as if they were in a parade. The Sara Rose acts the part of the leader in a marching band. The mast of the ship stands tall as the Union Jack claims the honour of being the Parade Marshal, and the full sails cheer everyone forward.

The two brothers, Martin and Matthew, are both in awe of the wonders of the sea. Coming from a small inland town, this is an adventure they could not have imagined a few months ago. Captain Mcbaine spots the two young men at the stern of the ship and approaches them.

"It's a great day to be at sea," says Captain Mcbaine. Martin and Matthew respond with a smile, and the Captain goes on to say, "I was wondering if the two of you would be interested in part-time work on the ship. The galley is short staffed and in need of help. The pay would help once you reach your destination and the work would take the boredom out of the voyage."

"Yes, Captain. Matthew and I accept your offer. The work would do us good, and the extra shillings would be much appreciated."

"Ship Ahoy, Mates!" calls Jimmy Brown from the crow's nest. The crew is alerted. The Captain returns to the deck and begins to speak with helmsman, Second Mate Quinn. They observe the oncoming ship.

Again, Jimmy Brown's voice calls from the crow's nest. "She's a fishing schooner and flies an Irish flag." The schooner is loaded with her catch and heading to the port of Dundalk. The two crews message back and forth with the aid of their signal flags as they pass on their port side. With great familiarity, they wave to each other, while the sea breeze puts distance between the two vessels.

* * *

The shimmering sea possesses magical colours of beauty that are beyond description. The Isle of Man slowly comes into view as the ship steadily gains new speeds. The Sara Rose remains at full sail and the approaching island creeps ever closer into view.

The town of Douglas and its harbour seem to be bustling with small ships and boats. Carriages can be seen on the dirt streets hauling cargo to and from the dock. Small shops are open for business. The board walkways are bustling with townsfolk and children running, followed by barking dogs - a very picturesque scene for the travellers and crew of the Rose. Smiles relax their hidden emotions; they feel as if they are being called home.

First-time travellers are in awe and marvel at the beauty of the Irish Sea. Its magically coloured waters possess a clarity that is beyond the description of man. The outcropped islands support forests that are home to all creatures of the wild. One only can suspect God himself played a hand in the creation of this untouched masterpiece. 'This is a great day to be at sea' enters the mind of all aboard the ship.

The golden sun slowly succumbs to the calls of the silent darkness. The first-class passengers begin seating for their evening meal, and stewards begin pouring tea, some call for stronger spirits.

The quiet little mouse waits for nightfall, anticipating the coming evening, wishing it had someone to share a meal with.

The second-class travellers enter the dining area and begin serving themselves. Everyone on board tonight is in a jovial mood after such a breathtaking day at sea.

Hardie Jenkins, the crew member who took ten lashes to his back just over a week ago, is aroused by the sight of the young Frances Cunningham. She's accompanied by her two brothers, Joey and Neil. Hardie follows the three youths in hopes they separate, thus giving him a chance to approach the pretty Frances. Third Mate Benjamin Johnson is the helmsman tonight and notices the suspicious actions of Hardie. In a piercing voice, he calls Hardie to the helm, where they get into a shouting match and begin to push each other back and forth. Jackal and the ageing Arthur witness the argument and quickly come to the aid of Benjie. Hardie, who knows better than to get into a fight with the Third Mate, quickly retreats to his bunk. The three men left at the helm know this is not the last they will hear from the vengeful Hardie Jenkins. They debate if the Captain should be informed of tonight's events. As true shipmates, they decide the matter will remain private for now.

From the crow's nest, Parker signals to the helmsman, Third Mate Benjamin Johnson, that all is clear ahead and to stay the course. The sun begins fading silently into the Irish coastline.

Lieutenant Rodgers begins his rounds this evening in the steerage section. He walks among the steerage passengers, hoping his nervousness is not evident. Having been born into upper-class society, he feels the steerage passengers are ordinary and beneath him, so idle chats with these travellers are to no advantage. The Lieutenant dreams of eventually becoming a Captain in the Royal Navy. He nods to First Mate Roddy Downing, who puffs on his pipe at the railing. The Lieutenant circles the stern area and is about to leave for other parts of the ship when he notices a young lady and two boys. The nervous Lieutenant approaches.

"Good evening, Lads. How are you tonight?" asks the Lieutenant. Neil and Joey smile back but refrain from answering.

The nervous Lieutenant makes eye contact with Frances. She hides her smile behind her hand. For a moment he is transfixed with the beauty of the young lady. Red-faced, the Lieutenant finds his thoughts and regains his confidence. He removes his cap, nods at Frances and continues on his way. The Lieutenant keeps looking back to see if Frances is looking at him. Much to his delight, Frances smiles back at the Lieutenant. The Lieutenant is smitten.

The ship's lanterns are lit with night descending on the ship, and the little mouse begins its evening rounds.

Some of the first and second-class travellers remain in the lounge area enjoying a game of chance and sip spirits. Their voices rise to a louder pitch. The mouse runs back across the deck to its safe home. The Lieutenant overhears the commotion and quickly approaches the guests. He moves between two men with his right hand positioned over the hilt of his sabre to prevent either from grasping the weapon and attacking the other.

The Lieutenant calms the two men, asking for an explanation. A second-class passenger accuses a first-class passenger of cheating in a game of chance. The other men in the game refuse to say anything to the Lieutenant and slowly remove themselves. The young Lieutenant takes brief statements from the two and seizes the money. "The Captain will want to speak with both of you tomorrow."

* * *

It is a cold, damp morning aboard the Sara Rose, as the ship slows in the North Channel. The winds constantly change direction, and heavy rain pounds the lone ship. The crew work hard moving the sails to match the strong winds. The high riggers reclaim a ripped sail and lower it with ropes. Two crewmen untie the ripped sail and attach a new one, hoisting it to the riggers above.

Jimmy Brown covers himself with a piece of canvas to avoid the dampness entering his clothing. From the crow's nest, he waves to the helmsman that all is well. The narrow North Channel can be a ship's demise if the winds increase. Heavy rain and gusts can cause giant waves to carry a vessel onto the rocky coast. Skeletons of abandoned shipwrecks are seen on the coastline and remind the crew not to leave anything to chance.

"All Stop!" suddenly shouts Jimmy Brown. "Man, overboard! All Stop, Man Overboard!"

Roddy Downing quickly turns the ship into the wind, and the rudder slows the Rose. The crew act instinctively. High riggers begin to lower the mainsails without orders. The deck crew turn the foremast and jiggermast to slow the Rose. The anchor anxiously finds its way to the seabed. Lieutenant Rodgers runs to the rear of the ship ordering jolly boats to be put into the water immediately.

The Captain rushes from his cabin to the starboard side of the ship. A jolly boat manned by five crew members fight the relentless rain. A second boat lowers with another six men. This boat is attached to the ship with a long rope and acts as a safety boat. It extends itself out to where the sailor fell to the cold, rough waves.

The talk quickly spreads that it is the young apprentice, Samuel, who fell from the spar to the raging waters below. The sailors in the small boats search, to no avail. Their small jolly crafts begin to fill with rain and sea water. The men tie the two boats together and call off the futile search. They paddle and pull themselves back to the waiting ship.

Captain Mcbaine orders the main sails lifted and the anchor raised. Roddy Downing releases the rudder as the jolly boats return to the deck of the ship. The ship slowly continues into the storm, returning to its original course, leaving the young sailor behind.

The sailors meet mid-ship and group together to bow their heads for a moment of silence for the young apprentice, Samuel. The rain washes clean all tears, but the memory of the lad remains.

Lieutenant Rodgers makes his way to the helm and reports to the Captain of the night's conflict between the two passengers. The Captain tells the Lieutenant the matter will have to wait until the ship clears the storm.

"Mr. Rodgers, do you know young Samuel's last name? I definitely must write a letter to his folks."

"I believe it was Howlyn. Samuel Howlyn."

"Yes, now I remember. Oh, Lieutenant. By the way, I asked Dr. Eden if he treated any new patients that had Katie's wrath passed to them. The doctor stated that he treated one new patient, Hazleton. Best keep an eye on him, Lieutenant."

In the dining area, the gossip focuses on the game of chance that erupted into an argument. One man accusing another of cheating soon becomes the main topic, and whispers overtake the sound of the rain. Fingers point to Jones, the first-class passenger being the one accused by a second-class traveller of cheating last night in the game of chance.

The tone of the passengers quiets as Jones enters the dining area and orders breakfast from a steward. Sneering, he displays his arrogance, walking past passengers to the corner of the dining area. Jones sits alone at a table puffing on his cigar. Ashes from his smouldering cigar drop onto the floor without regard.

Chapter 8

The Sara Rose struggles into the 'Firth of Clyde.' The rains, that earlier poured angrily from the sky, begin to recede and the gale-force winds that drove the sea to its rage during the day have calmed.

The Captain makes his way to his cabin, for he must tend to the matter of the game of chance that ended badly. He stops young Thomas Quinn, the apprentice on board and orders him to fetch Mr. Rodgers immediately.

The Lieutenant soon arrives at the Captain's cabin. He seats himself, and they begin to discuss the quarrel that led to the accusation of cheating.

The Captain shakes his head "I wish I didn't have to be the one to decide this matter. It's not the argument. It is the cheating accusation.

"Lieutenant Rodgers, give me the names of the two gentlemen who were involved, so I can proceed and enter the facts in the logbook."

The Lieutenant replies, "Mr. Peters from second-class and Mr. Jones from first-class."

The Captain quickly glances at Mr. Rodgers in surprise, "Oh, Mr. Jones! All right, Lieutenant. Find the two witnesses and Mr. Peters, and of course, Mr. Jones. Meet me back here in an hour."

The Lieutenant quickly leaves the Captain's cabin, and walks to the stern of the ship, hoping to catch a glimpse of the young lady that tickled his thoughts.

The Captain makes his way to the helm to speak to First Mate Roddy Downing. The two veterans of the sea discuss present conditions and their approach to Prestwick. The Firth of Clyde is a busy channel, and from the starboard side land is visible. The coastline is busy with smaller fishing vessels setting their nets. The Sara Rose is flanked on the port side by outgoing cargo ships, each supporting their country's flags. Parker is alert in the crow's nest. His keen eye must predict the movement of other ships to prevent a collision.

Parker has the perfect vantage point from which to view the beauty of this untouched land. Its mountains and forests have never had a man's footprints pressed in the soil to spoil the splendour of nature's magnificent touch. Parker's eyes witness the constant rush of streams and rivers as the sea calls for them to join together; like one calls their children, and they come running to open arms.

The Lieutenant taps on the open door, "Permission to enter, Sir? "The Captain nods and the Lieutenant enters with four men.

"Mr. Jones, Sir. It's good to see you again," remarks the Captain. Chairs are slid up to the desk, and everyone is seated, except the Lieutenant. He remains standing by the door, at full attention, with his hand on the hilt of his sabre. Jones sits directly across from the two witnesses, and stares at them with his smug smile, slowly puffing on his cigar. Captain Mcbaine opens the ship's logbook and asks the witnesses for their names.

"Nichol, Sir, Todderick Nichol" replies one of the gentlemen. The Captain enters his name in the logbook.

The Captain looks suspiciously at the other passenger who answers 'Flynn', in a muffled voice. The Captain also enters Mr. Flynn's name in the logbook.

"Now, gentlemen, please place your mark by your name in the logbook. Mr. Flynn, you will remain here. You other gentlemen, please go wait outside my cabin with the Lieutenant."

The Captain begins with a comment to Mr. Flynn, "Sir, I believe, through the years, that we have met at one time.

"Captain, I do not believe we have," replies Mr. Flynn.

"Sir, we have met before! Now, to the matter at hand. Was there any cheating or unethical card playing that evening?"

44

Flynn quickly replies, "No, Sir. There was not."

Captain Mcbaine looks up at Flynn and repeats the question in a louder tone of voice. Flynn answers, "No, Captain, I did not witness any cheating during the game of chance."

The Captain enters Flynn's comments in the logbook, telling him he is excused and asks for Mr. Nichol to come in.

Mr. Nichol removes his hat as he enters the cabin and stands by the large desk.

"Sir, please sit down. Tell me what you saw that night during the game of chance."

"Well, Sir, it's hard to say. Mr. Jones seems to be very quick with the cards and his hands. He has a manner about himself that distracts one from the game."

"But, Mr. Nichol, did you personally see any cheating during the game of chance?"

"No Sir," replies Mr. Nichol, looking down at the floor.

Captain Mcbaine excuses Nichol and asks him to close the door behind him. Captain remains at his desk, takes a sip of cold tea, and reviews his thoughts.

The tension has increased outside the Captain's cabin. Mr. Peters has become quite fidgety with Mr. Jones continually staring at him.

Captain Mcbaine opens his cabin door and calls in Lieutenant Rodgers and Mr. Jones. The Lieutenant closes the door and remains standing guard. Jones grins as he walks in without removing his top hat. He puffs on a cigar and blows the smoke toward the Lieutenant. The Captain reaches into the desk drawer. He pulls out a tin tray filled with money and slides it across the desk to Jones.

"Sir, count your money."

Jones, with an evil smirk, begins a count of the money. The ashes from his cigar fall to the desk and into the tin tray. Jones coughs, his shifty eyes burn into the money, as a child might get excited over the anticipated taste of chocolate.

"Yes, all the money is here," chuckles Jones.

Captain Mcbaine tells Jones he can leave with the money, "Oh, and Mr. Jones. Please refrain from any games of chance while on my ship." Jones quietly leaves, muttering to himself.

The Lieutenant is then asked to bring in Mr. Peters. Mr. Peters enters the room with his hat in his hand and his head lowered. The Captain asks Mr. Peters to seat himself. Mr. Rodgers stands at the door in a very uncomfortable stance.

"Mr. Peters, you have accused a man of cheating on my ship," states the Captain. "Perhaps you were cheated in a game of chance, but no evidence has come forth to support your case. Therefore, Sir, your accusation against another passenger is recorded as false. I must inform you that you will be asked to leave the ship at the next port. Do you understand, Mr. Peters?"

Mr. Peters nods and slumps in the chair with embarrassment. The Lieutenant is somewhat shocked at the Captain's comments and judgement and is about to give his opinion when the Captain looks at him. In a stern voice, the Captain says, "Lieutenant!"

Chapter 9

The Sara Rose enters into the Scottish harbour of Prestwick with the docks in sight as high riggers climb the mast of the ship. Third Mate Johnson is at the bow contacting the harbour with the signal flags. A reply returns from the Port Major of Prestwick, allowing the vessel to drop anchor and wait for instructions in the morning.

The Firth of Clyde remains a busy waterway with darkness sliding in and removing the light from a picturesque scene. The small fishing boats have made their way back to the docks with their catch of the day. Lanterns shine down to the quiet waters, and one can hear the echo of men talking in the distance. Their voices soon fade into the coming darkness, and a hush now exists.

* * *

There is an uneasy feeling in the lounge area tonight. The gossip focuses on a passenger being asked to leave the ship because of a game of chance gone wrong and an accusation of cheating. Most of the passengers enjoyed the honest company of Mr. Peters and his wife. A group of passengers discuss the possibility of forming a contingent on behalf of the Peters. Several of the female passengers are in tears as the issue is discussed.

"Mrs. Peters is a very humble lady and takes great pride in her three young children," says Carol Harris. Mrs. Harris, an attractive lady in her prime, places her hand gently on her husband's arm. Ronald Harris looks at the emotion in his wife's eyes and stands up boldly. "We all must help the Peters family."

Carol Harris now stands with her husband. She grasps his hand and tells the group that has gathered, "We must do this for the Peters, for they are penniless now." Mrs. Harris breaks down and begins to cry into her husband's evening jacket. His arms warmly console his wife, and they sit down. Everyone in the group has their head down in sorrow after Mrs. Harris's plea for support for the Peters family.

Murmurs can be heard throughout the gathered group; handkerchiefs catch the true emotions of everyone's heart. These precious tears from the heart give the group a stronger will to do what they can for the Peters family. Mrs. Harris takes off her evening hat and places it on the table; this is something a lady rarely does in public. She stands with tears rolling down her reddened cheeks and begins to say, "We must, we will support the Peters family. They are without a penny to their name now. I can't imagine what they are feeling. Mr. Peters may have been wrong in his actions, but we must think of his wife and the three children."

What were tears in Carol Harris's eyes now become cemented into a bridge of strength. The air she inhales gives her voice new confidence. "The Captain's actions may be the law of the sea, but we want the love of humanity for the Peters. We must all stand together and not allow this family to be put on the streets of an unknown city. They are penniless and heartbroken. Their dreams of a new life shall certainly be crushed."

The handkerchiefs, which held the desperate emotions and tears of the heart, now wave a newly found hope. A cheer of joy comes from the gathered group.

The Lieutenant, standing in the shadows, slowly backs away, as not to be seen by the crowd that has gathered. He walks the deck of the Sara Rose undecided about what to do. His duty is to the ship and the Captain. He looks up at the Union Jack hoping for an answer, but his country's flag is silent. The cool night air sends a chill down Mr. Rodgers's back, for he knows what he must do.

The ship's little mouse senses the tension in the air this night. It quickly scurries for its evening meal. The sound of footsteps on the planked deck makes its heart race, and the mouse leaves the meal behind.

* * *

The Sara Rose lies still in the waters of the Firth of Clyde. The morning sun takes its first peek over the rolling landscape. There is an evident nervousness on the decks this morning. Captain Mcbaine has not slept during the night; his decision sits uneasily with him.

In the lounge, first and second-class passengers regroup in the early morning. Their fellow travellers have told the Peters family that they want to help in any way they can and will speak to the Captain on their behalf.

Lieutenant Rogers approaches the Captain and salutes him. The salute is calmly returned.

"Yes Lieutenant, what can I do for you?"

"Captain, I must speak to you in private."

The Captain and Mr. Rodgers enter the Captain's cabin. The Lieutenant takes off his cap and is asked to be seated. Captain Mcbaine addresses the Lieutenant, "Mr. Rodgers, I sense this is a matter of great importance."

The Lieutenant comments in a low tone of voice, "Yes Sir, it is very important."

The Captain nods to Mr. Rodgers, "Sir, please continue."

The trembling Lieutenant lowers his head and is unsure of how to put his thoughts into words.

The Captain speaks again, "Lieutenant, is this matter to do with Mr. Peters and his having to leave the ship?"

"Yes," the Lieutenant replies. "Captain, may I speak freely?"

The Captain sits up in his chair. His hands firmly placed on the large desk. He pauses momentarily. "Mr. Rodgers, I will grant you this privilege, just this one time, Sir."

The Lieutenant shyly looks at the Captain, like a scolded puppy and says, "Captain, I heard the passengers talking that they support Mr. Peters and his family in this matter. Also, they stated they do not agree with your decision, and they plan to have an open discussion before the ship's docking at Prestwick."

The Captain slides back in his chair; his hands grasp the armrests. A knock on the door breaks the silence between the Captain and the

Lieutenant. The Captain nods to the Lieutenant who proceeds to open the door. It is the apprentice, Thomas Quinn.

"Sir, my father just got word from the Port Major that the ship is clear to proceed to the dock."

"Thank you, Thomas. I will be there shortly." The Captain, with Mr. Rodgers at his side steps onto the helm deck. Third Mate Benjamin Johnson is waiting to discuss the Port Major's orders on proceeding to the dock.

Captain Mcbaine orders the anchor lifted from the harbour bed. The high riggers go into action and begin to raise the sails. The deck bustles with sailors pulling ropes and setting trim to the sails. The stewards are clearing tables to prevent breakage of cups and dishes.

The ship's stowaway peeks out of the hole in the wall, knowing to stay home until silence returns to the deck.

The seagulls come alive and circle the sails. The cook orders Martin and Matthew to begin dumping the barrels of garbage overboard. Hundreds of birds flock towards the vessel in search of a free meal. Some are beaten back and leave with empty beaks. Others fly away with scraps hanging from their bulging beaks as the ship slowly advances towards the dock area.

The Sara Rose is now firmly secured against the Scottish dock. Captain Mcbaine turns to Mr. Johnson with a warm smile, and comments, "It's good to be in Scotland again."

The passengers stand and form a group as the Captain enters. He removes his cap, telling them to be seated. Before he can speak, Mrs. Harris addresses the Captain. "Captain, Sir, we cannot allow you to turn the Peters family into the streets of Prestwick, penniless and with only their personal belongings."

The Captain stands in the center of the lounge area. His eyes capture the look on the passengers' faces. The Captain struggles, "I am very sorry to inform you all that this is the law of the sea and that I must abide by my actions. There is nothing I can do to help the Peters family in this matter."

The Captain puts his cap back on with a firm grip, turns and begins to leave. He steps slowly across the planked floor with his head down. He stops suddenly and turns to face the silenced group of passengers.

"Ladies and gentlemen, as Captain I have to send the Lieutenant to remove Mr. Peters. Please! Pay careful attention to what Lieutenant Rodgers has to say. I trust the Lieutenant will be helpful."

Trying to hide his emotions, the Captain turns quickly away from the passengers. He briskly walks towards the galley, "Gentlemen, would someone give me a cup of tea." He continues to his cabin with the cup of tea and calls, "Thomas, get the Lieutenant. Be quick about it. Tell him to come directly to my cabin."

Chapter 10

The Sara Rose is firmly in her berth, well secured to the bollards. Thus, begins the unloading of the cargo from Liverpool, Brighton and the French port of St-Nazaire. The large covers from the cargo holds are removed, and the gangway lowered, but no one is leaving the ship.

Martin and Matthew are leaning on the starboard rail of the ship. Matthew notices a carriage drawn by two large black horses. He remains focused on the newly arrived carriage, and stares, like one would stare at a new-found treasure. A boyish smile warms his face. He tries to speak; his hand nudges Martin. The two young men lean over the railing of the ship, looking onto the wharf. Both are intrigued by the view.

There is a knock on the Captain's door. The Lieutenant enters the cabin and salutes, but the Captain does not return the courtesy. "Sit down Mr. Rodgers. We have a problem onboard ship. Now, Lieutenant, this is what I want you to do to resolve the matter, and I want you to act quickly."

* * *

The Lieutenant has been in the lounge area for some time now. He is speaking to the passengers, who are voicing their strong opinions against the Peters family leaving the ship. A few of the passengers begin leaving the vessel, but the group that supports the Peters remain to hear what the Lieutenant has to say. Even the little mouse is curious as its head sticks out of the hole in the wall to listen.

The Captain comes out of his cabin with the logbook and ship's manifest under his arm, stops, and salutes the First Mate before departing the ship. Steerage passengers are anxious to leave the ship, but the First Mate ignores their requests.

Martin and Matthew are still looking over the rail of the vessel when one of the cooks calls the two boys. Martin waves to the cook, giving a sign that he is on his way back to the galley. Matthew is motionless and continues to gaze down at the dock. He is in awe at what he sees.

There, on the busy pier, his stare is returned. Matthew feels an instant rush. He is momentarily frozen. The young lady on the dock smiles at him. She twirls her open white umbrella, edged in blue, over her shoulder. She is wearing a full-length white gown, with blue trimming on the sleeves and at the neckline that matches the twirling umbrella. Her mother, who is also a stunning lady, is dressed in an emerald green gown. She is standing on the pier looking up at the vastness of the Sara Rose. The young woman's father steps from the carriage and onto the dock. He is well-dressed in a dark suit, with the jacket reaching to his knees. A white shirt and white bow tie are visible at his neckline. His black top hat reflects the day's sun. He seems to be below average height and a bit stout; his well-fed stomach protrudes from the coat he wears.

Suddenly the young lady bursts into laughter, pointing upward to the ship. One of the cooks has grabbed Matthew by the ear, taking him back to the galley.

The Lieutenant walks Mr. Peters and his family to the walkway. Mr. Rodgers shakes Mr. Peters hand and tips his hat to Mrs. Peters. The Peters family is embarrassed as they descend to the dock, while onlookers tend to point fingers at them. Gossip runs wild on a closed ship, and now that gossip spreads to the dock.

Mr. and Mrs. Harris shake hands with the Lieutenant. They start to disembark when Carol Harris runs back to him, hugging him. The Lieutenant blushes and straightens himself. His warm grin turns into a smile. He continues to shake hands with the passengers, who slowly leave the ship.

The Lieutenant stands nervously as the steerage passengers make their way down the gangway. At last, he spots Frances Cunningham. The Lieutenant becomes flustered; he tips his hat to Frances. The young lady smiles and murmurs, "Thank you." She steps onto the walkway with Neil and Joey, her two brothers. Her father, Joseph Cunningham, the violin and mandolin maker from Brighton, nods to the Lieutenant.

* * *

It is late afternoon when a carriage pulled by a single grey horse arrives on the dock. The Captain steps out of the carriage and gives the carriage driver a shilling. The driver reaches into his pocket to return a few pence, but Captain Mcbaine shakes his head. The carriage driver tips his hat to the Captain who pats the horse's neck and proceeds to his ship. The Captain steps onto the deck of the Sara Rose and salutes the vessel; turns and salutes his Lieutenant. Captain Mcbaine instructs the Lieutenant to bring hot tea from the galley for both of them. He walks to his cabin, taking the logbook from under his arm and places it on the deck.

The dock and the deck crew work together, like a well-rehearsed play, without incident or error. At the stern of the ship, First Mate Roddy Downing calls for help. He has a young lad by the ear. Hardie Jenkins comes running to aid the First Mate. Jenkins then grabs the young man from the First Mate and throws him down on the planked deck. Hardie delivers a kick to the young man's stomach, and the First Mate runs after another boy. Hardie holds the lad down with his foot. After a few minutes, First Mate Downing returns with the lad he was chasing.

Hardie anxiously blurts out. "Shall I take care of these two stowaways?"

"No, Hardie, we better let the law deal with these two."

Young Matthew sneaks away from the galley. He looks over the starboard side of the ship to see if the young lady who captivated him is still on the dock. He grins as if he just has won a bet with himself. "Yes!" he quietly says, without the cook hearing him. Matthew is hoping the young lady can see him, but she is busy talking to her mother who is sitting beside her in the carriage. Her father is directing the carriage driver on the proper order for the luggage to be loaded onto the ship. The two black horses pulling the coach have become restless and are quickly calmed by the young lady's father.

The Lieutenant has returned with two cups of tea. After asking the Lieutenant to sit down, the Captain slides his chair back and crosses his legs in a more relaxed manner. The Lieutenant sips his tea and places the tin cup on the desk. The Captain is holding the tin cup of tea in both hands. He asks, "Lieutenant, the matter we discussed earlier today, is this taken care of?"

55

"Yes," replies the Lieutenant with a smug grin.

"Good," says the Captain.

Hardie and the First Mate can be seen pushing the two young stowaways down the walkway. Hardie has a billy club in his left hand and uses it at every available opportunity. They struggle with the youths down the gangway, until the four are on the dock. They then walk with the two stowaways to a holding area. Neither the port workers nor the public pay attention, for stowaways are caught daily on ships. Hardie guards the two youths while First Mate Downing searches the docks for the law that patrols the area.

Darkness begins to settle onto the docks. The large rope nets carry the baggage of the family onto the ship. The carriage now leaves the pier, with the young lady and her parents seeking lodging at a local inn for the night.

Matthew watches the carriage leave, taking the young lady who in an instant, won his heart. Matthew waits, holding the ship's railing, but she does not look back.

Hardie Jenkins holds a lantern in one hand, and his faithful billy club in the other. The two youths have settled down when the First Mate waves down a patrol wagon. The two youths' hands are bound with thin ropes and told to get in the barred patrol wagon, drawn by a team of Clydesdale horses.

Hardie and First Mate Downing return to the waiting ship. Only the flicker of the lanterns is seen when the two men board the ship. The Sara Rose will be a closed ship this night.

The little mouse is anxious this evening to find supper and quench its thirst from the dripping water barrel, where the cooks get their tea and drinking water.

Martin and Matthew are gathering the scraps and remains from the meal preparation and placing the waste in barrels. A strong odour is seeping from the barrels that have been holding waste in the warm sun for a full day. This putrid smell even keeps the steerage passengers away from searching for extra food. The barrels will be dumped at sea when the ship clears the harbour tomorrow. The seagulls and fish will again perform nature's magic in keeping its vast domain acceptable in this constant cycle of life.

Martin breaks into a coughing spell. He runs to the railing on the port side. Repeatedly he spits the phlegm he is coughing up. Martin turns pale and slides down to his knees to rest.

Chapter 11

The Sara Rose is suspended in the darkness this warm fall night. Lanterns can be seen lighting her planked deck, with the lights on the dock at a minimum. The odd rogue wave from the sea finds its way into the harbour causing the port side of the ship to creak and roll slightly.

The constant drip of the leaking water barrel has been calling the little mouse for hours. It breaks nature's rule and leaves the safety of its hole in the wall. The speedy mouse heads directly to the source of the water without paying attention to its instincts.

From nowhere there is a swoosh as an old corn broom knocks the little mouse over onto its back. It is in shock but quickly regains its balance in the poorly lit galley. The mouse hesitates, for it has nowhere to hide. Then suddenly it makes a break for the safety of the hole in the wall. The shaken mouse, now safe in its home backs into the corner afraid that its home will be found. The long seconds slowly turn to agonizing minutes, but the swooshing corn broom does not find the little mouse this night.

The advancing light slowly peels away the darkness to reveal a new day. The deck of the Sara Rose is thick with the morning dew, and the new day's sun slowly wipes Mother Nature's cleansing tears away.

Matthew is up early walking the dew-soaked deck, in hopes the young lady who caught his eye will return. Young Thomas Quinn, the apprentice aboard the ship, calls Matthew to lend him a hand in carrying the luggage that remains on the deck.

The two make several trips carrying luggage and large containers down the steps to the first-class rooms. Matthew grabs several lighter boxes that contain ladies' hats and notices a name on the containers, Miss Susannah Evens. He sets the boxes on the deck and begins to look at the names on the large trunks. The luggage looks the same as those he saw unloaded from the carriage of the young lady who smiled at him yesterday.

Matthew grins with delight, causing young Tom to become bewildered by Matthew's excitement and energy to get the luggage to the rooms. Matthew, now with a smile and a quickness in his step, picks up the boxes of bonnets and proceeds to the cabin of Susannah Evens. He places the boxes of hats on the shelves in Susannah's cabin and starts walking out of her room. Matthew suddenly stops, reaches into the pocket of his worn trousers and pulls out his lucky penny. His initial is deeply carved into this coin. Matthew then opens the box and touches the bonnet with his finger. The bonnet is violet-blue with a band around it to hold the decorative flowers. He places his lucky penny inside the band and closes the box.

The ship's bell rings into the morning air to call her travellers back to the dock. Captain Mcbaine and the Lieutenant are there to greet the new upper class passengers as they board. The steerage travellers form a group on the pier, and the normal pushing and shoving begins.

Officers of the law are present to stop fights from breaking out and to prevent thieving. A few young rascals manage to slip into the crowd and come running out with a purse. Times are hard. The working class help each other to survive, and when the crowd catches these young scoundrels, they are severely beaten.

At the bottom of the gangway, Mr. and Mrs. Harris, accompanied by Mr. and Mrs. Ogden, are engaged in conversation and are in no rush to board the ship. Floyd Ogden, a tall, grey-haired man who possesses an untamed charm, takes his wife, Diane's hand and winks to her. He leans towards the Harris's and whispers.

Soon, more of the upper class travellers gather with them. The Captain and the Lieutenant look down at the dock to see what the problem is. In the background, the Peters family can be seen approaching the group. Captain Mcbaine is anxious to get the Rose underway. The group now begins to proceed up the gangway. As they are stepping aboard the ship, the Ogden's greet the Captain and the Lieutenant. They are followed by the Harris's. The two couples stand aside. The Peters family nervously reach the top of the ship's deck with their three children.

Floyd Ogden removes his top hat and steps closer to the Captain. Mr. Ogden smiles as he says, "Captain, Sir, I would like to introduce you to the Peterson family."

The Captain and Lieutenant conceal their grins and shake hands with the entire Peterson family. The three children cling to their mother's dress. They are speechless and filled with fear. Tears roll off their sombre faces, not knowing if they will sleep on the ship or the streets of Prestwick tonight. The tension for the humbled family is extreme.

"Please pay the Collection Master for passage, Mr. Peterson," says the Captain with a smile.

Captain Mcbaine and the Lieutenant continue to welcome passengers. The group with the Peterson family proceeds to the Collection Officer, where they all take money out of their thick wallets, and contribute for the passage for the Peterson family. They shake hands, and the females offer hugs to each other. Mrs. Peterson, unable to contain herself, begins crying and is comforted by her husband.

Mr. and Mrs. Evens step onto the deck of the Sara Rose for the first time with their daughter. Mr. Evens introduces his daughter and his wife to the Captain and the Lieutenant. The Lieutenant is rather taken with the smiling Susannah. She closes her umbrella, and the two begin to talk. The Captain interrupts the conversation between the two.

"Lieutenant, please show the Evens to their cabins then report back to me."

Matthew is in the galley and notices the Evens family being shown to their cabin. He steps to the doorway. His eyes are entranced by Susannah. As she passes, Susannah looks back at Matthew and smiles. His admiring gaze is rewarded.

The Lieutenant returns in time to begin checking in the steerage passengers who are starting to board the ship. There is no idle chit chat as they board. The Lieutenant sees the pretty Frances on the gangway accompanied by her two younger brothers, followed by their father. Mr. Cunningham and his sons are carrying a few wrapped bundles of select wood. This material will be used in making violins and mandolins. The long voyage ahead will be an opportunity to get a few instruments made and perhaps sold.

The blushing Lieutenant is nervous; his mind is hard at work as he struggles to think of the right words to say to Frances before she steps on deck.

The moment has arrived. The internal jitters and racing emotions of the Lieutenant cause him embarrassment. He begins to tip his cap to Frances, but in his fidgety state when he reaches for his cap, he clumsily knocks it off his head to the deck. Flustered, the red-faced Lieutenant bends to pick up the cap, and his sabre hits Second Mate Quinn on the backside of his trousers. Mr. Quinn suddenly jumps and spins around as foul sailor language erupts from his lips.

The nearby crew and passengers next to the gangway burst out in a roar of laughter. Some begin to clap, for the precious moment has given the sailors a sense of belonging together. The crew quickly turns away from the red-faced Lieutenant as laughing at a commissioned officer is an offence. No crew member would want to be put over the waiting barrel because of this incident.

Frances covers her mouth, for she cannot contain her laughter. In the same instance, she feels for the young Lieutenant. She quickly kicks her brother Joey and gives Neil a stern look. The brothers' laughter quickly changes to grins. This unique young lady curtsies to the mortified Lieutenant. Everyone who witnessed the event is silenced. Miss Frances is a lady. Newly found emotions now pulse inside her.

Chapter 12

The Sara Rose begins to nudge away from her berth, and Captain Mcbaine salutes the Scottish flag. The St. Andrew's Cross is showing its bright blue and white colours in the morning breeze. Scotland is the Captain's country of birth and memories of his youth begin to flood his mind.

Traffic is hectic, with ships and fishing boats as the Sara Rose cautiously enters the waters of the Firth of Clyde. Captain Mcbaine approaches the Lieutenant. "Sir, hoist the green flag."

"Yes, Sir." The Lieutenant salutes the Captain and proceeds to the main mast waving to a crew member for help. The two men raise the green flag under the Union Jack. The coloured flag will warn other vessels that the Rose is in her proper sea lane and is loaded with cargo, thus having priority.

Captain Mcbaine returns to his cabin and begins to write in the ship's log: *Eighteen days into September, eighteen hundred and fifty-three. The Sara Rose is now leaving the port of Prestwick, Scotland and proceeding westerly on the Firth of Clyde.*

Martin and Matthew are told by the head cook to empty the foul-smelling barrels of kitchen waste into the sea. The two approach the rancid barrels, looking at each other with a disgusted look on their faces. The steerage passengers at the stern of the ship stay clear. Matthew and Martin are getting taunting comments from their fellow passengers.

The two 'barrel boys,' as they are now referred to by their travelling friends have created an instant following of seagulls. The crying gulls are practically eating out of the young men's hands as they toss the kitchen waste to the sea. The smell of the garbage is no longer offensive to the brothers. The gulls provide everyone at the stern with a fascinating sight, as the trail of gulls stretches out far beyond the stern of the ship.

An eagle swoops down from high above, snatching a seagull in mid-air, carrying it to land for its dinner. Groups of small blackbirds try to force the gulls off course, allowing their teammates a chance at the ship's waste. The gulls are well-trained at obtaining a free meal, and effortlessly catch the waste products in mid-air. The sea has come alive with schools of all different sizes of fish that hug the stern of the ship begging for a free meal.

The sea spurts up pockets of blood like a pulsing organ. Jealous fish attack each other for food, and others kill for spite. These bursts of bubbling blood now attract large sharks, like a meeting-at-sea, is called. The bustling waters leave pockets of red blending into a sea that once was the colour blue.

The sharks kill their prey at random, while the schools of smaller fish disperse into the surrounding waters and regroup into separate colonies, to feed on the sea bottom. The kings of the sea now have complete control of the area. Following nature's instinct, they begin to fight among themselves.

The barrel boys continue their thankless task. Three off duty crewmen come to the stern of the ship. Using the smelly kitchen waste as bait, they cast fishing lines into the lively sea.

The Sara Rose with birds trailing has become the main attraction on the sea. From a distance, it looks as if the Rose is pulling ribbons of squawking birds behind her. The stirring waters, caused by the schools of fish, attract small fishing boats to drop their nets in the ship's wake.

Crew members with their fishing poles have caught the evening meal for the ship's crew and passengers. Several sharks are cleaned and gutted on the deck, and the rhythm of nature will complete its cycle, with the fish entrails being returned to the sea as food.

The sun is directly over the Sara Rose reflecting a sea of sparkles that dance on the tips of the waves and roll quietly against the ship's hull. This sight continuously repeats with the sun retaining its height.

The Captain stands on the helm deck with the First Mate. "It's a great day to be at sea, Mr. Downing." The first mate smiles back as the Isle of Arran can be seen in the upcoming distance.

Mr. Peters, now known as Mr. Peterson, accidentally brushes against Mr. Jones in the gathering crowd to view the Isle. Jones turns and smiles at the nervous Peters, "Well, Peters, it's good to see you again." Peters, with his wife at his side, tips his hat to Jones. The Peters continue their stroll on the deck. Jones takes the cigar out of his mouth and chuckles loudly to make sure others hear him. Floyd Ogden and Ronald Harris happen to notice Jones' reaction to Peters. The two men shake their heads, for they know the issue between Jones and Peters has not been settled.

Matthew and Martin are busy carrying food supplies up from the lower decks for the preparation of the evening meal. Matthew is told by the head cook to get cleaned up and to put on a steward's uniform, for they are short-handed today. Matthew complains to the cook, claiming he is not suited for this position, but the cook overrules him. Martin snickers at Matthew.

* * *

The Sara Rose sails at seventeen knots loaded with cargo. She glides low in the waters of the Firth of Clyde with the winds in her favour. The small town of Whiting Bay can be seen advancing into sight. Her small port cannot accommodate a large ship like the Rose, but easily handles the smaller fishing boats and towed barges. The busy streets zigzag around rock formations. Some houses are built on rocks, while others have stilts under them to support the structures. The town is a pretty sight as seen from the deck of the ship. There is little industry, but it is home to all who live there.

The ship's speed accelerates, and high riggers are called on to perform their magical feat once again. The bow of the vessel splits the sea as if it is her divine right. The glass-like waters shower back to the sea with the vessel finding her stride. The high riggers have an unmatched view of the sea. The Isle of Arran disappears from their sight, and another island appears on the western horizon. Every passing hour brings this island closer. Parker climbs to the crow's nest; the Mull of Kintyre is now on the ship's course.

Third Mate Benjamin Johnson is at the helm of the ship. The coming darkness gradually swallows the setting sun. The Captain salutes the helmsman, and the two men glance over the charts. The Captain uses the ship's sextant to find and mark their position. The sextant is an instrument used by seamen to measure angles between objects to calculate their position. This instrument can also be used to measure the lunar distance of the moon and other objects in the skies, such as stars and planets. The sextant is a vital part of the ship's navigation system, but the crew tend to rely on the Captain's wisdom and experience.

Angelo, an apprentice aboard the ship, lights the lanterns on the railing giving the vessel a surreal appearance as the ship slows for night travel. Angelo stowed away on the Sara Rose when the ship docked in Sarnia, Italy three years ago. Angelo was physically injured when found aboard the Rose, telling the Captain and crew he ran away from home because he could no longer bear the wrath of his father's belt.

Captain Mcbaine appears on deck. He takes a lantern and swings it to attract Parker's attention. Parker calls down from the crow's nest, "All Clear, Captain!"

Captain Mcbaine turns, noticing Matthew and Martin doing chores on deck. He calls the boys over to him, "Well, lads, how are you enjoying your duties?"

"Sir, it is good to be of help, and the extra shillings will be needed once we land in America," answers Martin.

The Captain asks the young men where they are from in England. Matthew replies, "We are from the village of Blackburn in the County of Lancashire."

The Captain nods as he knows this is coal country and a coal town, owned by the mine. He then asks about their family,

"Our father works in the Lancashire mine along with our youngest brother. Mother sews work clothing for the company store. Our two sisters are married to coal miners and have children of their own. Matthew and I laboured in the Lancashire mines since the age of twelve, saving our pennies for passage to America," says Martin.

"What do you plan to do in America when you arrive?"

"We are going to Montana to work on a ranch. Miners whom we worked with told us stories of kin that went to Montana and became cowboys," excitedly says Matthew.

The Captain smiles at the young men, "You're on a great adventure." He takes his pipe in his hand, "Follow your dreams, lads. You will never regret it."

The Lieutenant is making his nightly rounds and says, 'Good Evening' to the Captain and the two young men when passing. Entering the galley, he pours himself a cup of tea and proceeds to the lounge area. A game of chance is being dealt. Peters stands near the players with his eyes piercing down at the table. His mind is captivated by the cards, and an intense desire rises from deep inside. Peters can almost feel his fingertips caressing the cards. The rush of emotions causes his pulse to race, and beads of perspiration form on his forehead. He requires air and opens his dry mouth. Peters is deaf to the sounds surrounding him. His mind continues to concentrate on the cards when suddenly he is startled by a tap on his shoulder. Peters guiltily turns to find Mrs. Peters standing there. He nervously straightens his hat and listens to her lively conversation.

Jones is sipping on a tall glass of spirits and watches from a distance. His keen mind is not on the cards, but on the players. His searing look memorizes the eyes of the cardholders. He jots down notes on each player in a notebook. The cigar ashes continually fall on his clothing and the floor, for it is seldom the cigar leaves his mouth.

The female passengers from the upper decks are in small groups in the lounge area. Some are knitting, while others walk the deck and speak of their positions in the community and their husbands' wealth. Most sip tea, although a few will whisper to the steward to add a touch of rum, to take away the chill of the night air.

The little mouse is very anxious this night to find its dinner. The activity on the decks of the Sara Rose has given the mouse little chance for exploration of the ship. Fears of the broom still haunt the mouse.

At the stern of the ship, Arthur plays his accordion and Jackal accompanies him. A crowd of steerage passengers gathers around to listen. The travellers clap to show their appreciation of the talents of the two men. A dark-haired lady in the crowd removes the rolled cigarette from her mouth. Only her front teeth are visible. She calls to Jackal, "Hey Matey, play, The Hangman's Jig."

The crowd encourages Arthur and Jackal to play the tune. Arthur stands to play the accordion, knowing this is a lively tune. Jackal's magic bow slides across the strings of the violin with speed and grace. The dark-haired lady begins to dance the jig. "Go, Molly, go!" calls out a steerage passenger as she grabs a shy middle-aged man. The crowds cheer them on. Molly, a feisty lady, is now doing The Hangman's Jig alone for her dance partner disappeared back into the group. The faster Arthur and Jackal play their instruments, the faster Molly dances. The crowd now surrounds her, and the braver men take turns dancing the jig with the spirited Molly.

Joey and Neil, along with Frances, come up from the lower deck. They can hear the excitement, but cannot see because of the people gathered. The crowd now lets out a loud cheer as the music stops. Molly, soaked with sweat, gives Arthur a big hug. Arthur, the ageing seaman, is delighted with Molly's reaction and hands her a drink of rum from his tin cup. The crowd slowly disperses, and the three youngsters greet Jackal when he puts his violin down. Neil cannot contain his excitement and tells Jackal that his father is now making him a mandolin and promises to make Joey a violin before they reach America.

"Where did you lads learn to play the violin and mandolin?" asks Jackal.

"As you know, our father makes string instruments, and he taught us," says Neil.

Jackal senses what Joey wants and hands over his violin to the youngster. Frances and Neil take a seat next to Jackal. Joey begins to play, **'Nearer My God to Thee.'** The notes bleed off the violin in the youngster's hands. The steerage passengers now regroup around Joey. The only sound heard is that of this magical instrument. This comforting perfection in Joeys hands calms the sea. The weeping violin causes tears in the travellers' minds, as thoughts of loved ones and the homeward winds stir emotions.

The strings of the violin in this talented youngster's hands have seduced the night, causing the darkness to paint its way into the surroundings. The dim moon sheds its tears in the form of rain and retracts its beauty behind the cover of a forest of clouds. The prism effect of the moonlight dazzles the steerage passengers into a subtle weakness.

Chapter 13

The little mouse makes its rounds in the darkness, closely hugging the walls. It drinks from the puddle on the deck as the dripping barrel continues to leak. Not enjoying the smelly fish that was laying on the floor at dinner, the rodent slowly creeps its way into the galley for a sweeter treat. Climbing in and out of the open cupboards it finds a brick of bread. The ship's little stowaway is now in its glory. It nibbles through the crust and enters the moist softness of the bread.

The morning finds the Sara Rose anchored off the coast of the Mull of Kintyre. The turn into the North Channel is a daylight venture, and the Captain is up at daybreak, calling for the great anchor to be raised. The high riggers perform their dangerous duties, with the morning dew clinging to the ship. Slowly awakening to a new day, the ship creaks and sways as it begins its trek in a northern direction.

The galley comes alive. Water is on the stove for tea, and tin cups jingle while being placed on the counter.

The little mouse awakens to the sound of the tin cups. Instantly it realizes that it fell asleep during its dinner. The mouse has nowhere to hide, for the open cupboards offer no protection. It can run across the deck and take a chance or wait until the sounds quiet. The clever rodent slips into the hole it made in the brick of bread. It hides there, thinking; if it sees no one, then no one can see it.

Matthew is wearing a steward's uniform while helping in the kitchen and dining areas. Martin continues to work in the galley and is sent to fetch food stocks from the storage lockers

Matthew cautiously peeks around the lounge corner to see if Susannah Evens is present. There is no sign of her or her family. The nervous Matthew places the chairs around the dining tables. He hears the sound of a sharp whistle and senses that Martin is calling for his attention. Matthew looks back to the galley area and sees Martin and one of the stewards making fun of him. All the galley workers know Matthew is smitten with the young lady in first-class.

The young Lieutenant enters the galley with his trusty sabre at his side and asks a steward for a cup of tea. He walks through the kitchen and dining area, sipping his tea as he inspects the stewards' uniforms and the table settings. He hands the empty teacup to Matthew. "Sir, button up your collar!"

The sound of the galley bell rings through the deck and lounge area. Breakfast is served in the dining room. The gentlemen help their wives to be seated. The children stay in the lounge area and play. A steward brings in a tray of breakfast samplings for the children.

Matthew turns, seeing Lieutenant Rodgers escorting the pretty Susannah to the Captain's table in the dining room. Mr. and Mrs. Evens follow them to the table.

The Lieutenant pulls out a chair for Miss Evens and then quickly seats her mother, Aggie. Now the dashing Lieutenant flashes a smile that lights up the entire dining room when Susannah and Mrs. Evens thank him. Donald Evens, a rugged individual and a very independent man, calls to the steward for tea before he sits down. The blue-eyed Lieutenant remains standing until Mr. Evens seats himself. He then removes his Lieutenant's cap and sits across the table from Miss Evens.

Susannah is very impressed with Lieutenant Rodgers and smiles at him. His blonde hair and captivating eyes hold her attention — the brass buttons on his uniform sparkle in the morning light. Aggie Evens notices her daughter's attraction to the Lieutenant. Donald Evens looks at his wife startled when he receives a slight kick from under the table.

Matthew's hopes are crushed, and his self-esteem is in a state of uncertainty. The stewards begin serving breakfast to the first-class passengers. Some have tea with a cut of bread, while others prefer a large meal. The tables have fresh fruit since restocking of the ship's supplies was just a day ago at Prestwick.

The Lieutenant is being polite and sips tea. He is truly delighted to be in the company of Miss Evens. Mr. and Mrs. Evens are having a cut of pork with roasted potatoes. Donald raises his hand and calls to a steward, "Bring me some bread, please, and more tea."

Haydn, one of the stewards working this area goes to the galley for the tea, "Matthew, grab that brick of bread and come with me."

Matthew, a bit uncomfortable in a steward's uniform, complies and follows Haydn. Matthew is surprised to arrive at the Evens' dining table, where he nervously stands. Haydn pours the tea.

Matthew's eyes are focused on Susannah. The scent of the perfume she is wearing excites his mind and coats his heart with an indescribable desire. There is a sudden weakness in his knees. His trembling hands set the brick of bread on the table. Susannah smiles at him, and their eyes connect. Matthew's eyes have become intoxicated with Susannah's beauty. The blood in his veins pulses to new heights.

Susannah is rather taken with Matthew. Her hand presses against her chest. She scarcely dares to breathe. For her, time has stopped. Then the little mouse jumps out from its hiding spot from inside the brick of bread. The mouse is terrified. In a courageous attempt to escape it suddenly jumps off the table. The Lieutenant lunges back in his chair and quickly stands to brush the mouse off his uniform. In the excitement, the Lieutenant's sabre catches the dining table and jars it enough to spill Miss Evens hot tea onto her lap.

The rodent falls hard to the floor. It quickly regains its balance and hides under the table. The frightened mouse is now staring at a dozen feet. It begins a chant as if it were saying its prayers for the last time.

Donald Evens cannot contain himself and breaks out into loud laughter. Mrs. Evens begins to giggle into her handkerchief like a school girl. Susannah is embarrassed by the spillage of tea on her lap and breaks out in tears.

Matthew is stunned by the event that just played out and backs into another dining table. He quickly runs into the kitchen for clean towels to wipe Susannah's dress. The red-faced Lieutenant stands motionless, not knowing what to do. He quickly picks his cap off the floor and attempts to apologize to Miss Evens for his clumsiness. Susannah begins to cry harder. Mrs. Evens, who is still snickering into her handkerchief, puts her arm around her daughter to console her.

Captain Mcbaine enters the room and is puzzled as to why everyone is laughing. He sees Susannah Evens in tears. His Lieutenant stands dumbfounded, with his face flushed. "Mr. Rodgers, report to the helmsman, immediately!"

Matthew arrives with the clean towels and stands awkwardly, not knowing what to do. On an impulse, Matthew drops to one knee. He gently wipes the tears off Susannah's cheeks with the clean towel, and for an instant, the world ceases to exist. The two are suddenly captivated by each other. Susannah's hand embraces Matthew's hand. In wonder, they gaze into each other's eyes, oblivious to everyone in the room. For a moment, they share only one heartbeat. The dining room suddenly quiets to a hush. Donald Evens gives his wife a gentle kick under the table. Aggie is silent and understands what her daughter is feeling.

Breaking the silence, the dining room passengers stand and clap for the young man in the steward's uniform, who aided the young lady in tears. Matthew straightens himself. He is surprised at what he has just done and quickly retreats to the kitchen. Haydn is there to greet him and gives Matthew a friendly slap on the back for his good deed.

The little mouse under the table knows it has to make a break for home. It ponders. Its instincts point the direction. The mouse's courage forces it to run across Mrs. Evens' foot, causing her to rise to her feet in a split second. Mrs. Evens lets out a nervous scream, grasping her dress in shock. The rodent scoots across the planked floor of the dining room. The mouse does not look back.

Again, Donald Evens breaks out into a mischievous laugh, pointing to his wife holding her dress and checking to see where the mouse ran. Susannah is caught up in the event and joins in the laughter.

Captain Mcbaine is not sure what to make of what has just happened. He joins the passengers in a moment of laughter as the little mouse runs off. The Captain seats himself with the Evens family. Donald, still not in full control of his laughter, continues to chuckle.

74

Susannah's eyes focus on the kitchen, but she cannot see Matthew anywhere. Haydn comes from the kitchen with a pot of fresh tea and a cup for the Captain. Susannah is anxious to ask where Matthew has gone, but instead, she holds her silence.

Matthew is on the starboard side of the ship. His mind is miles from him. He daydreams of reasons why a young lady like Susannah would desire him. He feels lost and empty inside, like an empty bottle thrown to the sea, drifting endlessly in search of an answer.

"Hey, Matthew, wait for me," requests Martin. "Haydn told me that you caused more than a bit of excitement in the dining room."

"Yes, I certainly did."

"You better go find that mouse and thank him before a broom gets him," chuckles Martin.

The two brothers joke together while walking away.

Chapter 14

The Captain and the First Mate plot a new course for the northern Isle of Lewis and the town of Stornoway, Scotland. The ship has fallen behind schedule, but the westerly winds are now in their favour. This will be a first voyage for the Sara Rose and her crew, other than Arthur, to the port of Stornoway. Captain Mcbaine knew in advance, that the vessel would venture to the northern Isle.

The rules of the sea are that only the Captain knows the next port of call prior to the ship's departure, but the cargo and inventory are written orders in a sealed envelope. The Captain's orders are opened a day later, when the ship returns to sea from the last port of call. Reading directives after leaving port prevents plots of mutiny, kidnapping or spying.

Captain Mcbaine closes his cabin door behind him and steps across the room to the ship's hidden safe. He opens the safe, taking out the orders marked 'Stornoway.' Breaking the seal, he opens the envelope and seats himself.

The Captain's orders are clear. He is to proceed directly to the port of Stornoway. The Sara Rose is commissioned by an unknown source to receive and deliver seven-sealed crates of Viking artifacts. The Isle of Lewis was once a critical Viking settlement, and now these precious artifacts will be in the care of Captain Mcbaine.

The warm sun and consistent sea breeze, this twentieth day into September, have the Sara Rose sailing in a northwesterly direction. The tip of Jura Islay is seen by Jimmy Brown from his post in the crow's nest. The ship meets the waters of the Sound of Jura, where the calm sea joins the Atlantic Ocean.

The warm autumn day has most of the passenger's topside to enjoy the sunshine. Neil Cunningham finally has the new mandolin that his father made for him. His father, Joseph, helps Neil tune the instrument. Joey and Frances sit and listen while Neil practises.

Molly, the dark-haired lady who had previously enjoyed dancing a jig, walks up to Neil. "Matey, will you play me a jig tonight?"

Neil looks up at Molly and smiles. Molly smiles back with only her two front teeth showing. She then walks to Joseph Cunningham and says, "You have a fine litter of young ones."

Joseph smiles back and says, "Thank you. My name is Joseph."

The happy-go-lucky Molly grabs Joseph's hand and shakes it heartily, "Most that like me, call me Molly."

Arthur approaches the Lieutenant. "Mr. Rodgers, Sir, I think I saw a stowaway in the food bin, in the hull of the ship."

"Get a few men together and find our stowaway." says the Lieutenant in a stern voice.

Arthur turns and walks toward the steps of the lower decks. On the way, he sees Thomas Quinn, the apprentice. Arthur asks young Thomas to join him. At the bottom of the stairwell, Hardie is talking to Randel, a crew member. Randel is a tall, lanky sailor who always looks out of place because of his height and thin body. He regularly has a pipe hanging from his mouth and wears a toque-shaped cap. His arms are always in motion, resembling a leafless tree standing in the wind.

Arthur and Thomas reach the bottom of the steps. Arthur begins to speak, "Matey, we have a stowaway on board the ship. Hardie, take the lanterns. You and Randel search the keel of the ship and the food storage bins. Thomas and I will head off to the cargo holding area."

Even with the help of lanterns, these areas of the ship are dark. There are many hiding places, and a stowaway can blend himself into the steerage section very quickly if need be. The ship's movement on the waters causes its keel and holding areas to creak in an eerie manner. The darkness in which the men are searching makes seeing anything or anyone almost impossible. They must rely on their senses of touch and hearing. Arthur and Thomas call to one another, for they must always know where the other is in this silent dungeon of darkness. They listen carefully to each other's sounds and footsteps as they slowly move around the large bundles of cargo.

Hardie and Randel are in the bow area at the keel of the ship. They try to be quiet, but Randel becomes tangled among the chains and leg irons that are piled in a corner. The tall, lanky Randel manages to get his foot out of the tangled chains. He now calls Hardie to bring over his lantern to help find his boot. The two men cannot contain themselves and begin to laugh. They both sit on the pile of chains, and Randel relights his pipe.

"Matey, this is hopeless. We can't see your big boot, never mind that stowaway," comments Hardie.

The excitable Randel swiftly replies, "And that big boot of mine is bigger than any stowaway. Now, help me find my boot, before the varmints down here eat my toes off."

The two men spread apart the chains that have concealed Randel's boot. Hardie hands his shipmate the boot, "Matey, here is that oversized boot of yours. Put it on before the stowaway or the ship's ghost trip over it," laughs Hardie. They give up the hunt for the stowaway and start for the stern of the ship. They hold their lanterns high, so as not to bump into any of the cargo or containers piled in the walk area. Randel calls out for Arthur and Thomas. The voice of young Thomas can be heard. "Over here, Matey!"

Randel and Hardie walk toward the voice.

"Arrr! Matey! Talk to me!" shouts Hardie into the darkness. The two men begin to feel uneasy. There is no one to be seen, and no one is answering them.

Randel quietly comments to Hardie, "Arrr! The Devil himself would not want to be here." The only sound heard is the creak of the ship, carving her way along the open sea.

The two men stop and hold their lanterns higher. Hardie calls out, "All right! Where are you devils?"

The light of the flickering lantern finds no one in its view. The two men become silenced by the stillness that surrounds them. Their minds race, the hair on the back of their necks stands on end and chills are sent down their backs. A sudden tap on Randel's shoulder sends him jumping into the darkness, and his lantern falls from his hand. Randel emits a boyish squeal as if his boots are on fire. The over-excited man gasps for air, as he turns to see Thomas standing there laughing at him. In an instant, Hardie's streak of meanness prevails. He cuffs the young Thomas across the face with his left hand.

Arthur comes from the darkness, "None of that, Hardie." Hardie walks towards the stairs with his lantern and returns to the top deck of the ship. Randel, who is now composed, helps Thomas to his feet. Arthur is upset and mutters to himself. "That damn Hardie! One day he will meet his justice, and I hope I am there to witness it."

The sun finds shade among the gathering clouds. The Rose continues to skim over the water on this warm fall day. Her graceful motion on the sea is a sight to behold, with Port Ellen seen from the ship's deck. The clean, fresh sea air sweeps among the passengers who are on deck absorbing the view. The racing breezes give the Union Jack a reason to wave its colours to the onlookers from the port.

The Lieutenant continues on his rounds of the ship. He is ever so watchful of the steerage section, looking for Miss Frances, but she is nowhere to be seen. Mr. Rodgers heads through the galley and takes a tin of tea. Entering the lounge area, he notices Matthew cleaning tables. He approaches Matthew calmly, "Sir, I must apologize for my behaviour the other day."

Matthew stops his work and replies, "It was all my fault. I should have checked the brick of bread before I brought it to the table."

The Lieutenant comments, "Yes, you should have, and I hope there will not be a next time, Sir."

"I will try my best Lieutenant," humbly says, Matthew.

"Good!" exclaims the Lieutenant, walking into the deck area of the upper class passengers. He sees Mr. Evens and his wife with their daughter, Susannah. In the hopes of not being seen by them, he turns back through the lounge area and continues down to the next level of the ship.

* * *

Port Ellen fades into the distance, and the coastline of Islay now holds the passenger's attention. Islay is sparsely populated, and there is no sign of homes or other dwellings. No wildlife is seen in the forests, nor are there any visible birds. Not even a gull trails the ship in these eerie waters. The skies hold the ghost-like clouds over the island. Islay is open to the Atlantic Ocean on three of her sides and supports a large bay open to the west. The great northerly and westerly winds show this small island no mercy come winter. From the deck of the ship, the passengers can see the vast forests of tall spruce, with protruding oak and ash trees. The rough shores of this island have an outline of large jagged rocks, all in a dull lifeless colour of grey. The harsh Atlantic waves seem to have cast a spell on this unprotected island, slamming time and time again into its cold coastline. This untamed landscape of Mother Nature sends a chill down everyone's spine, and loneliness sets in with the setting sun.

Islay is slowly fading into the darkness as the ship races to escape the clutches of this eerie island, with the calling of the open sea.

The usually happy-go-lucky Molly is concerned when she notices Martin bent over with his harsh cough. She hands him a handkerchief. "Martin, take this and breathe through it. Matthew, take Martin below. This night sea air is not good for your brother." says the motherly Molly.

"Yes, I've noticed he starts coughing more when night comes. I will find the ship's doctor once I get Martin settled down. Thank you, Molly."

Night has returned to the deck of the vessel. The Captain meets with the helmsman, Third Mate Johnson, to discuss the current route. This northern voyage to Stornoway is a first for all on board, except for the older Arthur. Captain Mcbaine calls on the young Thomas to fetch Arthur. The concern for the Captain this night is icebergs, for a rogue berg can destroy a ship in a matter of moments.

The night crew are on full alert, and Jimmy Brown is in the crow's nest. Jimmy is in constant communication with the helmsman. The men have fashioned long poles with lanterns tied to them. They are hoisted in the air at forty-five-degree angles over the edge of the ship to give the crew better vision at night. An approaching iceberg will reflect its ghostly appearance to the ship like a mirror. Every few minutes a crew member will call out to sea with a loud 'Ahoy!' If another vessel or iceberg is close, the sound will echo back to the Sara Rose. Hopefully, the helmsman would have time to turn the ship in a safe direction, thus avoiding a significant incident.

In the dining area, first-class passengers are seated for their evening meal. Second-class wait in the lounge area. Jones usually sits at a separate table, for his eating habits are closely aligned with his moral habits. He puffs on his cigar between bites of food, and there is often tea or rum dripping from his sneering face. The stewards are frustrated by the presence of Jones, for he constantly calls on them, and continually criticizes their efforts.

Children run in and out of the dining area, stopping at Jones table and making faces at him. Jones gives them an evil look that would scare Satin himself. Occasionally Jones will throw pieces of bread at them. The passengers in the dining area look upon the daily event as entertainment and chuckle to themselves.

Chapter 15

Tempting smells radiate in the air as the mouse remains backed into its favourite corner. It cannot let cravings control its behaviour. The little stowaway remains terrified by the memory of its last expedition that almost caused its demise.

Matthew returns to Martin's bunk with the ship's doctor. Dr. Eden asks, "How are you this evening, Martin? Did the medicine I gave you last week help at all?"

"Yes Doctor, the cough medicine did help," claims Martin in a raspy voice, sitting up in his bed. "But I ran out of medicine a few days ago."

Dr. Eden reaches into his bag for his stethoscope and listens to Martin's chest. The doctor begins to explain Martin's condition to him. "Martin, your lungs must heal. Avoid the cool, wet, sea air as much as possible. Always breathe slowly and into a clean handkerchief when you have a coughing spell. Take it easy on this last bottle of medicine. Hopefully, I can acquire more at our next port of call," calmly states the doctor, picking his bag up off the bed.

Dr. Eden finds his way back to the deck of the ship and knocks on the Captain's cabin door. Captain Mcbaine opens the door and greets the doctor.

"Good to see you, Doctor. What brings you this evening?" asks the Captain.

"Well, Sir, it's the young lad, Martin." comments the Doctor. "I am worried about him. His lungs are weak, and conditions in steerage are deplorable. It is not only the dampness, but the lack of cleanliness is a factor."

The Captain shakes his head slowly and replies, "Yes, I have noticed the young lad coughing several times, but Sir what can I do? Martin paid for a steerage passage, and there he must remain. All sick steerage would demand better accommodations when they are not feeling well, and this would result in an uproar from the first-class passengers. That would cause complete havoc on board my ship!" explains the Captain.

"Yes, I see your logic Captain; I will keep you posted on his condition," states the doctor.

"Doctor, what is the condition of my men who were in contact with, and serviced by the prisoner, Katie?"

"Well, Sir. As you know, I treated all the men, including Hazleton. He was the last visitor of Katie, and his infection was severe, the medicine had no effect."

"Why is that?"

"Hazleton's contact with Katie was more intense. He is infected with Katie's blood. There is nothing I can do for him; he is in the hallucinating state. It's just a matter of time before Katie's wrath takes Hazleton."

* * *

The Captain steps up on the helm deck; Third Mate Johnson is in control of the ship's wheel tonight. "Sir, how is the sea this night?"

"The sea has found its bed tonight and now rests," replies Johnson.

The Captain turns to Arthur, "Sir, you once told me you were aboard the 'Scarlett' when she sailed to Lewis and the port of Stornoway."

"Yes," replies Arthur with assurance and continues, "I reckon it was in eighteen hundred and thirty-nine, if I recall correctly, Captain. It was the Scarlett, and it was in the spring of that year, under the command of Captain Perkins."

"What was the route the Scarlett took to Stornoway that spring?" asks the Captain.

Arthur begins pointing out the route on the Captain's map, then pauses momentarily, "We sailed the coastline and stayed east of Coll. Then we anchored in the bay of Mull for the night to avoid the icebergs. We saved two days of travel by this route, instead of the Firth of Lorne passage."

"Very good, Arthur, thank you." says the Captain in his firm voice. "We will have to judge the sea winds come the morning." The Captain lights his pipe and continues, "We better get some rest tonight, for dawn's early light will be calling."

"Aye, Captain. A good night, Sir."

"Oh, by the way, Arthur. Have you captured the stowaway?"

"No Sir, but I'll get him," smiles Arthur.

* * *

Night once again descends upon the planked deck of the Sara Rose, and the cool air invites the darkness to join in and hide where the eyes of men fear to look. The sharp smell of tar seeps from the deck below where the crew had patched a leak at the stern. This nauseating smell causes the rodent's eyes to water, and the odour slowly drifts into its stomach. Now the unsure mouse moves out of the hole in the wall. Its shaky legs move clumsily, for the mouse is still terrified from its last experience. The mouse regains its self-confidence and makes its way among the legs of the chairs and tables. Its natural instincts return, and it stops every few seconds. Then it begins to nibble on a small piece of discarded cheese and bread. Quickly it stops eating, because its stomach seems to be revolving. Coughing out the cheese and bread; feeling weak and faint, it breathes faster. The wobbly little mouse returns to its home.

Matthew remains at Martin's bedside in the steerage area of the ship. The two are watching Joey and Neil Cunningham playoff in a game of checkers. The smell of stale smoke from men's pipes fills the sagging air and causes all to squint in the poorly lit area. The sound of snoring men echoes along the wooden beams. Those still awake try to block out this annoying symphony. A strange odour exuding from the steerage area is not spoken of as conditions are less than desirable.

Susannah is alone in her cabin and cannot find sleep. Tossing and turning, she seeks consolation from her pillow. Her constant thoughts are of Matthew and how he wiped the tears from her cheeks. Susannah is frustrated and dresses. She puts on a soft blue dress, knowing there is a matching bonnet in one of the boxes. She pulls down the box she believes contains a match to the dress. She removes the lid from the box and places the violet-blue bonnet on the bed. With a linen handkerchief in her hand, she softly brushes off the dust then pauses as if something is wrong. Her hand can feel something in the band that holds the flowered arrangement together. Susannah's fingertips fumble, finding a penny in the band of her bonnet. Puzzled, she moves closer to the lantern. An old worn penny is in her hand with the initial 'M' inscribed on it. She rolls the penny in her hand, recalling the last time she wore this bonnet. She remembers it was the day they arrived at the dock at Prescott.

Susannah holds the engraved coin tighter in her hand. The slow rocking of the ship puts her at ease. Her internal emotions begin to embrace the moment. The flickering lantern dims and her heart knows from whom the worn coin came.

Susannah sits on the bed. Her heart is racing in a manner to which she is unaccustomed. She squeezes the coin in both hands against her chest and looks at her hat on the bed. This special moment takes her into womanhood. Silent thoughts romance her mind, and a teardrop finds her cheek.

Susannah returns the bonnet to its box. She puts a light blue shawl over her hair and shoulders, leaving the warmth of her cabin. Climbing the stairs to the main deck of the ship, her left hand grasps the linen handkerchief with the engraved penny wrapped tightly in it. She walks through the empty lounge, in the dim light to the starboard side of the ship. Holding the railing of the ship with her right hand, Susannah stares at the moonlit sea, night dreaming of what the future has in store for her.

The reflecting waters cast a continuous glow on this young beauty. Her golden hair flirts with the night breezes. Her hand clasps the engraved penny, as one would hold a diamond. Perhaps she has found the diamond that will sparkle in her thoughts and life forever. Susannah closes her eyes as tears find her cheeks. The Heavens open and release a falling star.

* * *

The grey dawn slowly yields to the oncoming light, and the dull skies begin to rule the morning. The air is fresh with dampness soaking into the aged, worn wood of the vessel.

The Captain orders his First Mate to prepare the ship. First Mate Downing relays the orders to Parker in the crow's nest. Parker shouts the orders to each rigger. Their work this morning is slowed by the damp conditions. These fearless men seldom worry about safety, but the lingering dew has them tying themselves to the masts and cross arms of sails.

The cold, choppy waters this early morning prompt the crew to work quickly to get the ship to her maximum speed. Parker remains in the crow's nest scanning the sea for icebergs. Acting on Arthur's advice, the Captain's plans to sail to the island group of Mulls, where the Islands of Tiree and Coll will offer them protection during the night.

The Sara Rose is far out to sea, coastlines have disappeared like an illusion, leaving a shroud of fog where land once was. Angelo climbs to the crow's nest, allowing Parker to take a break from his post. Parker enters into the galley, pours himself a fresh tin of hot tea, rips a large chunk off a brick of bread, then proceeds to the stern of the ship. There he sits with Jackal and young Thomas Quinn. A discussion of the morning's weather quickly ensues.

Jackal comments to Parker, "Mate, I suppose you saw me hanging like a fish out of water when the wind slipped me off the spar."

Parker observes the nervous Jackal, whose hands are slightly trembling, holding his tin cup close to his lips. "Yes Jackal, this is your lucky day for the Devil himself almost had you. You best be keeping an eye out for him," smiles Parker. "Thomas, go climb to the nest and check on Angelo. This is Angelo's first time to be alone looking to the sea. Ring the bell if there is trouble looking back to you."

Most of the first and second-class passengers are in the lounge area when the lunch bell sounds. Martin and Matthew are on their way to the ship's stern for the unpleasant duty of cleaning fish.

Matthew suddenly stops; a violet-blue umbrella has captured his attention. His eyes widen, his mind wants this to be Susannah. His heart races and he begins to feel faint. Susannah turns, the umbrella immediately stops twirling. Matthew and Susannah have their eyes focused on one another from across the ship. They are both motionless and time has stopped. Their minds are in awe, silence prevails, and uncontrolled emotions enter.

Aggie Evens is watching from a distance and approaches Susannah. Understanding what just took place between the two, she places her hand gently on her daughter's forearm. Susannah's fluttering heart floods her mind with warm thoughts and desires. She struggles to compose herself. Her cheeks glow, and her eyes sparkle. She turns to her mother with an innocent smile, and the words are lost in her girlish giggle. Aggie grasps her daughter's arm tighter in approval of what she has witnessed. Mother and daughter make their way to the dining area, followed by Donald Evens, who is unaware of the scene that has just unfolded.

Donald Evens tips his hat to Jones, who sits at a corner table by himself. Nodding back, as if he were in pain, Jones has an irritable look about him. The cigar in his mouth is short and is burning his lips. He tosses it to the floor of the deck and waves to a steward to light his fresh one.

Matthew daydreams while he helps Martin with the cleaning of the freshly caught shark. The smell from the fish saturates the air. Martin begins to cough, and he backs away when the fish is cut open. Matthew quickly guts the shark and disposes of the waste over the stern's edge; then the two young men carry off the cleaned fish to the galley. Matthew's eyes scan the deck for Susannah, but she is nowhere to be seen.

Chapter 16

The crow's nest bell suddenly rings out, sending the crew members into a state of panic. They run to the port and starboard sides of the ship to see what lies in their path. Parker hurries to the mast and quickly climbs the spar to the crow's nest. The two young apprentices, Angelo and Thomas, cannot control their anxiety as they point in the direction of an iceberg. Parker calls out, "Iceberg ahead. Iceberg ahead."

The Captain rushes to the helm. First Mate Downing and the Captain go over their options. The Lieutenant rushes to the walkway on the bow of the ship and views the single iceberg in his spyglass. The Lieutenant calls back to the helm, "She's a beauty, and she's alone."

"Turn the Rose to the north and into the wind," briskly orders Captain Mcbaine.

Parker slaps Angelo on the back, "Good eye, Lad. The two of you go down to the deck. You will be needed. I will take the watch now."

The Sara Rose slowly begins to turn into the wind as Helmsman Downing manoeuvres the ship's wheel. The high riggers take their positions. "Lieutenant," shouts the Captain, "Are we running north or sliding?"

"Sliding, Captain," calls back the Lieutenant in a high-pitched voice.

The ship is slowly sliding on the sea to the northeast, in the direction of the iceberg. The turn to the north and into the wind is a correct move by the ship's handlers, but the undercurrents of the Atlantic now control the Rose. Only an experienced Captain realizes what the seas are capable of and how to overcome the situation.

The upper class passengers peer over the starboard side of the ship to catch a glimpse of the iceberg. Matthew and Martin are in the galley carving the shark into steaks when they hear of the excitement. Matthew knows this is his chance to mingle with the first-class guests and perhaps speak to Susannah. He quickly washes and puts on his steward uniform. Matthew takes a tray and a pot of tea and walks among the guests.

Jones, puffing on a cigar, is quietly talking to his friend Flynn. Both men are standing and looking out to sea, keeping their conversation private. Flynn tips his hat and backs away from Jones, quietly disappearing into the crowd. The devious Jones stands alone with his walking cane, blowing smoke into the restless northern wind. He calls to the steward for a cup of rum and Matthew answers his call. Matthew weaves his way through the crowd with Jones' order, continually scanning the deck for a glimpse of Susannah.

* * *

"Lieutenant, what is our progress?" calls out the Captain.

"The Sara Rose is still on her slide, Sir," replies the nervous Lieutenant.

Captain Mcbaine now steps off the helm hurriedly and shouts to the crow's nest, "Parker, what is your observation?"

"The Rose is still into her slide Sir," answers Parker.

The Captain quickly commands to the crew, "All hands-on deck! All hands-on deck! Now!"

This Master of the Sea strokes his bearded face with his left hand and nervously steps towards the helm. His years at sea tell him that the vessel is in danger. The sliding effect of the sea continually takes the ship in a direct line toward the iceberg. The Captain calls out in a firm voice, "Turn the foremast to a degree of forty-five and hold her there! Riggers, drop sails one and two from the spar on the port side! Be quick! Mr. Downing, turn the Rose into the berg!"

These rapid actions enforced on the Sara Rose cause the ship to sway suddenly. Most of the passengers lose their balance momentarily. This movement of the ship brings the steerage passengers to the stern area to see what is taking place. The Cunningham family is topside, along with their steerage friends. Everyone stands silent, in awe of the iceberg, the Sara Rose is trying to avoid.

"Mates, bring the foremast back slowly! Back to a degree of thirty. Parker, get them riggers to lower the port mizzenmast to half!" orders the Captain in a calmer voice.

"Aye Aye, Sir!" calls back Parker.

The passengers of the Sara Rose do not realize the possible danger that the ship may be in as the iceberg looms closer. The berg is massive. On the open sea, there is nothing in which to compare its enormous size. From the passengers' vantage point, the berg would tower over the Rose ten-fold in height and has a length that perhaps is twenty-fold that of the ship. From the starboard side of the ship, passengers can see the gigantic berg occasionally release huge pieces of itself back to the sea. These large sections of ice break off and fall, causing the sea to spew a massive surge of water hundreds of feet into the air. Then this shower hovers momentarily over the sea like a rainstorm, making this a magnificent sight to behold. The passengers cheer at this wonder of the sea. The excitement builds as the ship gets closer to the iceberg.

"She's a big berg," calls Parker from the top of the crow's nest to Jimmy Brown, who is on his way up the mast for a view. The two men have the perfect view of this monster on the sea. The Sara Rose continues to claw her way into new water, keeping her distance from the berg.

The Captain loudly asks the Lieutenant, "Are we still sliding, Lieutenant?"

"No, Sir, we are heading due north."

"Good! Lieutenant stay the course and pray that northern wind does not change its mind."

Matthew wanders in and out of the crowd serving tea to the upper deck passengers. "Steward. Steward!" Matthew turns. He is overjoyed to see Susannah. Her eyes instantly widen as her thoughts become jumbled. She is breathless and her left hand unconsciously presses against her chest. Matthew is dumb-struck with his stalled mind incapable of thought.

Susannah's emotions suddenly cause her to feel faint. Matthew puts out his hand to steady her. Susannah grasps his left wrist, then quickly releases her grip and backs away. "I am sorry," she quietly utters.

"No, I am sorry, Miss Evens." A long pause ensues before Matthew replies, "You called for a steward. May I help you?"

Susannah places her hand over her racing heart and softly replies, "Yes, you can help, I would like some tea, please."

Matthew smiles. He holds a tray in front of him and pours a cup of tea for Susannah, "Here you go, Miss Evens."

She takes the teacup in her left hand and slowly sips the tea. Her eyes remain focused on Matthew. "Thank you, Matthew, for the cold tea," giggles Susannah. The seed which has just been planted, will grow into love.

* * *

Aggie Evens tugs at Donald's arm. "See Donald. I told you there was a spark between those two."

"Spark!" Donald exclaims. "I knew it from the beginning when I saw him staring at Susannah over the edge of the boat on the dock in Prestwick."

"You did?" Aggie asks in an excited voice.

"Yes, Aggie, it was the same look I had when I first saw you."

"Oh Donald, now I know why I married you."

The Sara Rose is now directly north of the gigantic iceberg, and the Captain's inner fears have settled. He knows only a small percentage of the iceberg is showing itself. The greater volume of the berg is hiding below the surface of the water.

The Captain calls out, "Take the foremast back to position Mates." He then points up to the riggers, "Ahoy, pull up the mizzenmast to the spar." The Captain strolls over to the starboard side, looking at the impressive iceberg. He can hear the passengers cheer when more of the huge blocks break off the iceberg. The deep sound echoes back to the ship when the blocks of ice collide with the sea. They hold their breath in anticipation of the explosion of massive bursts of water shooting up from the depths of the sea. The passengers raise their hands in time with the motion of the rising rainbows of water shooting upwards. This massive volume of water seems to hang in midair, suspended in time. Then, with perfect timing, the millions of droplets taste the sea air for the first time and shower downward as they are called home.

The curious rodent wakes to the shouting and cheering on deck. It promptly sticks its nose out of the hole in the wall to see what the excitement is about. The rodent ventures out of its secure home clinging to the walls and up onto the railing of the ship. The little stowaway perches itself on its hindquarters, watching in awe as the mystery unfolds.

The Captain looks up at his riggers performing their graceful tasks. "Good work Gentlemen. Now get the port sail up the mast."

"Aye Aye,!" is shouted back from the high riggers.

Captain Mcbaine makes his way to the galley, where he takes two tins of hot tea and proceeds to the helm. "I think you can use a tin of tea, Mr. Downing."

The steerage passengers at times have little about which to cheer, but seeing the breathtaking iceberg has raised their spirits. The Cunningham children are still pointing and jumping up and down while the berg continually sheds its many coats of ice. The excitable Molly approaches Joseph Cunningham. Her smile warms him, and he moves closer to her. He grins to himself as Molly's hand joins his. The ship becomes quiet. Passengers stare at the disappearing iceberg, as one would look at a departing loved one. The joy the moment has brought them will soon fade, but the lasting memory will remain.

Matthew and Susannah are engaged in small talk, standing side by side looking out at the sea. The spectacular performance of this massive iceberg has captured everyone's full attention, and Matthew does not look out of place talking to Susannah. Aggie and Donald occasionally peer over their shoulder in a manner as not to be noticed by their daughter. Aggie takes Donald's hand and whispers into his ear. "He is the one." Donald squeezes Aggie's hand in a way that shows approval of his daughter's choice.

Matthew and Susannah are smitten with each other, and the small talk is more giggles than conversation. The faces of both are flushed, and their bodies sway as they speak. Their minds are a mix of emotions and thoughts. They are hesitant to reveal their inner thoughts to each other.

Matthew knows he could get into trouble for talking to Susannah while on duty, especially if the Lieutenant should notice him. As the moments pass, his nervousness increases. The crowd on the deck is slowly dispersing into the lounge area. Matthew quickly says, "Can you meet me here tonight, at this very spot?"

"I am not sure," says Susannah slightly confused, pausing momentarily then softly saying, "Yes I can. Yes, I will meet you here tonight."

"All right. See you tonight." excitedly replies Matthew, turning to scan the deck to see if anyone has noticed him. He slowly walks back to the lounge area, stopping and turning to see if she is looking back at him. His heart begins sinking to unknown depths. He wants to walk back to her to see her smile again, to hear her voice again. His mind is telling him that he is missing her already. He stops, turns and looks in her direction. Susannah remains looking out to the sea. His chest becomes tight; it seems all his emotions are knotted inside of his stomach.

Susannah has vanished into the crowd without looking back at him. Matthew's mind fills with thoughts of what he should have said to Susannah, instead of what he'd blurted out without thinking.

Chapter 17

"Aye, Captain, we had us a beautiful view of the iceberg this afternoon. It was a sight I shall not soon forget," comments Doctor Eden, and goes on to say. "Sir, regarding Hazleton. He seems to have disappeared. The crew is rather tight-lipped about his vanishing, and I never pursued the matter."

"Somehow Doctor, these matters seem to resolve themselves," says Captain Mcbaine with a slight grin.

"I believe you're right, Captain. Katie got her revenge. When will we reach port? My supplies are running very short. The cold weather and damp nights are taking their toll on the passengers, I as well."

The Captain ponders for a moment, "Well Doctor, we are now twenty-four days into September. With good weather and God willing, perhaps the twenty-seventh day of this month, we will arrive at Stornoway."

* * *

There is a quiet knock on Susannah's cabin door. She opens it and sees her mother standing there. "Come in Mother. Come in and sit down." Both mother and daughter are grinning to the point where they cover their mouths to keep from breaking out in a laugh. They look at each other, each lets out a small burst of joy, and the words get lost in the happiness.

Aggie composes herself and says to Susannah, "It's him? It's Matthew?"

Susannah, still with her hand over her mouth, excitedly announces, "Yes, mother, it's Matthew. I do not know what is happening, but when I am near him, I feel faint."

Aggie smiles, placing her hands on Susannah's arms giving them a loving squeeze. Mother and daughter embrace each other. Susannah's eyes begin to fill with tears of joy. She cannot compose herself. Aggie passes her daughter a silk handkerchief. Now a collection of tears of joy are gently wiped together into tears of love. The silk handkerchief, which holds the emotions of the heart, is now tucked into Susannah's sleeve.

"Mother, tell me what is happening? I miss Matthew, and I don't even know him? I feel funny inside. It is like a tingle that rushes around and around inside of me. My stomach is in knots, and I have a hard time concentrating." Aggie's smile turns to a grin, "Susannah, you are falling in love."

* * *

Martin lies down on his uncomfortable bunk bed. His canvas luggage bag serves as his pillow. He covers himself with his blanket, which is an assortment of worn clothing sewn together by his mother. Martin jokingly says to his younger brother, "You're as nervous as the old cat we got down from the ash tree last year."

"Yes," replies Matthew. "I am meeting Susannah on deck tonight, and I don't have a clean shirt. I smell like that old shark we carved up." Matthew twists and turns, pulling out clothing from his faded suitcase that is held together with a thin leather strap.

"Yes, I noticed you and that shark smell the same. Some seawater and soap might cure that." Martin jokes and laughs as Matthew throws a bundle of soiled clothing at him. The laughter is contagious, causing Matthew and fellow passengers who are nearby to join in.

Matthew gathers up the clothing he has thrown at his brother and stuffs it into the worn suitcase. He takes the shirt he will be wearing tonight and a well-used chunk of lye soap to the washing area.

Martin lies down on his bunk bed and realigns the luggage bag to a more comfortable position.

The Lieutenant is on duty this night and is strolling among the steerage passengers. The young Lieutenant works his way in and out of the standing crowd hoping for a glimpse of Frances. He turns, suddenly stopping. There directly in front of him, stands Hardie. The Lieutenant's hand spontaneously grasps his sabre nervously. He feels a rush of fear, for he's caught off guard. With great self-control, he does not remove his sabre from its sheath.

The burly Hardie takes another step directly toward the Lieutenant. Hardie glares at Mr. Rodgers young face, with a look that would cause anyone's soul to tremble. The Lieutenant steps back abruptly, assaulted by the strong smell of stale rum escaping with Hardie's breath.

"Arrr! Matey!" are the words that seep from Hardie's intoxicated mouth. Hardie slurs, wiping his drooling mouth on his sleeve. "I have you now." A vengeful gleam glows in Hardie's eyes. He begins to raise his hands to strike Mr. Rodgers. The Lieutenant's instincts take over, and his hand begins to remove the sabre from its sheath.

Hardie hurls a clenched fist at Timothy Rodgers. The Lieutenant sharply twists and turns to avoid the punch to his face. This unexpected movement by the Lieutenant causes Hardie to lose his balance. The Lieutenant takes a step back, and the sheath that held the sabre is now empty.

The blade the Lieutenant is now at Hardie's throat. The daring Lieutenant pushes the sabre hard against the throat of his victim, a thin stream of blood dribbles along the blade. Hardie's head is forced sideways, as the pressure from the sabre will not allow him to turn. He stands in a weakened position, knowing any sudden movement he makes enables Timothy Rodgers to win the day. Hardie's hand slowly rises to the blade of the sabre to take the pressure off his throat. With calmness, the Lieutenant pushes the blade harder against Hardie's throat, causing his intoxicated blood to squirt. The blood streams onto Hardie's shirt; then it runs onto the planked deck. Hardie's hands rise slowly in the form of surrender.

Mr. Rodgers, now in control, loudly commands, "On your knees, Hardie!"

"I will never get on my knees to you! Never!" comes the gagging voice of Hardie.

The Lieutenant, in a single heartbeat, pulls the sabre away from Hardie's throat. He turns the blade in a swift motion and strikes Hardie on the side of his head. Hardie falls like a side of pork to the bloodied deck. Officers of the ship quickly come to the aid of Timothy Rodgers.

The officers roll the unconscious body of Hardie onto his back, then begin placing him in chains. Randel is among the spectators in the crowd and gives the Lieutenant a nod, acknowledging a job well done. While the officer's chain Hardie, Mr. Rodgers composes himself. The Lieutenant still has his sabre in his hand. He wipes the blade of his sabre across the shirt of the unconscious Hardie before returning the weapon to its sheath.

Proudly, he straightens his uniform and turns to report the incident to the Captain. The passengers, who were witness to the event backed away in fear. The Lieutenant glances toward the crowd and notices the Cunningham family looking at him. Frances Cunningham has her hands together, clutching her handkerchief. She hesitates. Then giving in to her internal feelings, she impulsively rushes to the Lieutenant. Frances's behaviour silences her father and her two brothers. From a distance, they can see Frances in the Lieutenant's arms. Gazing into each other's eyes, neither speaks. Finally, Mr. Rodgers turns and exits the stern of the ship. Frances remains standing in the same spot. Her father walks up to her and places his arm protectively around her.

* * *

The hands of time slowly take their natural course, giving way to the seductive darkness that makes its way onto the deck of the Sara Rose. Now the dimming daylight is escorted into the darkened corners. The resisting sea is severed in two by the bow, with the ship finding its course into the shadows of the calling darkness. Constant sounds of the splitting waves echo along the decks of the vessel. The massive sails embrace the night air and extend their beauty to the watching full moon. Lanterns on the ship flicker their acknowledgement, and the moon, in turn, releases a glow upon the sea guiding the Sara Rose this night.

Crew members on the port and starboard side of the ship are lowering sounding weights into the sea. "Report!" calls out Third Mate Johnson.

"Twenty-four fathoms," is heard from the port side.

"Twenty-six fathoms," is the call from the starboard side.

The Captain and Third Mate know this is too deep to anchor the ship for the night. "Take her in, Mr. Johnson."

"Aye Aye, Sir." Mr. Johnson turns the great wheel of the ship into the protected bay of Coll.

The high riggers return to duty and lower the sails for the night. The ship will anchor in the bay.

"Release the anchor! Riggers! Drop them sails!" shouts the Captain. Parker makes his way down from the crow's nest and lends a hand to the deck crew.

"Good job, men. It's a good day to be at sea. Extra rations of rum for you all," says Captain Mcbaine. A cheer sounds out from the crew.

The vessel is anchored in a quiet bay at the northeast tip of the Island of Coll. The ship was blessed with calm waters and favourable sea winds this day. The Sara Rose is safe from the sea in the quiet bay, and no lanterns will be lit on her decks during the night to attract any attention. Only a skeleton crew will keep watch because the possibility of pirates does exist.

The decline in temperature the last few evenings gives the ship's little stowaway a larger appetite. The stillness of the ship and the hush along the decks tells the little mouse it is time to seek out food and water.

Matthew returns to his bunk, finding Martin asleep. He changes into the dry shirt he washed earlier. His hair has become rigid from the seawater, and he rubs his head with his fingers trying to soften his hair. Taking the bottle of tonic water, he splashes it on one hand, rubbing it onto his face. Matthew finds a brush among Martin's supplies and runs it through his hair several times to rid the stiffness. He sits on his bunk and goes over in his mind what to say to Susannah. His thoughts filled with reasons why he should not go to meet her and the reasons why she would not want him in her life.

Johnnie, a passenger in the bunk next to Martin's, offers Matthew words of advice. "Matthew, sprinkle a bit of this cologne on your neck, it attracts the ladies like flies," says Johnnie as he passes the cologne to Matthew.

Chapter 18

The little mouse scampers excitedly among the crusts of bread, rolling each to find a bit of butter. The dripping water barrel provides the mouse with a drinking source, and it laps up the water to quench its thirst. Now the rodent does something unusual. Putting its head down on the planked floor, it pushes itself through the puddle. Then it turns, placing the other side of its head on the floor, it pushes itself through the water. The silly little mouse rolls onto its back in the puddle of freshwater, twisting and turning its body, as if it has an itch. A drop of water from the barrel hits the mouse in the face; the mouse shakes its head and sneezes to release the water that seeped into its nose.

The mouse remains hungry but needs to rest and dry its wet coat. Slowly making its way home, the rodent looks back and sees a trail of wet imprints on the floor. Curiously circling the wet footprints, the mouse wonders where the wet spots came from.

Susannah's newly found emotions fill her mind with thoughts. She gazes at the engraved penny she found in her bonnet, and she slowly traces the letter M with her fingertips. A knock on the door startles her. Susannah opens the door to see her father standing there. "Father, come in."

Donald Evens enters his daughter's cabin. He places his finger vertically over his lips and whispers, "Your mother is not to know of this." Mr. Evens closes the cabin door and stands nervously with his hat in his hand. He gets up his nerve and says, "You're rather taken with that young Matthew. Have you thought about what kind of life you would have with him? His only possessions are the clothes on his back."

"Father, I don't understand any of this, but I want to see him again. Something inside of me wants this very much." Susannah shyly covers her mouth with her hand and looks down.

Mr. Evens does not seem to be disturbed by his daughter's comments. He takes her into his arms and whispers to her. "Follow your heart, my dear. I will support you no matter what you may do."

Susannah bursts into tears with her father holding her. Regaining control of her mixed emotions, she kisses her father on the cheek and says, "Thank you, Father."

The Rose is lit by the light of the moon tonight, and Matthew has been in the shadows of the upper deck for over an hour. He grows impatient for Susannah's arrival as the night air dips to freezing temperatures. His mind begins to race with thoughts, and now his biggest fear is that Susannah will not honour their agreement to meet.

Randel slips quietly into the depths of the keel of the ship. He carries a lantern, for this area of the vessel is darker than the night. Randel makes his way along the cargo holds. He stops to get his bearings, then raises his lantern and turns. From a distance, he can see movement. He instinctively becomes more aware of his surroundings in the darkness. Randel knows he is not alone. He slowly moves along on the bottom of the ship, being careful not to trip over unseen obstacles. Randel extends his arm holding the lantern. In the eerie darkness, Hardie, is chained to a beam that supports the keel to the next deck. The shackles, which were on Hardie's legs when dragged to the keel have been removed. Hardie covers his eyes as the lantern light is too bright for the captured man. There is an odour that reeks from him. His canvas pants are soiled, and what last he ate clings to his clothes.

"Hardie, how are you? Are they feeding you?" asks Randel.

"Arrr! Aye, them devils tried feeding me. I fooled them and spat it all back on them. I tell you, Randel, I will get even. That I will Matey," answers Hardie with a shriek of evilness in his voice.

"That was a ridiculous thing you tried with the Lieutenant. You're lucky he never stuck you in the throat like an old boar," chuckles Randel. Randel pulls out a partial brick of bread and sets it on the floor for Hardie. He then says, "I see you have company down here. I bet that stowaway has become a friend."

"Yes, we were looking for him, now he looks out for me. He brings me water and food that he steals from the upper decks," quickly replies Hardie.

"All right, I best get out of here before I'm missed on deck. I'll try and get down here tomorrow if I can sneak away."

Waking up from a nap, the little mouse stretches. It comes out from its hole in the wall realizing that something is not quite right and follows its frozen tail round and round. It stops, tries to roll onto its back to control the itch it feels, but the frozen fur will not let it turn over. The puzzled rodent forgets its problems and scurries into the kitchen in search of crumbs.

* * *

Matthew continues to wait in the dark; the unknown controls his thoughts. With his heart surging to new speeds, his warm breath releases into the cold air. The envious moon reflects off the silent sea, and suddenly, Susannah's shadow falls on the planked deck.

Matthew steps into the moonlight, stopping before he reaches her. He is speechless with Susannah walking toward him. She extends her right hand, and Matthew instantly takes it in his. On an impulse, he takes her other closed hand and gently presses her hands together. While gazing into Matthew's eyes, Susannah breaks this tranquil moment and shyly says, "Matthew, I was not sure you would meet me tonight."

Matthew nervously whispers, "I was not sure if you wanted to meet me." The two smile at each other in the moonlight, while Matthew holds Susannah's hands. They walk to the railing on the starboard side and look out to the sea. Each star glitters tonight, and the moon reveals Susannah's face, prompting Matthew to kiss her cheek.

They are unaware of two voices whispering to each other in the distance. "Damn! It's cold out here tonight," says the shivering Donald.

"Be quiet Donald. They will hear us," says Aggie in a quiet voice.

"Did you see that Aggie? He kissed her already! What do you make of that?" excitedly exclaims Donald. "We better get over there and break this up."

"No, don't be silly Donald! She wanted him to kiss her. You seem to have forgotten a lot."

The cool moonlight tugs at the young couple's heartstrings and their feelings intensify. Susannah is wearing the full-length dress that Matthew first saw her in at the dock of Prestwick. Matthew's eyes notice the blue trimming on the neckline of the dress and the violet-blue bonnet that Susannah is wearing. His eyes are focused on the bonnet. Matthew wonders if Susannah has found the lucky penny that he placed in the band. Susannah knows what Matthew is thinking. Matthew can feel Susannah's left hand begin to open in his. His heart skips a beat. His trembling hand touches the lucky penny that drops onto his hand. Matthew looks at his open hand to see the deeply carved initial in the penny. He wraps his arm around Susannah and lovingly kisses her wanting lips.

Donald and Aggie Evens are still peering from around the corner. "Come on Donald. Let's go back to our cabin. She is safe with Matthew. We have nothing to worry about."

"Yes dear, it's too cold to keep standing here, and I believe you're right about Matthew," comments Donald. "So, Aggie, tell me. When you give me that look of yours, does it mean you want me to kiss you?"

Aggie's eyes light up. Her smile warms Donald's thoughts; he grins and says, "This cold weather makes one's soul frisky."

Chapter 19

Reddish orange rays of sun pierce the horizon this frosty morning. The deck of the Sara Rose lies in silence, and the sounds of the sea have disappeared. The Union Jack is frozen in time, high on the main mast of the ship. The usual rocking of the vessel is not felt, nor are the moans and groans heard which accompany an anchored ship.

* * *

The shivering little stowaway wakes to a layer of white, powdery snow. From the safety of the hole in the wall, the confused mouse slides its whiskers into the soft snow. The mouse creeps, pushing snow with its face as if it were sneaking up on its prey. Its facial whiskers cannot detect if this strange material is food or a plot to capture the rodent. The mouse trusts its instincts and backs into the corner and the safety of home.

A knock on the door of the Captain's cabin is the first sound to be heard this dark, bleak morning. "Captain, Captain!" excitedly calls the Lieutenant. "The Sara Rose is frozen to the sea. Come quick!"

"Lieutenant Rodgers, I see the weather has caught us off guard! Sound the bell and get all hands-on deck! Now, Lieutenant!"

The sharp sound of the ship's bell rings into the frozen bay, alerting the sleeping crew and the awakening groggy sun. The Lieutenant waits for the crew's arrival on deck for the morning roll call. "All present and accounted for Captain," says the Lieutenant.

The Captain orders six men to get out the brooms and shovels and start clearing the deck of the snow.

"Arthur, you go down to the keel and check on our friend Hardie. Jackal, you take your crew and start breaking the ice off the spars and mast poles. Make sure you are all tied to the spars while up there. We need every one of you. Randel, get the ropes and the sounding weights. Drop them through the ice and see how thick it is. Continue to break the ice around the ship with the weights. Lieutenant, tie a rope to Angelo and lower him with an axe to chop the anchor chains free. Parker, climb the mast pole to the crow's nest and see just how far the ice is out to sea."

The vessel comes alive with the movement of the crew as they swiftly hurry along the decks. The sun is slow to show itself and the dull darkness of the morning hinders the men's work.

Randel and four crew members drop the sounding weights to the frozen waters. The Captain looks down at their progress, "Randel, keep it going. Get your crew to break the ice completely around the Rose. I will get someone to clean off the jolly boats and ready them."

Martin and Matthew are the first passengers on deck. "Captain, can we help?" asks Martin.

"Yes, the two of you can help. Start getting hot tea to the men. We must keep them warm. Martin, you should not be out in the cold air. Tie a scarf over your mouth," suggests the concerned Captain.

Walking from the port to the starboard side of the ship, the Captain quickly checks the progress of his crew. First Mate Downing is at the helm and is slowly turning the large wheel back and forth to free the rudder from the locked jaws of the ice.

 Angelo has freed the anchor chains from the sea's clutches. "Good work Angelo! Now, you and Thomas ready the jolly boats." commands the Captain. The Lieutenant walks with the Captain to the galley. Each man warms his hands on a hot tin of tea. The Lieutenant is surprised when the Captain calmly states, "This is not a nice day to be at sea."

The Lieutenant smiles back at the Captain and questions him, "Is this the first time the Rose has been captured by ice?"

"No, Lieutenant, we froze in the harbour one fall on a voyage to Canada. It was while we waited in the harbour at Halifax for our berth to be readied. A great northern blew in with a vengeance and locked us for a week. I recall it was in forty-six and late into October. We had snow piled on the deck, and all the ropes were icebound. The men pulled two jolly boats across the ice and over the drifts of snow. They would paddle the boats when the ice gave way. The Port Major of Halifax allowed the crew to venture into the town and get some much-needed supplies for the passengers. They came back with axes and ice chisels and many thick long ropes." The Captain stops speaking and sips his tea.

The Lieutenant is giving his full attention to the Captain's story. The Captain gets another tin of tea, and the interested Lieutenant asks, "Captain, it sounds like it was quite the ordeal. Are there any of the crew members from forty-six still serving on the Rose?"

"Yes Mr. Rodgers, it was indeed an ordeal, and one I often think about. I believe Mr. Quinn and Jackal were mates on the Rose at that time. Well, Lieutenant, we may have to continue this conversation later. Let's go see what we can do."

The morning sun has climbed its way onto the horizon. A silent, hazy ring surrounds the sluggish sun. This can only mean colder weather ahead. The full moon has set the weather pattern until the next lunar change.

The Captain and Lieutenant walk the snow-covered deck to the stern where the jolly boats are kept. They proceed carefully; the high riggers continue to chip ice off the spars with their hammers.

"Lieutenant, get a few more crew members here and let's get these jolly boats on the ice."

Angelo and Thomas help in getting the small jolly boats over the stern and onto the ice. Randel's crew continues to break the ice with the sounding weights.

A few of the steerage passengers come up from the lower deck for fresh air. They quickly go back, as the cold air is not agreeable this early in the morning. The upper class passengers, who are inquisitive, look over the port and starboard side to see what is happening and quickly return to their cabins.

"All right men, push these boats down the ice, four of you to a boat. Climb aboard the boat when the ice starts to break. Then paddle the boat till you come to the next ice flow. When you know that the ship can punch her way through, turn your boats around, and tie the long ropes to the Rose. You will be able to pull yourselves back in the boats and break the ice with axes as you go. This will give the ship a channel to get to the open sea. You lads be careful out there."

The Captain now walks to the bow of the ship with the Lieutenant. "Mr. Rodgers, is the anchor free from the ice and ready on my order to come up?"

"Yes, it is Captain."

"Mr. Downing, is the rudder now free?" asks the Captain walking toward the helm.

"Aye Captain."

"I am glad to hear that Mr. Downing." Captain Mcbaine looks up at the high riggers chipping at the ice and removing snow off the downed sails. Parker is in the crow's nest giving direction to the riggers and keeping an eye on the men working the jolly boats.

The little mouse is backed into a corner with its tail tucked underneath its body. The colder weather has naturally slowed its heart rate, and its shivers keep time with each breath. The rodent's sensing whiskers are covered in frost, and its eyes have a buildup of frozen tears crusted around them.

Donald and Aggie stop at Susannah's cabin door. Donald knocks. Susannah opens the door to them, and Aggie hands her daughter a cup of hot tea. "Here you are Susannah, and take a warm biscuit. How did you sleep last night?" asks Mrs. Evens.

Susannah is still wearing the dress she wore last night. "I never slept at all. I just sat in the corner of the bed wrapped in a blanket all night."

"You should have come to our cabin if you could not sleep and were cold," says Aggie.

"No mother, I had to be alone last night. I needed to think."

Captain Mcbaine is standing at the stern of the ship and checking on the progress of the men in the jolly boats. The Lieutenant joins him to discuss the readiness of the ship and the next steps to be taken.

"Lieutenant, I never had a chance to commend you on your handling of Hardie."

The Lieutenant blushes and humbly says, "Thank you, Captain."

"Yes, from what I heard; you are a very lucky man. Hardie can be extremely vicious when he is so inclined. You're very good with your sabre, and you put a quick end to the incident. You had the right to take his life. Perhaps you should have, but you showed restraint. I admire that in an officer."

The Lieutenant warms the morning air with his smile. His chest puffs up as he thanks the Captain again.

"Captain, what will become of Hardie, now that he has offended the Sara Rose and his fellow crew members?"

"I think you know the answer to that question, Lieutenant!"

* * *

The sun has mystical rings surrounding it, and the orange-tinged sky is free of clouds. The cool rays of this wonder begin to warm the crystallizing air.

Captain Mcbaine walks towards the crow's nest and shouts. "Parker, get Jackal down here!"

"Aye Aye, Sir."

"Randel, how is the task coming along?"

"Good, Sir. We have the Rose free. She awaits the call of the sea."

Jackal makes his way to the deck and walks with the Captain towards the galley. He pours tins of tea for Jackal and himself. Arthur walks into the room, and the Captain calls to him, "Arthur, did you see to our guest?"

"Yes Captain, I gave him a biscuit and water," replies Arthur.

"All right. Jackal, I see you and your crew worked hard, and the mast and spars are free of ice. Are the sails free and ready to be deployed on command?"

"Aye Aye! That they are!" answers Jackal chewing on a biscuit.

"Fine. Jackal, ready your men but get them warmed up first and a biscuit or two in them. The lot of you may be on them spars for a fair while. It will be a challenge to get the Rose back to the sea."

It's now mid-morning in the bay off the Isle of Coll. The morning sun has done little to warm the air. The Sara Rose is within a quarter-mile of the Isle. Coll is a combination of jagged rock and sparse evergreen trees. There seems to be a quantity of browning grasses on the island that make this a haven for wildlife. One can see a variety of bird species taking flight, circling the ship in hopes of a free meal.

On the frozen edge of the bay, where the sand meets the frozen waters, there is a silver fox that seems undisturbed by the ship. It is digging in the snow-covered beach, perhaps looking for clams. Three young pups, waiting for their lunch, are hiding among the naked willows. The tops of the stunted evergreens begin to sway with the cold wind descending on this lonely island.

Martin and Matthew have retreated to their bunks in the steerage section. Both are looking for a change of dry clothes.

"Well, Matthew, you haven't said a word about last night. I never heard you come back to your bunk during the night!"

Matthew twists and turns as if he wants to avoid the question, "Well, she is very attractive, and I am penniless, with nothing to offer her. When I am with her, I cannot think. Everything I want to say to her comes out wrong."

"Do you like her?"

"Yes, Yes, I do. Very much. And last night we kissed."

Martin is shocked by Matthew's words. He takes his wet shirt, coils it into a ball and throws it at Matthew. Together they laugh. Martin pulls the covers over himself, making himself comfortable.

The men in the jolly boats have managed to carve a small channel through the ice to the open waters. They return to a warm welcome from the Captain and the Lieutenant. The jolly boats are pulled back onto the ship and set on the deck for now. They may be needed again if the vessel cannot dislodge herself from the imprisoning bay. The Captain tells the men who manned the boats to warm themselves in the galley. "Be quick men. Our wind has arrived."

Jackal and his crew position themselves on the spars and tie safety ropes around their midriffs. If the Captain's plan works, the ship will suddenly leap seaward. Jimmy Brown waits in the crow's nest. From his vantage point, he will conduct this preplanned escape from the frozen bay. The Captain orders all extra hands to the bow of the ship to help lift the great anchor.

The Captain takes his pipe from the buttoned pocket of his uniform. Reaching into his pocket again for his tobacco pouch, he fills his pipe, and strikes a match on the railing of the helm. The eyes of the crew are locked on the Captain as he walks to the starboard side of the ship. The planked deck remains covered with packed snow and ice. The smoke from the Captain's pipe funnels its way into the cold morning air and rises to greet a breeze.

The entire crew watch their Captain as he taps the pipe on the hand railing to empty the pipe of tobacco. He begins walking to the helm of the ship, where Second Mate Quinn awaits his orders.

"Mr. Quinn, I believe all is in order."

"Yes Sir, Captain." The excitement in the Second Mate's voice offers his approval to the Captain.

"All right then. Mr. Quinn, let us begin! Pull the bow of the ship down with the anchor toward the sea bed. Give the order now, Mr. Quinn."

The Captain gives commands to Arthur, who relays the orders to the crow's nest and riggers. "Turn the foremast to the northwest and the jigger mast to the northeast, and we shall create a circling turbulence inside the sails. High riggers, do your part and raise the mainsail to full position on the mast, now! You, riggers. Do the same for the mizzenmast. Let's go men! Hurry! Be quick!"

The Sara Rose is awakening, coming to life. Creaking sounds are heard on the planked deck. There is a snapping sound. The newly formed winds expand in the frozen canvas sails. The great anchor is true and holds the bow of the Rose tight as the sails fill with strength. The mighty masts bend into the wind as the pressure builds on the sails.

The ship is in a tug of war with itself. It claws at the sea, looking for release. The frozen Union Jack now responds to the morning breeze and does its part. The crew cheer the flag and colours of their homeland.

The Captain stands at the helm with his hand raised toward the cold sky. This moment is suspended in time. Crew prepare themselves for the upcoming task. The Captain looks upward to the full sails retaining the ship's strength. Suddenly the Captain drops his arm. Every able man pulls the great chains. The cranks and pulleys are worked to their maximum. The stern of the ship is beginning to rise from the force of the anchor being pulled at the bow of the vessel. The great anchor that rested on the seabed during the cold night starts to rise. The men use brute strength to turn the pulleys and cranks. The stern of the ship suddenly lowers into the water, helping to move the anchor up.

In a slingshot effect, the Rose, with her rigged sails, finds the new waters. The riggers cheer and hang on to their safety ropes. The helmsman turns the great wheel of the ship, allowing the rudder to find the channel carved for the vessel. The men at the bow continue to raise the anchor to the deck of the ship. Jimmy Brown gives the Captain a wave, a sign that the ship has found her route to freedom. The Captain waves back to the crow's nest in acknowledgement. The high riggers keep their positions; they will be needed soon to realign the sails when the Rose tastes the new waters.

"Well done Sir! We did it!" happily shouts Arthur.

"Extra rum rations for everyone tonight Arthur," says the Captain.

All the crew join in with a loud 'Hurrah!' The Sara Rose finds her stride.

Chapter 20

The sun is in its morning phase and slowly begins its vertical climb. The mysterious ring surrounding the sun continually rises like a protective halo. The sailors have named this a 'Phantom Sun.'

The crew inhales the cold air while they work, expelling it in a crystallized form. There is a continual dropping of ice and snow pellets to the deck from the sails and ropes. The ship stretches herself further out to sea, reaching for the horizon. The large sails fill with new-found breezes that are pulsing in the wind and bursts of snowflakes descend from the grey sky.

The Captain returns to the helm with a map. "Mr. Quinn let us set the course for the northern tip of the Isle of Skye. I believe by late afternoon we will be protected from icebergs, for the Islands of North and South Uist stand in their way."

Captain Mcbaine takes the ship's map to his cabin and begins charting the new route. With the speed of the vessel now determined, the Captain can calculate the time they will arrive at a set destination. He takes the ship's logbook and enters the position and date. The Captain then records the actions of Hardie in the ship's log. Captain Mcbaine leans back in his chair and takes his pipe from his pocket, considering what he should do about the matter of Hardie Jenkins.

The cooks are busy preparing the midday meal for the passengers and crew. Again, all will have another light meal eaten in their cabins. No passenger would want to be seated in the cold dining and lounge areas this afternoon. The cooks are roasting large sides of pork, while bricks of bread are being taken out of the ovens and cut into slices for sandwiches. This day, all first and second-class passengers, along with crew and steerage, will eat the same meal.

Matthew finds his brother sound asleep in his bunk. Since the passengers will not be having lunch in the dining room, Matthew is not needed. He was told to report to the kitchen later in the day, for the large barrels holding the kitchen wastes will need emptying. He does not think about this unpleasant task, for he is concerned about Martin's health and hopes he does not offer to help. Matthew's thoughts go back to Susannah. They agreed to meet tonight on the deck after dark. The weather's drastic change has left him wondering if she will be there this evening.

* * *

It is early afternoon; passengers on deck are greeted with cold air and a dull overcast sky as they stroll. They are bundled up with extra clothing and carefully walk the partially snow-covered deck, avoiding the forming puddles.

Jones barks at one of the stewards, demanding a cup of hot tea, "Hurry up! It's damn cold standing here! Make sure you add more rum to my cup this time. I will be watching you!"

The steward passes Jones his tea and rum mixture. The cigar in Jones' mouth is short, and his eyes are drowning in smoke. Jones quickly spits the butt to the floor. He stops in front of a table and puts his walking cane and tin cup on the table. He takes out another cigar and calls the steward to light it for him. While Jones is waiting, Mr. Peters walks in for tea to take to his wife in their cabin. "Peters, come here," orders Jones. "How about a small game of chance in my cabin tonight?" The shocked Peters stops. "Steward, where is the light for my cigar?" shouts Jones. Then Jones growls with a snarly voice. "Well, Peters, let's say an hour after dinner tonight. I will be in my cabin waiting. Perhaps I can get Mr. Flynn to join in the game with us."

Peters thinks for a second and turns to Jones. His inner voice is telling him to walk away, but his inner craving answers. "I just may take you up on your offer Mr. Jones."

The Captain gets up from his comfortable chair; he is not thinking about comfort at the moment. He takes his empty tin cup and leaves the cabin. He proceeds along the port side with his hand sliding along the railing. The tin cup is held in his left hand and taps against his uniform in time with each step. The galley bustles with the crew members going in and out warming themselves. They use the galley to thaw equipment, for this is the only area which has heat. The cooks are a surly bunch this day, for their territory has been invaded by the crew. Haydn notices the Captain and fills his tin with hot tea. The Captain returns to his cabin where the Lieutenant meets him, and motions Mr. Rodgers to follow him inside.

"Mr. Rodgers, here is the sextant. You can see the Isle of Skye on the map! I charted the course already. You and Mr. Quinn set the vessel toward it." The Lieutenant takes his finger and follows the line the Captain has marked on the map.

"Mr. Rodgers sit down for a moment. I need your input on the issue regarding Hardie Jenkins."

The Lieutenant positions the sabre he wears to the side and seats himself. He removes his hat and slides the chair closer to the desk. The Captain sits down with his elbows placed on the arms of the chair. He takes his pipe and relights the remaining tobacco. He ponders for a moment while stroking his beard.

"Lieutenant, you were the officer involved in the altercation with Hardie Jenkins. He is now chained to the keel of the ship, as you know. If the Rose were in the Royal Navy and if we were at war, Mr. Jenkins would have been put on the walking plank, bringing an end to the issue. His outburst could be looked upon as an act of treason. Captain Mcbaine draws smoke from his pipe and ponders for a moment. We cannot return him to England for trial until spring when we have completed the tour to the Americas and Caribbean Islands. Do you have any suggestions Lieutenant?"

"Well Captain, we could hand him over to the authorities when we reach Stornoway. However, the crime was committed on the Sara Rose, a British ship, so they would be powerless to punish Hardie. Or, we could have a trial on the Rose and deal with Hardie Jenkins ourselves."

"Yes, I agree with you, Mr. Rodgers. So be it." The two men are quiet, considering their options. The Captain puffs on his pipe again, and then says, "We will set the trial after we leave the port of Stornoway. Dr. Eden will head the trial. All right then. Thank you, Lieutenant."

Matthew slips quietly from his bunk so as not to disturb Martin, who is fast asleep. Matthew leaves the confines of the steerage section and climbs the steps to the top deck of the ship. The weather has not changed, leaving the deck icy. The cold winds off the sea are continually increasing. There are few passengers on deck in these frigid conditions. Matthew continues to the galley and spots the dreaded barrels holding the kitchen waste. He slips between the cooks, takes a tin and dips it into the pail of hot tea.

"Haydn, can you give me a hand to roll the barrels to the stern once I put the barrel covers on?"

"I will only help you roll them there and stand them up, but I will not help you empty or clean them." laughs Haydn.

Haydn and Matthew roll the wooden barrels to the stern of the ship and remove the tops. "Haydn, where are you going?"

"Sorry Matthew. I only promised to help get the barrels here, not to help empty and clean them. Matthew, I am in my uniform, and I can't get it dirty."

Matthew pouts to himself. Reaching in the barrel, and begins throwing the wastes overboard. The scraps in the barrel have started to ferment, and the odour is causing Matthew's stomach to turn. Stepping back, he waits for a moment. Becoming accustomed to the smell, he continues with the nasty task. He then begins to remove the top of the second barrel. Suddenly, he hears Martin's voice.

"Matthew, why didn't you call me?"

"You get back to your bunk. This cold air is not good for your lungs. I can manage this on my own."

On this cold, late afternoon, no crew members come with their fishing poles to try their luck. The dreaded northern wind continues to unleash its wrath upon the sea. The ship remains in control and carves her way through the chilled waters, taking all on board further northward to the unknown. The Phantom Sun with its circling halo, keeps its promise.

118

* * *

The cold air has woven a blanket of darkness over the ship. The colour of night conceals the daytime hiding spots. The decks have a layer of frozen snow on them, on which the moonlight sends its scarce light. The ropes and sails release clinging pieces of ice that sporadically fall onto the deck. The cold night allows the sounds to escape through the cracks of the frigid air.

Parker is in the crow's nest and will be relieved several times throughout the night by Angelo. This allows each a turn to warm up, as the temperature is descending even lower. All lanterns are lit on the ship, thus allowing the night crew to keep watch for icebergs. They believe they are protected by the North and South Isles of Uist, but cannot let this go to chance. The night crew ties lanterns on long poles stretching out to sea to provide a better view. Third Mate Benjamin Johnson controls the helm along with the apprentice, Thomas Quinn. Young Quinn stands on his tiptoes peering into the darkness.

Matthew managed to get a small bucket of warm water from the kitchen to wash and shave the day-old stubble on his face. He dabs a few drops of the cologne that Johnnie suggested he use.

"Martin, did you eat anything tonight?"

"No, I didn't. I just took the last of the medicine I had. Are you off to see Susannah again tonight?" asks Martin.

"Yes, I am. Now be quiet about it. If I can sneak into the kitchen, I will get you a biscuit or two."

"I think you better wipe the soap out of your ear before you go," chuckles Martin, along with a few of his steerage mates.

Matthew steps onto the top deck of the ship and looks about. He is not worried about being seen by the crew but is concerned if observed by the Captain or Lieutenant. He makes his way along the slippery floor to the kitchen and puts a few biscuits for Martin in his pocket.

The moon is full, without a cloud to hide its bright stare. It peers down with its chilly gaze at the deck of the Sara Rose. Parker calls out, "All clear." The sudden announcement by Parker startles Matthew, who was in deep thought of what to say to Susannah tonight. The sailors on night duty walk the decks with their lanterns and look into the cold night for a reflection. The relentless, choppy waves of the sea sound harsh, slapping the cold water against the Rose. The ship pounds the waters and is continuously being pushed forward by the twisting wind against the canvas sails.

The sound of footsteps in the dark causes Matthew to panic. The darkness plays with his mind, and he is unsure of what he hears. Susannah steps out of the shadows. She stands silent in the moonlight, while her breath warms the night air. Instead of wearing a bonnet this evening, her head is covered with a dark hooded cape. Her long blondish hair and her contagious smile render Matthew spellbound. The two are speechless and cannot take their eyes off each other.

Suddenly, without hesitation, Susannah kisses him on the lips. The watching moon is shocked — Matthew trembles where he stands. His motionless body is transformed, and a new rush courses through his veins. Neither is aware of the cold enveloping them. Their stares melt into each other's eyes. Their craving lips beg, becoming sealed in a passionate kiss.

Chapter 21

The Captain is seated at his desk with the cabin door closed. He takes off his hat and opens the ship's logbook to its last entry. Removing the top from the ink bottle, he dips his pen into the black ink. Captain Mcbaine begins to write the date:

This, the twenty-sixth day of the month of September;

The Captain details the events that resulted in Hardie Jenkins being confined. In a separate entry, the Captain notes the vessel's position and weather conditions along with her expected arrival date in Stornoway.

The Captain puts down his pen and leaves the cabin. He strolls to the starboard side of the ship. The moonlight reveals treetops in the distance. He knows this is the outer edge of the Isle of Skye. The Sara Rose is on course and soon will turn to the northeast, into the waters of Little Minch.

* * *

The cold darkness is hushed away and the rhythm of the night is lost. First signs of a new day are emerging from the horizon. Like a curtain opening to display a new dawn, the morning sun slides the black night away.

The newly risen sun no longer supports what the sailors call a 'Phantom Sun'. The rings, which the sun wore, dissipate beneath the horizon and break with nature's rule. There is new warmth with the advancing sun and the frigid morning air leaves its crystallizing forms behind.

Skimming the protected waters of the North Minch, the ship continues claiming new strides on the sea. For the crew on the deck, the morning light is adding new colours to the spectacular view of the Isle of Skye. The Isle juts in and out to meet the great sea in several locations, providing many hiding areas and safe harbours from the weather.

Jimmy Brown makes his way down from the crow's nest. The vast Isle of Skye slowly disappears, leaving only the tops of the trees visible. The young Lieutenant walks the deck and communicates with Third Mate Johnson before his shift ends. The two study the charts and maps for the Rose will be in Stornoway this day.

The little mouse has been held hostage by the snow and ice on deck. It had ventured into the snow during the night but was forced back as the soles of its feet were getting cut on the jagged ice formations. Nightfall will have to make another appearance before a meal is found.

The travellers are looking forward to a meal in the dining room. Sandwiches in their cabins are not an experience to which the first-class passengers are accustomed. Her daughter accompanies Mrs. Evens to the preset table. Mr. Evens is delayed again, continually stopping to talk to other passengers. Susannah is nervous and fidgety, glancing around the room for Matthew. Aggie is not fooled and knows what her daughter is doing.

Donald Evens eventually makes his way to the table, seats himself and calls for tea. In an excited voice, he comments, "That Jones character, again he asked me to join in a game of chance in his cabin. I told him I was not interested."

"Good for you, Donald! You know I don't want you involved with games of chance anymore. The last time remains fresh in my mind," says Aggie.

Jones is in the back of the room seated by himself. There is a cloud of cigar smoke hovering around him as if he were sitting in fog. The stewards try to avoid Jones, but Matthew is caught in his view. "You! Bring me a plate of sliced pork and roasted potatoes, along with a few biscuits and gravy. But none of those soggy green things you call vegetables. Send someone over with a new cup of tea. This one has ashes in it. Be quick about it, young man!"

From the corner of her eye, Susannah is watching Matthew. Aggie senses the tension. Matthew can feel himself being watched and feels uncomfortable being in this situation. His self-esteem slowly erodes, feeling he is looked upon as a commoner.

Donald is only concerned with his meal and pays no attention to his wife and daughter. In a bold moment, Susannah raises her cup when Matthew is directly in her view. Matthew is caught off guard and stops. He steps slowly to the table where the Evens family is seated.

With a generous smile, Susannah looks at Matthew. "Matthew, I would like you to meet my mother, Mrs. Evens."

Matthew's body instantly weakens. His face reddens, and the pot of tea shakes in his hand. His mind races into a new realm as Mrs. Evens smiles and extends her hand to Matthew. Bewildered, he stands holding the teapot, puts out his left hand, then withdraws it. He places the teapot on the table. With his right free, he gently shakes her hand.

"It's a pleasure to finally meet you, Matthew."

"Yes, Ma'am," are the only words that the flustered Matthew can utter.

Susannah can sense Matthew's nervousness and quickly begins to make small talk about the cold weather. She tries to get the panicked Matthew into the conversation, but he only nods and agrees with Susannah while she talks.

"Who's this?" Donald Evens, suddenly questions.

"Oh, father, I want you to meet Matthew, a friend of mine."

Mr. Evens suppresses his chuckle. He gets up from his chair, reaches for Matthew's hand and shakes it vigorously.

"Hello, Matthew. It is nice to meet a friend of Susannah's."

Donald sits down and gives his wife a slight jab with his elbow. Aggie covers her mouth as the tea she just sipped almost spurts from her mouth, in reaction to Donald's elbow. Susannah picks up the pot of tea, pouring more tea for her mother and herself. Matthew quickly comes to Susannah's side of the table, taking the teapot and excusing himself.

The Cunningham children are on deck with their father, Joseph. Frances Cunningham can see Timothy Rodgers in the distance consulting with the Captain. She continually keeps glancing in his direction, hoping he will turn and see her. The two officers salute each other and go their separate ways. The Lieutenant notices Frances, steps down to the steerage section and walks along the railing of the stern. Mr. Rodgers does not want to appear to be too obvious. He stops and looks out to the sea, trying to work up the nerve to approach the young Frances. He places both hands on the railing staring down at the ship's wake. The relaxing motion and view give the Lieutenant the inspiration to approach Frances and her family. The Lieutenant turns. Frances is standing by his side. "How are you today, Lieutenant?" asks Frances.

"Ah, fine. I am fine, Miss Frances," stutters the Lieutenant, looking downward. He is caught off guard but quickly regains his aristocratic manners. "Thank you for asking, Miss Frances. It's a lovely day and a great day to be at sea."

"Yes, yes, it is. It's a grand day, and we all welcome the warmth."

The infatuation intensifies between the two as they continue to talk and smile at each other, standing by the railing of the ship.

The sun finds its strength and begins to shine, melting the snow and ice from the ship's decks. The wind, which fills the sails, has a softer sound and the stretching of the ropes creates a calming sensation. The smooth motion of the Sara Rose gliding on the sea waters soothes many of the upper class. Some succumb to sleep in the deck chairs, and the warm sun covers them like a favourite blanket.

Captain Mcbaine and First Mate Downing are at the helm studying the maps and charts. Neither has been to Stornoway, and are not sure what to expect. Captain Mcbaine puts out a call for Arthur.

Arthur soon makes an appearance at the helm, "Reporting as ordered, Sir."

"Arthur, have you seen Hardie Jenkins lately?"

"Yes," replies Arthur, "I was down at the keel some time ago and gave him his dinner."

"Good, Arthur. We are on the path to Stornoway. My charting tells me we should be arriving in a few hours. Do you recall the harbour?"

"Yes. I do, Captain."

"Please continue, Arthur."

"Well, Sir, she has a long arm that reaches from the mainland. It is on the port side." Arthur points on the map. "Stay out on the sea till you see her inland channel. This will save time instead of following the mainland. The port has a deep harbour. Reckon it was twenty-four fathoms."

The Captain and Mr. Downing are paying close attention to Arthur speaking, following his finger as he shows the route on the map.

"When we get into the harbour, Lewis Castle will be looking down at us. The castle is a sight to behold from the sea. They say it was built some seven or eight hundred years ago."

"Thank you again, Arthur. I am looking forward to the port of Stornoway," smiles the Captain.

It is mid-afternoon in the North Minch when the Sara Rose enters the channel to the Port of Stornoway. The image of Lewis Castle is seen on the horizon and brings the passengers to the ship's railing. The Captain tells Third Mate Johnson to proceed to the bow of the ship with the signal flags. The Lieutenant calls for all hands-on deck. The crew begins dropping the sounding weights from the port side of the vessel.

"Twenty-seven fathoms on the port, Sir."

"Good, Mr. Downing. Arthur was right about the deep harbour. I see the docks are quiet. Perhaps we can go straight to the ship's berth."

The Lieutenant shouts to the high riggers to get in position and to begin lowering the mainsails. Third Mate Johnson uses the signal flags to contact the port.

"Captain!" shouts Mr. Johnson. "We are ordered to drop anchor and await further instructions."

"Aye, Mr. Johnson. All stop! All stop!" orders the Captain.

The high riggers go to work, displaying their incredible skill, and grace. They swing from rope to rope, dropping the sails to the spars. The anchor of the ship is lowered. The Lieutenant counts the chain links as the anchor settles to the sea bed.

"Nineteen fathoms, Sir," shouts the Lieutenant. The ship comes to a stop. The passengers delight in the view they witness and cross back and forth from the port to the starboard sides of the ship. They point excitedly to Lewis Castle. It stands like a pyramid peering down on the Sara Rose. It makes them feel as if somehow, the castle is silently watching them.

Third Mate Johnson is busy receiving messages from the Port of Stornoway. He quickly repeats the messages to Angelo who writes them down. Mr. Johnson takes what Angelo has written down to the Captain.

Captain Mcbaine is puzzled and strokes his beard as he reads the message, "Gentlemen, we have cannon pointed at our ship. We will comply with their wishes. The Port Major wants more proof from the Rose that she is a British ship, and the Union Jack is true."

The Captain leaves the helm with the Third Mate following him. He waves at the Lieutenant to join them. "Mr. Johnson, get one of the jolly boats down to the sea. Lieutenant, I will give you the ship's manifest and a list of supplies we need from the port. Take Mr. Johnson and four other sailors. Meet the port officials in the harbour. Do not take any firearms with you, and Lieutenant, leave your sabre in my cabin till you return."

The Captain steps into the kitchen, taking a tin of water and drinks quickly. He strolls to the dining room where a few children are running around the tables. His uniform and warm smile bring the children closer to him. They stand by his table in awe, as if they were in front of royalty. Their mouths are open, and their active minds fill with questions. Captain Mcbaine tells the children to sit down, and he asks their names. The children answer politely. A few of the children twist and turn as they talk. The Captain raises his hand to his face to hide his amusement. Haydn approaches with a cup and pot of tea.

"Anything else, Captain?"

"Yes, find some of that hidden chocolate for my guests and bring a piece for me." The children continue talking. One boy, perhaps six years of age, comes around the table and touches the medals and ribbons on the Captain's jacket. A mother looking for her child walks in, and the Captain nods to her, suggesting that everything is fine. The young boy asks the Captain what the medals and ribbons represent. The Captain takes a sip of tea and then begins to answer the youngster.

"Well, I was a seaman for several years and served with many great men. Then I commanded a ship in the Royal Navy. The medals and ribbons were presented to me from the Admiral of the Royal Navy, for my service."

The young boy turns his head sideways and is confused by the Captain's answer. "Captain, Captain," says the youngster raising his hand, wishing to speak. "If we are all good, can we get ribbons and all those kinds of medals too?"

The Captain smiles at the boy. "You can be or do anything you want."

Haydn returns with five pieces of chocolate on a platter. The children excitedly reach for the chocolate and quickly begin smacking their lips, enjoying the unexpected treat.

A little girl points to the one remaining piece of chocolate.

"That is your piece, Captain, Sir." He smiles, joins in, and eats the chocolate. The children lick their fingers and wipe their faces with their hands. Then, with laughter, they point at each other and make faces. The amused Captain stands and tells the children he must get back to work. The little girl, who reminded the Captain about his piece of the chocolate, stands and says, "Thank you, Captain."

Captain Mcbaine, having thoroughly enjoyed his brief encounter with the children leaves the dining room in smiles. He makes his way to the helm and politely greets Mr. Downing. From the helm two men watch the Lieutenant and the small crew in the jolly boat meeting with the harbour representatives.

Chapter 22

Jimmy Brown, from his perch in the crow's nest has the perfect position to view the harbour and Lewis Castle. He can see several fishing boats at the docks unloading their catch. There are a few smaller ships anchored, which appear to be local vessels. He notices the meeting in the harbour has been completed and the jolly boat is returning to the Sara Rose.

The Captain is there to greet the Lieutenant. They salute and the Lieutenant hands the ship's manifest back to the Captain. The Lieutenant, proud of the mission he just completed, says to the Captain, "Sir, they no longer think we are a pirate ship and believe we do not fly a Jolly Roger flag."

"Thank you for the good news Lieutenant. Let us proceed."

The Sara Rose slowly moves towards her berth, led by a small boat sent by the Port Major. Four sailors work the jigger mast helping the helmsman steer the ship. Another group of sailors turn the foremast, assisting the vessel to rest against the pier.

With the Sara Rose firmly against the dock at Stornoway, Lewis Castle appears to stare down at the ship and the harbour. Those who dare to gaze at the imposing stone structure for an extended period soon acquire a feeling of uneasiness. The walkway lowers onto the pier. Captain Mcbaine takes the ship's manifest and his orders from the ship's safe.

"Mr. Rodgers, you are in charge of the vessel until my return. No one is permitted to board or leave the ship. Do you understand, Lieutenant?"

"Yes, Sir."

The Captain now turns, salutes the ship, and then disembarks. On the dock, he is directed to the Port Major's office. He continues his walk to the office of the Port Major located high above the wharf. He climbs the several flights of stairs to the flat walkway and turns to look at Lewis

Castle before knocking on the door. The Port Major steps onto the walkway to greet the Captain. The two men salute each other, then shake hands.

"Glad to meet you, Captain. My name is William Brett. I am the Port Major here at Stornoway. Don't let my uniform confuse you. I also hold a position in our army. You may call me William."

Captain Mcbaine points to Lewis Castle and says, "It's a very impressive sight from the sea, but the view from here is breathtaking."

"Yes," exclaims the Port Major. "I have been here for many years, and I am still amazed at the Castle. It's solid as the day it was built, almost eight hundred years ago."

The two men enter the office of the Port Major and begin business over a cup of tea. A short time later, the Captain emerges from the office with the Port Major. The Captain walks back to his ship, continually looking up at the Castle as if it were constantly calling him.

The Captain will allow passengers who have expressed a desire to explore Lewis Castle to leave the ship and visit the shops and inns. They are instructed to return when the ship's bell rings out.

It is late afternoon, and the Captain now believes they will return to the sea by nightfall as planned. Daylight hours in this northern port are limited at this time of the year. Soon the winter winds and cold temperatures will lock this harbour into an isolated island. The only visits will be from the bitter north wind and the skies' dropping layers of snow downward on this silent part of Scotland.

Most of the upper deck passengers disembark from the ship to visit the castle and pick up personal supplies from the small shops. As the Cunningham family groups together, the blushing Lieutenant tips his hat to Frances and bids her a pleasant day. Joey and Neil are playing swordsmen with sticks they found on the dock. The happy-go-lucky Molly makes her way down the walkway hurriedly, calling to Joseph to wait for her.

Susannah is walking the deck in search of Matthew. She approaches Martin. "Martin, where can I find Matthew?"

Martin is surprised by the sudden question. He stops and looks around for the whereabouts of his brother. "I'm not sure, Miss Evens. I have not seen him for some time. Shall I go look for him or can I help you?" asks Martin.

"I must talk to him. It's important. Martin, my family and I are leaving the ship to tour the town and Lewis Castle. Would you and Matthew like to join us when we visit the castle?"

"Ah, I am not sure, Miss Evens. I will ask Matthew when I find him," answers the puzzled Martin.

"Fine, then. Tell you what, Martin. You and Matthew meet us at the entrance to the castle. Let's say in an hour?"

Martin nods his head in agreement and goes to the steerage section in search of his brother.

On the dock, the large crane stretches upward from its platform. It is made of hefty cross poles, all bound with ropes and hand-drilled holes, where iron rods keep the structure together. The unloading from the cargo holds has begun. Occasionally a team of horses is spooked by the sounds and sudden movement on the docks. Young boys are running with shovels and buckets, trying to keep the dock clean of manure.

Dr. Eden, with his supply bag in hand, asks the Captain if he wants to join him on a visit to the town and to look for medical supplies. Captain apologizes to the Doctor, stating he cannot leave at this time. He goes on to say that he must remain on the ship for the delivery of the expected cargo. The Captain walks the Doctor to the gangway of the ship and wishes him luck in his search for medical supplies.

* * *

From the shadowy depths of the ship, come the words, which echo along every board and railing. "Dead man down! Dead man down!" Those dreaded words are what no Captain or member of a ship ever wants to hear.

The Captain paces the planked deck waiting for word of what happened. He waves his arms for all the work to cease. "Lieutenant, lift the gangway from the dock. No one will be allowed on or off the ship till we find what has taken place."

"Arthur, what is going on down there?" shouts the Captain from the open hatch.

"Sir, you may want to come down here and see for yourself!" says Arthur as his voice cracks with emotion.

The crew on deck stare down the open hatch, trying to see what has happened. The Captain takes off his cap and wipes his forehead. He walks down the stairs to view the scene below. Most holding bins are empty, making the bottom of the ship eerie and hollow.

"Over here, Captain." calls a crew member.

Carrying a lantern to where the men gather, the Captain walks to the keel of the ship. The speechless crew moves aside for him. He stands and pauses for a brief second. The entire crew remains quiet. The Captain crosses himself, and the men follow his lead.

"I believe we found our stowaway," comments the Captain in a softer tone of voice. No crew member replies, but they all keep looking at the motionless body of a young man. He lies on the chains that once held Hardie Jenkins.

The blood from the youth has dripped over the chains and onto the planks on the floor. There is a sizable pool of blood which remains, but most of the blood made its way into the gaps and joints of the boards. The bloody open gash, on the sandy-haired young man, runs from the top of his head down to his right ear. His right eye remains open, and the body lies motionless on the rusted chains. Some of the blood was diverted around his ear and formed a pathway under his plaid green and black shirt. The pockets of his brown pants are pulled out as if someone were looking for something. The inside of his left hand is bruised and covered with dried blood, and his right hand is blackened with a tar-like substance. Amongst the rusting chains lies a stone head hammer with signs of blood on it. The lost look that the young man held in that dying moment will forever be carved in the minds of the crew.

"We can see Hardie befriended this young soul. Hardie must have talked the lad into helping him escape the chains. But the lad never escaped the evilness of Hardie Jenkins. Someone get a blanket and cover up this young man."

The crew is overwhelmed by this gruesome scene. Randel turns and makes his way to an empty bin where he shouts up to the waiting crew members to drop down a blanket. Backing away from the body, the men are deep in thought. A crew member points to the floor where he was standing. Arthur kneels with a lantern.

"Captain, look! Look here! Hardie used the blood of this lad to draw us a picture of the skull and bones. Sir, it is the Jolly Roger."

The crew knows without question that this is a death threat. An instant rush of cold shivers climbs along the spines of the sailors. These hardened seamen tremble in their worn uniforms, fearing the wrath of Hardie Jenkins. Now their minds run wild with thoughts of why Hardie may want each of them dead. The Captain knows he is losing the confidence of his men, who fear the unknown.

Chapter 23

Martin and Matthew are waiting at the entrance to Lewis Castle. The Evens family walk the cobblestone walkway with Susannah in the lead. Susannah's smile catches Matthew's attention. The pink bonnet she wears enhances her blonde hair. She is in a full-length pink dress, with white trim on the hem, and on the cuffs of the long sleeves. Susannah has a matching umbrella, folded under her right arm.

Mrs. Evens wears a full-length, grey coloured dress. Her dress has black trim on the bottom and at the neckline, to match her bonnet. Donald Evens follows behind the two ladies carrying a bag of supplies he purchased from one of the shops. Holding his walking stick in his right hand, he stops and unbuttons his brown leather jacket. His high-top boots are the same colour as the jacket. He has on a beige woollen sweater and grey pants.

"Hello, Matthew. Hello, Martin. Thank you for meeting us here," says Susannah beaming with a smile.

The nervous, but happy, Matthew replies quickly. "We are honoured to be asked to join you and your family this fine day."

"Mother, Father, you have met Matthew before. This is Martin, Matthew's brother."

Donald and Aggie both shake hands with Martin. "Well, let's get on with the tour of the castle. Maybe we can find a place to sit down soon. My feet are killing me," says Donald.

They walk on a narrow cobblestone road to a lowered drawbridge. It is approximately thirty feet long and has two large chains running from the castle to the open end of the bridge. The old iron chains on each side of the drawbridge are moss-covered indicating that the bridge has not been lifted in years. Stagnant water in the moat surrounding the castle gives off a stale odour. A group of ducks glide on the tranquil waters causing the floating lilies to bobble. Sensing that winter is approaching, the wild grasses and plants have begun to turn brown.

As they stroll along the enormous walls of the castle, Martin and Matthew are amazed, touching every block of stone they pass. Aggie can see the excitement in their daughter's eyes, due to Matthew being there. Martin begins to run ahead and climbs the steps to the top of the castle wall. Susannah turns to her parents with a look that only her mother would understand. Mr. Evens tells them to go on ahead, while he and Aggie look for a place to sit down.

"Donald, do you see how happy Susannah looks?"

"The only thing I want to see right now is a chair to sit on, and a glass of whiskey."

"Oh Donald, look at her and Matthew together."

Susannah, Matthew, and Martin are on the top of the castle wall and look down toward the sea. They can see the ship and the Union Jack waving in the late afternoon breeze. The dock area is in constant motion with men and horse-drawn carriages. Large and small containers align the dock area. The crane used to lift supplies to the Sara Rose is motionless. Martin points to the deck of the ship where they notice all the men gathered in a circle. They wonder what is happening and can see that the gangway has been lifted, thus denying access to the ship. The three make their way down the stone stairway to the grounds of the castle. They share their news with Mr. and Mrs. Evens, Donald suggests there is no need to worry.

The Captain has called all the members of the crew together. They have gathered around him in a circle. "Men, first of all, let's join in prayer for the young man." The crew remove their caps and bow their heads. The Captain recites a short prayer for the stowaway.

"We have a serious situation on board the ship. We have, not only a dead man but a man who committed murder aboard the ship. Now, we must find Hardie Jenkins, and soon. The Lieutenant will unlock the door to where the firearms are stored. All those who know how to use a weapon, take one. We will split into groups and search the ship from the keel to the crow's nest. We don't know if Hardie is onboard or if he crawled into one of the cargo lifts and is on dry land by now. Mr. Downing, you take four armed men with you and search the bottom of the boat in the bow section.

Mr. Quinn, arm a group of men and search the stern bottom area. Mr. Johnson, take a few men and search the steerage section. Arthur, you and Randel, carry weapons and guard the stairwells. Lieutenant, you look in the upper class cabins and take armed men with you. All right, let's get our firearms and begin the search. You three men, follow me. Men, remember if you have to shoot, shoot to kill."

* * *

Matthew and Susannah walk among the rows of fruit trees. Susannah grasps the trunk of a small tree in her left hand and swings around in front of Matthew. Their breath mingles; their eyes crave the other, and their bodies silently beg to touch. Matthew quickly looks over his right shoulder to see if anyone is looking. Without hesitation, he kisses her on the lips. They both pull back and take each other's hand under the leafless apple tree.

Aggie notices the two from the corner of her eye and calls them over. They walk back slowly, chatting as their feelings intensify for each other. Each walk on the opposite side of the trees. When they get close to the trunk of a tree, they reach out and touch each other's hand. The tree trunk hides the touch and the two giggle every time their hands meet. Donald and Aggie look at Susannah and Matthew in amusement.

Donald takes his wife aside and whispers in her ear, "Were we like that?"

Aggie looks at Donald and grins. "Donald, you've forgotten how mischievous you were. Hmm, Donald, you still are, at times."

Donald blushes and chuckles to himself. His steps have found a new stride.

Deep in the bottom of the ship, the search for Hardie has begun. First Mate Downing and his small team of men are in the darkest part of the vessel. A few men hold lanterns tied to broom handles. This enables them to see further ahead when they come to the corner of the cargo. The groups call back and forth for safety reasons.

The Lieutenant approaches the Captain with his group of men staying close to him. "Captain, we searched all the cabins and opened every door, but no sign of Hardie or any mischief."

"Thank you, Lieutenant. We did the same. We even checked my cabin and the crow's nest. Let's go to the stern and look in the jolly boats."

The group of men advances toward the stern. The canvas covers that protect the jolly boats are taken off and the boats inspected for any signs of Hardie having hidden there. The Lieutenant calls the Captain over, and they both look down at the water. They are surprised to see a rope hanging over the edge of the stern, swaying in the wind.

First Mate Downing and Second Mate Quinn come to the stern of the ship with their respective groups of men. They both salute the Captain. "Sir, we have found nothing at all. There is no sign of Hardie, or any cargo being disturbed. We've searched every inch of the bottom of the ship."

"Thank you, Mr. Downing. Let's go back to the galley area; I see Mr. Johnson and his men. Someone check on Arthur and Randel."

"Lieutenant, we have to resume the unloading of the ship, but the darkness has beaten us this day. I must make a report to the Port Major on the incident, and arrange burial for the murdered lad. Don't allow anyone on or off the ship till I return."

The Captain is questioned by the passengers when he steps on the dock. He tells them he will return soon and they will be allowed to board the ship at that time. They move aside for the Captain as he walks towards the Port Major's office. He knocks on the door and is greeted with the customary salute. The Captain informs him of the current situation regarding Hardie, and Hardie's earlier actions toward the Lieutenant. They discuss the murder of the young stowaway and the futile search of the ship for Hardie Jenkins.

The Port Major gets up from this chair and heads towards the closed door. He exits the room and waves his assistant to enter the office.

"Captain, I will get my assistant to inform our local police. In Stornoway, we only have three officers of the law. They have no jurisdiction aboard your ship. Only you do, Sir. It is a good assumption that Hardie Jenkins may be among us in the town."

"Yes, it's possible he may be hiding in Stornoway and will surface once the Sara Rose is out to sea. There is also the matter of burial for the young stowaway," comments the Captain.

"That should not be a problem. I will notify the local clergy on my way home this evening. We have a Potter's Field outside Stornoway. Did the young man have a name?"

"Only Hardie Jenkins and Our Lord now know the name of the youth," says the Captain as he lowers his head.

"Captain, I don't know your Hardie Jenkins, but the Jolly Roger sign in blood tells me this man seeks vengeance and is still aboard your ship."

"Yes, I believe you're right," says the Captain as the two men salute each other.

The Captain leaves the office of the Port Major and begins his descent to the pier. He informs the passengers on the dock of what occurred on the ship, assuring them they have nothing to worry about and can board the ship now. The Captain is faced with a barrage of questions. Floyd Ogden announces that they will take a room at the local inn for the night. Carol Harris says they will do the same. The Captain waves for the gangway to be lowered and leads the group of passengers up the walkway to where the Lieutenant is waiting to greet him. Captain Mcbaine salutes the ship before stepping onto the deck.

"Lieutenant, inform Mr. Johnson he will be in charge of the passengers boarding and leaving the ship. Then meet me in my cabin as soon as possible."

The Captain goes to his cabin, throwing his cap on the desk, and opens the bottom drawer, taking out a bottle of rum. He pours a generous quantity of rum in his tin cup and sits in his chair. The Lieutenant knocks on the open door and the Captain waves to him to come in.

"Sit down, Mr. Rodgers. Would you like a tin of rum, Lieutenant?"

"Sir, I am on duty."

"Yes, you're right, Lieutenant. So am I." The Captain opens the bottle that held the rum and pours the contents of his cup back in. He opens the drawer of the desk and returns the rum to its original spot.

Chapter 24

Darkness begins to descend on the town of Stornoway. Two men, on either side of the street, walk with a long pole. A large candle made from whale fat is fastened to the end of the pole. They begin to light each street lantern. Following the men, while they continue with this nightly chore, is a parade of stray dogs. The dogs follow in this evening ritual till they pick up the scent of a cat, and then the chase is on. The dogs can be heard barking in the distance as the pursuit continues. The more they bark, the more dogs gather and join in. Finally, the pack of dogs realizes the cat has disappeared. The dogs scatter and head in different directions.

Matthew and Martin, along with the Evens family, walk the cobblestone streets of Stornoway where the darkness quickly joins them. They notice Dr. Eden coming down a side street and wait for him. The doctor greets the group, and they all walk to the dock together. The doctor asks Martin how he has been feeling lately. Martin replies that he has been feeling much better since the weather warmed.

The Evens, along with Doctor Eden, Matthew and Martin enter the dock area. They can see the Ogden's and Harris's coming at a hurried pace. Donald Evens asks them where they are going at such a late hour. They reveal what has happened on the Sara Rose, and state they are not spending the night on the ship and will seek lodging at the inn. They ask Mr. Evens if he and his family want to join them at the inn tonight. Donald thinks for a second and kindly says no. The families bid each other a good night and continue their separate ways.

Two armed men stand at the top of the gangway while the group comes on board. Dr. Eden says goodnight and proceeds to the Captain's cabin. Donald shakes hands with the two brothers and thanks them for accompanying them on the tour of Lewis Castle. Aggie Evens smiles at Matthew and Martin, then walks off with her husband. Susannah has a tear in her eye, knowing she has to leave Matthew. She touches his right hand. He takes her fingers in his hand and gives them a gentle squeeze. She smiles and walks away.

Susannah stops after a few steps. She looks back at Matthew. A yearning, a desire to run back to him overwhelms her. She controls her emotions and joins her parents.

The doctor knocks on the Captain's door. A pause ensues. The Captain is writing in the ship's logbook. He closes the book and walks to the door. "Good evening, Doctor. Come in and take a seat. How did you enjoy the afternoon in Stornoway?"

Dr. Eden enters the room with his bag of supplies. "Captain, it's a unique town. I did manage a quick look at the Castle. It's an amazing structure, and I am glad I had a chance to see it. I hope you get a chance to visit it!"

"I don't think I will have time. A lot has happened since I last saw you, which you probably heard already! Did you manage to get the medical supplies you needed?"

"I was only able to purchase two bottles of medicine. Captain, is there any more information on the whereabouts of Hardie Jenkins?" asks the doctor while preparing to leave the Captain's cabin.

The Captain slides back his chair and stands. "No, Doctor, no one has seen him." He walks the doctor to his cabin door. The two men shake hands and bid each other a good evening.

* * *

From the hole in the wall, the mouse can view all the activity on the deck of the ship. It is suspicious of everyone tonight, for the footsteps are louder and much quicker. The mouse can hear the dripping sound of water as it falls to the planked deck from the freshwater barrel. The rodent knows it must be patient and wait till later.

Aggie Evens turns to her daughter. "Susannah, I insist you stay with us tonight. We will get a few things from your cabin, and I will get a steward to bring a cot into our room for you." Susannah agrees quickly, without argument.

The rumours of the murdered stowaway have the passengers in fear, and many bring their blankets to sleep on the lounge chairs as a group.

Martin has been asleep since he came back from the tour of Lewis Castle. The steerage section is alive with the sleeping sounds of snoring men. They seem to shake the cobwebs free from the wooden beams faster than the night spiders can build them. Some of the sounds cannot be described, and the smell of these weary travellers causes one's eyes to squint in this poorly lit area containing little to no ventilation.

It is late, but Matthew cannot sleep. He continually turns from side to side on his uncomfortable bunk bed. He knows the guards will send him back if he attempts to go on deck this evening.

The sounds of footsteps are heard on deck as the armed crew maintain a continuous patrol. From time to time, they peer over the railing of the ship, for the shadows and reflections cause imaginary visions. It is a haunting feeling with the lantern's flickering in the eerie darkness. Suddenly, a light will vanish from sight, when a breeze teases the air and extinguishes the flame.

Two men on patrol stop and aim their firearms into the darkness, calling, "Who goes there?" The silent night does not respond. They call again, "Who goes there?" A chill trickles down the backbone of each man. Their minds run wild. Their eyes are staring sightlessly into the darkness. The fingers that hold the triggers are frozen. The creak of the ship against the wharf breaks the spell, and the men advance into the blackened night, realizing it was their imagination.

* * *

The ships little stowaway peers into the night sky, dropping the crust of bread from its mouth. The mouse knows not what it is seeing, realizing its demise may be near.

143

The night has suppressed what little light had remained. The nervous moon in its quarterly phase, acts as if it holds a secret. It tips downward, possibly pointing to the hiding spot of Hardie Jenkins. The ghost-like clouds wipe the face of the moon, not allowing it to fall asleep this night. Even the night skies now fear the wrath of this evil man. The tragedy aboard the Sara Rose has caused the stars to join hands in the night. The Heavens open to display a wondrous light show. Perhaps this is in remembrance of the nameless youth who was murdered. The sailors aboard the ship look upward in astonishment, removing their caps. They have never witnessed an event such as this, calling the inspiring scene, 'The Northern Lights.'

Chapter 25

The agonizing night does not give up its claim on the darkness, and now an empty eeriness is instilled into the souls of the passengers and crew. The slow rocking rhythm of the ship keeps time with the night's heartbeat. The imagination of all onboard has climaxed to a point where each can visualize being murdered by Hardie Jenkins.

The ships little stowaway backs into the corner of its home. The hole in the wall offers the terrified mouse the personal protection it needs from the dreaded ships broom and the constant nightmares of becoming a victim of Hardie Jenkins. The rodent knows it must escape the clutches which blanket the vessel in horrors and must devise a plan to sneak off the docked ship, before the Sara Rose sails.

* * *

The morning sun edges its way into the Port of Stornoway. In the lounge, passengers are bundled in blankets trying to sleep on the uncomfortable deck chairs. They have their eyes closed, but none is truly sleeping, only going in and out of trancelike dreams. Their nervous bodies twitch as if they are witnessing an ordeal that the Devil himself has initiated.

Their elusive thoughts are waiting for the morning sun to erode the shroud which surrounds them. Only the children were blessed by a sprinkling of magic from the Sandman when he performed his sacred duty.

Dawn has regained its strength and advances, beginning to remove all signs of the night. The tension that gripped all is slowly released with the arrival of daylight.

The Captain and crew have been awake throughout the long night. He tells every second man to go to get a few hours of sleep. The Captain knows they are all at risk of being on the end of Hardie's sword, and he particularly fears for the Lieutenant. If Hardie is to draw blood again, it is the Lieutenant's blood he wishes to see pooling on the deck of the Sara Rose.

"Mr. Downing, Mr. Quinn, join me as I walk to the galley. Gentlemen, it was one of the longest nights I can recall. The two of you likely feel the same. There was no sign of Hardie during the night. I believe he remains on the ship. Are you in agreement with me?"

"Yes, Captain, Hardie seeks blood, and I can sense his presence on board. We all do," nervously comments First Mate Downing.

"I believe you're right, Mr. Downing, his first victim would be the Lieutenant. So, I want you and Mr. Quinn to keep a constant watch on our Lieutenant."

The Captain knows he must get some sleep, and wearily proceeds to his cabin. Sitting in his chair, he takes a sip of cold tea to relax his tired body before he closes his eyes. His mind tells him it is safe to fall asleep, but his eyes keep opening to see if the door to his cabin is locked. His mind's internal struggle leads him into a dreamless sleep.

Jones uses his walking stick to push the lounge door open and enters where the passengers sleep. He grumbles while passing the deck chairs, making sure his presence is known, as a trail of cigar smoke follows him. He noisily makes his way to the dining room, calling for a steward to bring him tea. Looking around, he notices a few families sitting at tables, including the Peters family.

"Peters, you look like you saw a ghost in the night," chuckles Jones as he passes. Mrs. Peters puts her hand on her husband's hand as a sign not to comment to this taunting man.

Matthew is up early, waiting to be called to work in the galley. Martin remains asleep in his bunk. Joey and Neil Cunningham are making their way to the stairwell and up to the deck at the stern. Two youngsters are full of questions about Hardie, when Matthew joins them at the table. The lads have their theories as to where Hardie may be hiding. Thinking of this as an unsolved mystery, they are playing detective.

Matthew cannot keep up with the questions Neil and Joey are asking him. They bring up the event which led to Hardie being chained; describing the bravery the Lieutenant showed, and how their sister thinks of the Lieutenant as a Knight in shining armour.

The flamboyant Molly comes to the table and joins in the conversation. She offers her opinion as to where Hardie may be, claiming he slid down a rope when the Sara Rose was settling into her berth.

Molly goes on to say that in all probability with everyone busy tying the ship to the mooring, Hardie lowered himself into the waters and swam along the dock. Molly points to the dock and tells them he swam around the corner, crawled onto the pier and disappeared into the town. Joey and Neil sit at the table with their mouths gaping. Their eyes widen in size as they listen to Molly. Intrigued, the boys are quiet for a moment, then their inquisitive thoughts come alive, and they bombard Molly with a volley of questions.

"Molly, do you think Hardie will come back to the ship and murder the Lieutenant?"

"Why would he leave the ship, if there are so many hiding places onboard?"

"Why did he kill the stowaway?"

"Will he try and kill the Captain?

"Molly, are we all in danger too?"

Molly smiles at the youngsters. She calmly gets up from the table and says, "No, we are not in danger children. The brave crew will protect everyone." She walks to the railing of the ship rolling a cigarette.

There are a small number of dockworkers gathered on the pier this morning. A few repack tobacco in their pipes, lighting them while they talk. Pockets of smoke join the morning air as they point in different directions, discussing the cargo before the work begins. The workers bid a good morning to the Port Major of Stornoway, as he makes his way to the Rose.

The Port Major identifies himself to the guard on the wharf, who is protecting the entrance to the vessel. He allows the Port Major to proceed up the gangway where two armed sailors ask his business. One of the guards goes to the Captain's cabin and knocks. The Captain quickly rising to his feet. Taking his cap in hand, the Captain opens the door, wiping his eyes on his sleeve. He proceeds to the entrance of the walkway and shakes hands with William Brett, the Port Major.

"Sir, join me for a quick cup of tea," says the Captain. "Let's sit over here. It will be private."

"Captain, I see your crew is rather restless. I take it, there is no sign of Hardie Jenkins. I talked to our local police, and they spread the word that Hardie may be hiding in the town. A few of the local men went from door to door with the law last night checking on everyone. There was no sign of any intruders or disturbances during the night," claims the Port Major.

William Brett takes a sip of tea and continues. "I took the liberty of speaking to the church clergy about the murdered young lad. They said there would not be an issue with laying the young man to rest in Potter's Field, but the cost would have to be incurred by your ship."

"Yes," says the Captain. "The cost is the least we can do to give this unfortunate soul a final resting place."

"The clergy told me they would send someone with a carriage later in the day to pick up the body. I expect you will accompany the body to the cemetery when it is called for later today?" asks the Port Major.

"Yes, I will. Perhaps a few of the crew may accompany me as well. I will also take care of the costs for the burial."

The Captain and William Brett continue the conversation as they proceed to the walkway. "Thank you, Captain. We still have a few loose ends to wrap up. The seven cases of Viking artifacts that the Sara Rose has been chartered to deliver to the Americas will be loaded on the ship last. They are stored under guard in the armoury, and I will be present for the loading. We have to itemize each article, then reseal the cases."

The Port Major begins his descent to the dock to oversee the unloading of the remainder of the ship's cargo. The Captain returns to his men.

The dockworkers swing the large derrick over the ship's cargo area and wait for instructions. There seems to be some confusion about who is to go to the bottom of the ship to load the cargo into the nets. The Captain can understand the crew's reluctance to enter the cargo hold this morning.

"Lieutenant, you will be in charge of the crew on deck, and I will go below and help in the cargo hold."

Captain Mcbaine takes a lantern in his hand and tells Randel to follow him with the six other men. The men follow the Captain down the steps to the mysterious bowels of the ship. He calls for the sling to be lowered. The Captain knows he must lead his men by doing what the crew fear to do. His actions of entering the dreaded bottom of the ship inspire confidence in his men, yet his inner fears remain.

Chapter 26

The little mouse cannot control its hunger any longer and makes a desperate dash for the dining room. Again, the rodent ignores its natural instincts and runs into the middle of the room, using the legs of the tables and chairs as hiding spots.

The mouse retains its belief, if it cannot see anyone while it hides behind a table or chair leg, then no one can see it. The sound of footsteps approaching on the wooden floor sends the mouse scampering into a nearby cupboard. The little stowaway waits for the sounds to subside before emerging.

* * *

A single greyish horse, pulling a two-wheeled cart approaches the dock. An elderly man with a pipe in his mouth stands in the cart, continually coaxing the horse to keep moving. The driver of the wagon is wearing a flat grey cap and warmly wrapped in a heavy wool jacket. The horse steps sideways at the sound of its hoofs on the wooden dock, and the driver can be heard calming the horse, repeating, "Come on Genny. Come on girl."

Behind the cart walks a Priest, wearing a long black robe with a rope tied around his waist. His black hat is shaped like a crown and appears to be approximately four inches in height. A pair of small rimmed glasses rests tightly against his face. In his left hand, he holds a Bible close to his chest. The Priest walks a short distance behind the cart with his head down, continuously chanting prayers.

The grey horse is nervous, making her way along the stacks of cargo on the dock. Dockworkers stop their work when they notice the Priest walking behind the cart. The driver coaxes the horse near the gangway, calling out that he is there to pick up a body. The Priest remains behind the cart. Opening the Bible, he begins to read to himself.

The Captain leans over the railing, calling down to the driver of the cart. "Sir, we will be down shortly with the body."

"Lieutenant, get the First Mate over here. The two of you carry the lad onto the dock."

"Me, Sir? You want me to help carry the body down?" questions the shocked Lieutenant.

"Lieutenant, I will only say this once more! Get the First Mate and help him carry the body to the dock!" shouts the agitated Captain.

The body of the murdered young lad is wrapped in a grey blanket. An offensive odour seeps through the blanket. The Captain pulls off the canvas cover which keeps the wheel of the ship dry while they are in port. They lay the youth on the canvas, tying it snugly around him with thin ropes, creating a makeshift coffin.

They are observed by the silent crew, who stand with their caps in their hands. Captain Mcbaine reaches into his pocket, pulling out a bundle of keys tied with a leather strap. He unties the leather strap to slide off a key. Kneeling next to the body, he tucks the key inside the canvas coffin and offers a few words, "This nameless youth is sent to you, Our God. Now, he has the key to enter your Kingdom of Heaven as he wishes."

First Mate Downing and the Lieutenant pick up the body. They slowly carry the young man to the dock, followed by the Captain with his cap in his hand. The crew and passengers look down to the wharf, crossing themselves. The lifeless body is placed in the cart, and the Priest begins to read a prayer, making the sign of a cross. All the dock workers remove their caps and stand, showing respect for the young stowaway who lost his life aboard the Sara Rose.

The Captain salutes the Lieutenant and tells him he is in charge of the ship.

The elderly man takes the grey horse by the bridle, calling, "Come on Genny. Come on girl." Driver and horse walk together off the dock proceeding onto the streets of Stornoway. Captain Mcbaine follows the Priest, who walks a short distance behind the cart.

From the deck of the Rose, the sacred sound of a lone violin is weeping the solemn tune, **A Closer Walk with Thee**, calming the restless morning air. The women on the ship begin to cry. The men turn away from their wives, to wipe away their own tears.

The planked boardwalks of Stornoway begin to fill with the town's citizens carrying flowers, and rosaries in their hands. The small children timidly hide behind their mothers' skirts.

The Port Major joins the Captain in the walk to Potter's Field, as the grey horse leads the saddened crowd down the centre of the street. The Captain looks back at his ship, while sounds of the violin echo between the empty houses. He sees a line of people stepping off the vessel. Dockworkers have joined the line of mourners, and the citizens on the sidewalks now join in the walk to Potter's Cemetery.

The stray dogs that run the boarded walkways of Stornoway by night emit a lonely howl along the empty streets.

The cart driver and his grey horse continue the walk to the edge of town, making their way carefully across the hallowed ground. Most of the souls beneath this sacred soil have neither markers nor stones. A deep emptiness comes to all who now enter this consecrated part of town with its secrets.

The vast cemetery is overgrown with small shrubs and long grass, now turning to the winter colours. In places, the abandoned graves have sunk into the ground. One can see where wild animals and birds have used the lonely, sunken graves for sleeping and nesting.

In the centre of Potter's Field is an old wooden cross that may have been erected when the island was first inhabited. Its rugged crosspiece has lost all strength, but not its will and is a sad reminder of the ravages of time. A few of the graves closer to the old cross have stone markers with dates chiselled into them. One reads twelve hundred thirty- four; another eleven hundred ninety-one.

"Whoa Genny," softly says the driver. The grey horse stops as followers form a large circle in this desolate cemetery. The Captain and the Port Major each remove a shovel from the cart. Matthew leaves Susannah's side and takes a shovel to lend a hand. A dockworker takes another, and the men prepare the final resting spot for the young man. The ladies in the crowd begin to sing the hymn **'A Closer Walk with Thee,'** and the crowd joins in. First Mate Downing takes the shovel from the Captain, and a townsman relieves the Port Major. The men take turns, for everyone wants to help.

Then under the watching eyes of the Heavens, six men lower the unknown young man to his final resting spot. The Priest says one last prayer and a choir of voices join to sing **Amazing Grace**, while the humbled crowd crosses themselves. The rugged, old wooden cross retains its silent thoughts.

Chapter 27

The returning crowd silently walks down the centre of the dirt-covered street. The stray dogs that rule the town when the darkness falls, come running to meet the townspeople. From a distance, the Sara Rose can be seen with her Union Jack lowered to half-mast.

The mouse lays sleeping on the railing of the ship sunning itself. Its sleep is disturbed when a flock of squawking seagulls fly overhead and land on the wharf in search of a free meal.

The woken rodent notices the crowd of people walking toward the ship and is startled. The little stowaway quickly jumps from the railing and scoots to its home in the wall, in fear that the crowd may be after it.

The grey horse and its driver accompany Captain Mcbaine to the church inside the town. The Captain pays the Priest for the service and the resting spot in Potter's Field for the unknown young man.

"Sir, would you like a ride back to your ship?"

"Yes, I think that would be an excellent idea. It's getting late."

"Come on Genny. Come on girl." says the cart driver as he motions the grey horse forward.

From the dining room, Jones shouts, "Where is everybody? Pour me a flask of rum and add a bit of tea to it. I have been here for hours waiting for someone to fix my dinner."

"Sorry, Sir. We were at the burial for the stowaway," replies the steward.

"The burial! What burial?" shrieks Jones, "No one told me! Now, where is my dinner?"

The two-wheeled cart makes its way across the dock to the gangway where it stops. The Captain reaches into his pocket for a few shillings, but the cart driver shakes his head, refusing any payment. Captain Mcbaine tips his hat to the cart driver in appreciation. He takes the horse by its bridle and rubs its mane a few times. Giving the horse gentle pats on the neck, he says, "Good girl, Genny!"

The Lieutenant hurriedly approaches the Captain the moment he steps foot on the deck, "Sir, you must come with me."

"Perfect, Lieutenant. What's the problem?"

"Follow me to the bottom of the ship, Sir. The crew and I have found a place where Hardie may have been hiding. I told the crew to keep their silence till they heard from you."

"Very good, Lieutenant. Let us see the hiding place you found. Are the men still guarding the area?"

"Yes, they are," says the Lieutenant, descending the steps to the bottom of the ship with the Captain.

Four of the crew members bear firearms and are guarding the area. The eager Lieutenant holding a lantern, says, "Look, Captain, when they built the ship, they made her very strong. Extra ribs were added to reinforce the hull and the main mast. The Rose has a larger cargo capacity, and she has a false area where the next deck begins. I am sure the stowaway was hiding in here and in all probability told Hardie about this spot."

"Thank you, Mr. Rodgers. I believe you could be right. That would have given Hardie a motive for murder. He could be anywhere up there, and is probably listening to us now."

An eerie rush of fear envelops the men while looking at all the possible spots for concealment. The thought of Hardie listening to them causes their toes to curl and their souls to quiver.

The Captain now uses hand signals, in the event Hardie may be near and listening. He motions the Lieutenant and two guards to come to the main deck, leaving two men to stand their posts.

"Well, we still can't be sure Hardie is even on the ship, or if he is hiding in the area we have just seen. Whoever crawls up into that cavity will be a dead man, for Hardie will have a knife in his throat before he has time to scream. We do not have any idea of all the exit places where he could come out. We are expecting cargo soon and must prepare for it. You two men, go for a bite to eat, then relieve your mates who are on guard now. Shoot to kill if he appears. Let's keep this to ourselves gentlemen. We will deal with this later."

"Lieutenant, the Port Major will be here soon, and we have to ready the ship for the cargo. We are expecting seven sealed cases of Viking artifacts. The crates must be opened and the artifacts itemized. We are responsible for every piece inside the boxes. We will not make the sea tonight as time has left us."

* * *

Susannah is in a world of her own, sitting in the late afternoon sun on the port side of the vessel. Her mind is a stirring bundle of emotions. The magical poetry in 'After Midnight' is taking her beyond the deck of the ship and into mesmerizing daydreams. The author has her spellbound as she reads. Her lips move with every written word, and her left hand is pressed against her chest, retaining each word, not allowing them to escape.

Entranced, Susannah cannot hear the footsteps around her, nor the giggling of her mother next to her. Aggie Evens is thoroughly enjoying 'The Jolly Beggars' by her favourite author, Robert Burns. She bursts into an occasional laugh and nudges Donald to look at what she is reading. Donald ignores her, for he is slumped in his deck chair with only one eye partially open. He goes in and out of consciousness with the slight rocking of the ship lulling him into slumber.

Mrs. Peters and a group of ladies are deep in conversation, while their children run up and down the deck. Jones is agitated and annoyed as the children stop and stare at him, then run away pretending to be terrified of this outspoken individual. They make childish gestures to him from a safe distance, which in turn infuriates Jones. He tends to puff harder on his beloved cigar, the more he is taunted.

Finally, the outspoken Mrs. Harris stands up and threateningly addresses the children. The scolded children break up their little group and run to hide behind their mothers' skirts.

The easily embarrassed Ronald Harris puts his head down and turns in another direction. The conversation quickly changes with the appearance of armed guards walking alongside the cargo in a horse-drawn wagon.

Standing at attention, in the dulling sunshine, the men's faded red uniforms almost appear to be an orange colour. Out of eight men in this company, the one who is in charge carries a sword at his side and is a Corporal. His uniform has a single blue stripe across the shoulder area and at the end of his sleeves. A thin ribbon of blue fabric is sewn around the cuff. The other seven men have firearms and hold them as if they were on parade.

"Captain, I have the cargo waiting on the dock," says the Port Major walking up to the Captain at the railing of the ship.

"All right, let's bring the containers aboard. Lieutenant, get the men ready."

The crew of the Sara Rose have the cargo bin swept clean of cobwebs. They scraped the mildew off the moulding lumber -- sunlight has never shone on this part of the vessel. The Lieutenant waves to the dock crew to begin work. The soldiers are ordered to step back from the wagon by the ranking officer.

A team of well-groomed, sorrel Eriskey ponies pull the four-wheeled wagon on which the cargo rests. Two men step down from the driver's seat; each holds a horse by its bridle and continuously talks to the patient horses. The sling of the large crane lowers beside the four-wheeled wagon. Four dockworkers climb onto the cart and begin to slide the crates onto the sling. The precious cargo is loaded onto the ship and placed in a secluded area of the vessel.

The Port Major calls down to the dock and dismisses the two men who hauled the cargo. One man climbs onto the wagon, while the other walks the team of horses onto the dirt streets. The armed guards reposition themselves to protect the entrance to the ship.

"Captain, I want you and your most trusted men to be present when we open the five crates. Sir, I insist that only you and the Lieutenant bear witness to what is in the two small boxes," says William Brett.

"Lieutenant, go fetch Mr. Downing, Mr. Quinn, and Mr. Johnson if he is about. Ask them to join us. Be quick now!" requests the Captain.

The Port Major picks up a long round bar of steel which is flattened on one end like a chisel. He pounds on the larger unsharpened end of the chisel with a hammer. The flattened end finds its way between the layers of boards. William Brett applies pressure downward with his body as one corner begins to inch open slowly. The Captain helps and the two keep moving the pry bar around until the top is free. The Lieutenant arrives with the three men, they stand over the open crate astonished at what they see.

William Brett calmly says, "Gentlemen, here is a look back to a thousand years ago. Count yourselves blessed. You are among a handful of people who have seen these great pieces of our past."

"This is amazing! Some of the artifacts we are about to touch may have belonged to one of our ancestors," says the excited Lieutenant.

"You're correct, Lieutenant. Now, each box has an inventory slate inside. Every time the box was opened, a complete inventory was done. The slate was signed and dated, along with the copy I have."

The Captain takes the slate, and the crew begins removing each piece carefully. They start with a sword that is still within its sheath. This priceless piece is gently set on an unopened crate. There are three loose swords without sheaths; their chipped blades indicate they were well-used in fierce battles. Captain Mcbaine is checking off each piece, while William Brett makes sure that nothing is broken, and places the items back into the crate. The Captain signs his name to the slate as does William Brett while Mr. Quinn nails the container closed.

"I am anxious to see the next crate opened," declares the Lieutenant.

Mr. Downing picks up the bar with the flattened end and holds it against the crate for Mr. Johnson to hit with the hammer. The two men work their way around the crate. The Lieutenant bends down to take the top of the crate in his hands. "Oh my God!" gasps the Lieutenant. He is shocked at what he sees. The lid slips from his hands and falls back onto the crate.

"What is it, Lieutenant?" asks the surprised Second Mate as he steps back. The red-faced Lieutenant bites his lip, closes his eyes, and again removes the cover. Captain Mcbaine steadies himself and peers into the crates, as does the burly Mr. Johnson. The Port Major places his hand over his mouth. The five men are trying to contain themselves, but cannot. They laugh loudly in a way that offends the young Mr. Rodgers.

"Lieutenant, the poor soul in the crate surprised us also. Please excuse our behaviour," politely states the Captain.

"Sir, look at the skull. It looks like this victim was hit with an axe."

Captain Mcbaine kneels by the opened box, pausing as if he were talking to an old friend. He crosses himself, and the onlookers follow his lead.

Chapter 28

The stray dogs chase a sand-coloured cat onto the planked dock for amusement. Frightened, the cat runs around the large crates of cargo, seeking a hiding place. The homeless band of canine brothers finally corners the cat. It positions itself ready for the attack and hisses at the dogs.

Some of the strays begin barking in opposite directions, claiming victory for this is a game they played several times. The cat does not agree and digs its sharp claws into the wooden planks. The barking clan has had their fun and move on to a new adventure. The hissing cat is not amused by its treatment and slithers away.

* * *

"Port Major, shall we proceed and get this last crate opened and inspected. Then, I insist you join us for dinner on the ship tonight."

"Thank you, Captain. I am looking forward to a meal on the Sara Rose," smiles William Brett.

Mr. Johnson now takes the round bar of steel in his hands. Mr. Quinn picks up the hammer and begins pounding the chisel bar to open the last big crate. The Lieutenant keeps his distance while First Mate Downing pulls the wooden top loose. The six men are like children on a Christmas morning, viewing the secrets that lie within the box.

"These artifacts are very different from those in the other four boxes. Look at the shape of this sword. It is thinner and lighter, having a protective covering for the hand," excitedly says the Captain. Astonished, he continues. "There are diamonds embedded in the handle. I count seventeen small diamonds adorning in the handle. Do you think this represents the number of people who found their death by this blade?" asks the Captain.

"I am not sure Captain, but it certainly looks that way. I agree these artifacts do not resemble those in the first four cases. I was informed at the time, that all the items were found in the same area on the Isle of Lewis," states William Brett. "Look at the battle shields. They are smaller than the ones we saw in the last crate and made of a different type of metal. Both of the shields have scenes engraved in them and are divided into four sections that start at the centre."

"Would the engraved scenes be the seasons of the year?" asks the Lieutenant stepping back from the open crate.

The Captain takes the sword in his hand again. "Sir, these rare pieces may have been in the Viking arsenal, but I think they have a Mediterranean look and style about them," comments the Captain to the Port Major, placing the precious weapons back in the box. He picks up the slate and checks off the artifacts, allowing the Second Mate to repack the remarkable find. He then signs his name to the slate, as does William Brett. The slate is set into the box with the artifacts and Mr. Johnson begins nailing the cover back on.

"Well, gentlemen, I want all of you to join me for dinner at my table. Mr. Downing, place a guard over our precious cargo, then join us for dinner."

It is a rare occasion when the First, Second, and Third Mates are asked to dine at the Captain's table. Captain Mcbaine must unite his crew, for the Hardie episode has the sailors somewhat divided. Loyalty to the ship is essential, and the Captain must command by divine right. Once again, the Lieutenant pays close attention to how the Captain gains respect from the crew.

Mr. Downing joins his shipmates at the Captain's table. There is a cup of hot tea waiting for the First Mate as he seats himself. Most of the guests have left, and are either in the lounge area or strolling on the deck.

Jones is quiet, sitting at his corner table with his cigar. Smoke from his cigar gives him such pleasure, hanging in the air like a fog. The men at the Captain's table try to contain their excitement over the contents of the crates they inspected, whispering about the artifacts so as not to be overheard. Jones purposely stretches his neck to hear the conversation at the Captain's table.

A large roast of sliced pork and a tray of roasted potatoes with a pork gravy are set on the table. A brick of sliced bread and a pot of steaming beets follow.

"Port Major, would it be a violation if a few biscuits and hot tea are sent to the docks for your men guarding the Rose?" asks the Captain.

"They are on duty Captain and will remain on the dock until the ship is out to sea. When I have finished this delicious dinner, I will personally take my men biscuits and tea."

The little mouse, hiding in the hole in the wall can smell the harsh cigar odour and begins to sneeze. With tearing eyes, the rodent circles its small home looking for fresher air. Finally, in desperation, the mouse slides its nose out of the hole in the wall in search of fresh air. The scent of fresh bread tantalizes the mind of the rodent, and its fierce hunger prevails.

Arthur and Jackal are having a late supper at the stern and are joined by the tall, lanky Randel. Randel sits with his mates and they discuss the possibility of Hardie still being aboard the ship.

Arthur voices his opinion, "Hardie had no motive to kill the young lad. Why did he have to kill him? I did not understand Hardie this last month. It seems like he was on a mission of sorts!"

"Aye, mates, I recall now, when we docked in Brighton, we were raising a few flasks of rum in the inn. Hardie wasn't there but came into the inn later that night. His chest was puffed out, and he was bragging of earlier deeds and soon to be acquired riches, but that was Hardie. As the night went on and the rum tasted much better, Hardie's shillings kept the drinks coming," explains Jackal.

* * *

From the deck of the Sara Rose, the darkening streets of Stornoway can still be seen. A man from the town begins his evening routine. He walks on the boardwalk with a large lit candle tied onto a long pole and reaches upward to give life to the waiting street lanterns.

163

The band of stray dogs gathers on the dirt street of the town, waiting for street lanterns to be lit. Once the flickering flame stirs the candle into its duty, the strays go into a communal state. They all begin wagging their tails rapidly and rub against each other. Then, in harmony, they howl into the coming night as if they have completed an important task and now are taking credit for it. They follow the candle man to the next waiting street light.

The scent of the sea rushes in as darkness calls. The Port Major slowly makes his way back to the deck of the Rose after delivering tea and biscuits to his men. From the vantage point of the deck, the Port Major looks out at the dirt streets of the town and the dock area. Lewis Castle can be seen with its majestic stare, while the dimming skies surround the fortress with a ghost-like aura. Lanterns are lit, chasing the darkness away and the accompanied hush which lurks.

Martin is packing the unwanted scraps into the big wooden barrels, from which unpleasant odours seep. Matthew, along with another steward is busy cleaning up the dishes and utensils. Matthew works his way to the table where the mysterious Jones sat, finding the table and floor covered in ashes.

Going to find a broom to clean up the mess, Matthew pauses at the opened door to the lounge area and notices Susannah. Matthew is captivated by her smile and her mannerisms. He stands in the open doorway, hoping she will look back and smile at him, but she is engrossed in conversation with a male passenger. The male passenger has her full attention. His legs are crossed and his body is turned sideways on the chair facing her. From a distance, he can tell the two are enjoying their conversation. Matthew's heart sinks and jealously drives him out of the dining room, directly to the stern of the ship -- in a pout.

* * *

William Brett knocks on the Captain's door. "Come in, Sir. I hope your men found some comfort in the tea and biscuits?" asks the Captain.

"Yes, they did. The men thank you very much for thinking of them," replies the Port Major, pulling up a chair to the Captain's desk. The Lieutenant closes the door before returning to his chair.

"Well, gentlemen, shall we open the two small crates? You will understand the need for complete secrecy regarding the items you are about to see. This is why I insisted that only you, and the Lieutenant bear witness to the contents of these two smaller crates."

The Captain retrieves one of the boxes hidden under a blanket in the corner of the room. He places the small wooden crate on his desk, William Brett takes a chisel and begins to pry the cover open. He hands the top to the Lieutenant and reaches into the wooden crate.

The suspense of the moment heightens with the three men peering into the opened crate. Inside the box, there is a moss-like webbing of fabric to protect the valuable cargo from being damaged in transport.

The Port Major's hands tremble slightly holding the wrapped item over the Captain's desk. The Captain slides the empty crate to the side of his desk, allowing room for the object. William Brett sets the precious artifact down and carefully unwraps the piece. In a hesitant, crackled voice, he says, "Gentlemen, the missing Crown of Egbert, King of Wessex."

The room fills with reverence; a silence prevails. The men are humbled and remove their caps. The Captain and Lieutenant gaze in awe at what they see. Instinctively both reach out to touch the precious Crown, but stop themselves. They look at each other, yet are unsure if they should speak.

This hallowed moment is broken by the Captain. "Can this be? Is it possible that this is the missing Crown of Egbert?"

Chapter 29

A serene silence overcomes the three humbled men staring at the Crown of Egbert. Their minds have succumbed to thoughts that they cannot comprehend. Their eyes dilate and their hearts race. Their fingertips want to touch the Crown, but they remain motionless, afraid and speechless.

The tranquil waves slowly rock the Sara Rose against the dock and the mellow ripples fold into the seawater. A prism of light is dropped down from the night skies. The glass-like waters reflect the view to the watching heavens, with the Rose at the centre of this glow.

A deafening thunderbolt erupts in the skies over the ship, and the streets of Stornoway fill with townsfolk. The lonely street lights have lost their flicker as a gust of wind extinguishes their flames. The stray dogs that roam the night streets become silent and cower under the boarded sidewalks.

The upper deck passengers rush to the starboard side of the ship, while steerage travellers group at the stern. They all look upward and search the night sky to see what has aggravated the watching heavens.

* * *

The Captain sits and composes himself. The men are astonished to have the Crown of King Egbert, King of Wessex in front of them.

"Gentlemen, I am at a loss for words," says the Captain quietly.

"Yes, I feel the same way. I feel powerless and very insignificant at this moment. We have the missing Crown of Egbert in front of us. There are many who would want this piece of history. They will do whatever it takes or pay dearly to have this for their own. The harbour has been attacked twice by pirate ships, just this year alone. This is why all the cannon were pointed at the ship when she entered the harbour. It would not have been the first time the Jolly Roger was covered over with the Union Jack," explains William Brett. He continues, "The lost Crown was discovered six years ago, along with the other artifacts on the Isle of Lewis. The artifacts have been locked in the armoury since that time. The articles were purchased by an undisclosed buyer in the Americas."

The Captain listens to the Port Major very carefully and then remarks, "This puts the Sara Rose and her passengers in grave danger. This is a peacetime passenger and cargo ship, even though the ship is equipped with cannon. Only once, since I became Captain of the vessel, were we fired upon by pirates. Thanks to the Rose's speed, we outran their Jolly Roger."

The little mouse that rules the deck at night ignores its inhibitions and pokes its nose whiskers out from the safety of its home. The dripping sound coming from the water barrel stirs the mouse's wants. Again, the little rodent's desires are stronger than its instincts. It zigs and zags between the many table and chair legs to find the water it desperately craves. The puddle forming on the planked deck is an oasis to the little mouse. It thirstily laps up the freshwater. The more it ingests, the more it desires.

The water-logged mouse begins to feel uncomfortable. Perhaps the cigar smoke is coming back to haunt the rodent's stomach. It moans and groans until it expels its stomach contents on the planked floor.

Matthew is lying in his bunk bed with his head high on the canvas bag he uses for a pillow. He repeats over and over to Martin that he saw Susannah talking to another man in the lounge area.

"Matthew, it is you Susannah likes. I've seen it in her eyes when she looks at you," says Martin, trying to console his younger brother.

"Why was she seated next to some man and talking with him? She never even looked in my direction," sulks Matthew.

"Oh, Matthew, you're making too much of this. Go to sleep," snickers Martin.

At the bottom of the ship, armed sailors take shifts watching for the elusive Hardie Jenkins. The men standing guard claim they can hear noises from the boards above and feeling as though they are being watched. This eerie feeling could unhinge any man's mind in a very short time, and the dreaded guard duty is taking a toll on the crew.

The two apprentices, Thomas Quinn and Angelo, are on duty tonight swabbing the deck of the ship. Arthur is making his rounds, lighting the ship's lanterns and stopping to chat with the young crewmen. Thomas asks, "Arthur, do you think we will be at sea tomorrow?"

Arthur stands where he is and lights his pipe. "Yes, I believe we will. The Captain suggested that we may be underway before high noon if all goes well."

"I am glad I had a chance to see Lewis Castle. Arthur, did you get to see the castle?" asks Angelo.

"Yes, I did lads. It was in thirty-nine when I served on the Scarlett under the command of Captain Perkins. I don't think the Castle has changed since then. Now get this deck swabbed."

* * *

"Lieutenant, set the other box on the desk so we can open it," asks William Brett as he picks up the chiselling tool.

The Lieutenant holds the small crate while William Brett pries the lid off the box. The Captain takes the top in his hands and the three men peer into the box. The Captain and the Lieutenant are both puzzled. There are five leather bags set in the fabric to prevent movement. Each leather sack has a strip of rawhide woven in and out to keep it closed, preventing the contents from spilling. William Brett removes one of the sacks from the open box.

"Gentlemen, each one of these bags contain one hundred coins from the same era as Egbert's Crown. Except for one; it has seventy-three coins in it. So there is a total of four hundred and seventy-three coins here. You can see the sacks are sealed and they shall remain this way till they are handed over to the proper owners," states the Port Major.

"I cannot even imagine what kind of value would be put on the coins, never mind the lost Crown of Egbert, and the five crates of Viking artifacts. This is a marvellous find for history. A true treasure!" comments the Captain excitedly.

Susannah quietly closes the door to her cabin. She stands in the hallway looking in both directions. There are armed guards at each end of the hall. She places her shawl over her shoulders, proceeds to the stairwell of the ship and quietly climbs to the deck before stopping. The ship rolls slowly against the dock and the occasional cracking sound that releases into the night air unsettles Susannah. The rumours of Hardie Jenkins rush through her terrified mind, instilling a new fear in her.

Susannah softly walks along the planked deck as if she were afraid to wake the sleeping ship. Her irrational thoughts hint to her that she is being watched. Her heart is pulsating at an uncontrolled speed and her spine tingles. The visions in her mind compete with what she sees, but her blind suspicions have no proof. Finally, her hand touches the railing of the ship. Feeling relieved, she looks down at the poorly lit dock.

Turning in the direction of her imagined horror, Susannah now composes herself. She wipes her mind clean of the self-imposed girlish fears. Her slightly shaking body begins to relax while waiting for Matthew.

In the Captain's cabin, the Port Major makes a startling comment. "Gentlemen, I am not comfortable with the situation we have aboard the vessel. I have performed my duty in delivering the artifacts onto the ship. We have checked and double-checked the contents of the crates, and the issue of Hardie Jenkins leaves a sour taste in my mouth. Captain, is it possible Hardie plans to take control of the ship eventually?"

"Sir, I hardly think Jenkins himself could overpower my crew and gain control of the ship. He would have to kill one man at a time to complete his task," swiftly replies the Captain.

"Captain, Stornoway has been attacked by pirates twice, and they could not gain control of the harbour. Therefore, I strongly believe we are being watched and the Sara Rose will be attacked for the treasure she carries." William Brett pauses, places his hands behind his back, and chooses his words carefully so as not to offend the Captain, "Captain, is it possible Jenkins knew of the cargo the ship would be transporting to the Americas, and her route?"

The Captain quickly responds to William Brett's question, "Definitely not, Port Major. I was the only person to read the orders and they are locked in the ship's safe, here in my cabin."

The Lieutenant steps back. The Captain is enraged and continues, "I am the Captain of the Sara Rose and your accusation is uncalled for. You may outrank me, Sir, but your rank on my ship is invalid."

"Sorry to question your authority, Captain. I did not mean to offend you or your ship. Please accept my apology."

"Yes, Port Major, we are all a bit edgy the last few days. Lieutenant, go fetch us a container of tea."

* * *

"Matthew, are you planning on meeting Susannah tonight," asks Martin in a subtle manner.

"The last time I saw her, we hadn't made plans to meet."

"Oh, so you're going to sulk in your bunk all night and whine to everyone here that you are not good enough for her. You better get dressed and get on deck to see if she is there. What if she is waiting for you?" says Martin sternly.

Matthew grumbles to himself, turning to face the other direction in his bunk. His mind is replaying the incident in which he had seen Susannah seated next to another man talking to him.

"Get dressed and get up to the deck of the ship. You will regret this moment for the rest of your life if you do not," insists Martin.

Time slowly passes while Susannah quietly waits for Matthew. The sailors with firearms patrolling the deck have noticed Susannah, but her presence on the deck of the ship is never questioned. Susannah knows it's late and begins her way to the stairwell. Stopping, she looks around hoping that Matthew will arrive before she goes down the steps.

Susannah regretfully retreats to her cabin and is surprised to see her mother waiting for her in the room.

"I wondered where you went. I heard you leave your room. Thinking you may have gone deck side to meet Matthew, I took it upon myself to wait up for you."

"Oh Mother, Matthew never came to meet me tonight. I prayed he would."

"Do not worry about Matthew not meeting you tonight. Perhaps he was sleeping after a long day, or the guards would not allow him on deck," suggests Aggie. "Now you get some rest. Everything will look better in the morning."

Chapter 30

The Lieutenant returns with a container of tea and the conversation turns to lighter matters. Lieutenant Rodgers tells the Captain that all is quiet onboard the ship, joking that he almost tripped over a mop handle while returning with the tea.

The Captain smiles, "That young Angelo! I reprimanded him once before, for leaving a mess behind. I will give his ear a tug when I see him." The three men chuckle.

"Captain, is it possible someone made contact with Hardie at Prestwick?" asks William Brett, reaching for more tea.

"No, Port Major, there was no crew allowed off the ship when we docked at the Scottish port, nor Liverpool," says the Captain. "In Brighton, the sailors were allowed to leave the vessel for the evening. I recall that Hardie never came back to the ship that night. We had the crew go and find him. They said he was drunk, sleeping in a chair at the inn when they found him."

The Captain thinks momentarily. "Lieutenant was Arthur out with the crew that night in Brighton?" he asks.

"I'm not sure, but I do know that Randel and Jackal were on leave that night. I was on the walkway that morning when the two came aboard. I recall Randel had a hard time navigating the gangway."

"Lieutenant, go get the two men, even if you have to wake them. Bring them to me. The Port Major and I will seal this crate and cover it, so they do not see it," says the Captain.

The little mouse wakes by the freshwater barrel, hypnotized by the constant dripping of water. The foul smell of its stomach contents lying in front of the sick mouse motivates it to find the safety of the hole in the wall.

Matthew climbs the stairwell, fighting his earlier jealousy and continually blaming himself for not arriving earlier. His upward gaze at the moon and stars tonight does not give him any answers. Leaning over the deck, he looks out at the sleeping town, watching the street lights flicker.

The town's boardwalks are empty under the dim light. Only a cat can be seen in the distance crossing the dirt-covered street. The fearless band of stray dogs that call the night theirs are nowhere in view.

* * *

A knock on the door causes the Captain to rise from his chair and proceed to unlock the door. "Come in, Gentlemen." Randel removes his toque-like cap as does Jackal. The two men enter, but remain standing, while the Lieutenant closes the door behind them.

"At ease men. This is William Brett, the Port Major here at Stornoway. We are trying to trace Hardie's steps in Brighton. I understand the two of you were with Hardie that night?" asks the Captain.

"Yes, we were with Hardie. He was in a cheerful mood when he came to the inn. We enjoyed his banter that night; for he kept the innkeeper busy bringing us drinks of rum the entire time. The crew appreciated the drinks on Hardie's shillings."

"Jackal, I do not know what you meant when you said, when he came into the inn? Did not all of you go to the inn together that evening?"

"Captain, if I recall correctly, we were in the inn for some time before Hardie came in, hollering for rum. Is this not so, Randel?"

"Yes, we had a few drinks of rum before I saw Hardie enter the inn. He called for drinks for the crew of the Sara Rose when he came in. The drinks flowed all night. We left the inn, and our drinks, when we heard the ship's bell ring in the morning. Hardie said he'd have one quick rum and he would be along. I recall him pulling out a pouch of shillings several times to pay the innkeeper." explains Randel.

174

"Thank you, Gentlemen. You are free to leave." The Captain salutes his men. They return the salute and bid everyone a good night.

"Well, Port Major, we may have an answer to the puzzle concerning Hardie Jenkins. It may be possible that someone at the Brighton harbour bought Hardie before he reached the inn. In all probability, it was someone he sailed with before joining the crew of the Rose. They would know his weak spots and his extreme need for revenge. I gather we all have come to the same conclusion. Hardie is among us."

"Yes, Captain. I believe he is present on this vessel as we speak. If attacked by pirates on the sea, he will show himself and do what he can to aid in the capture of the Rose. There is a fortune aboard the ship just in the artifacts alone. The right buyer would pay dearly for the lost Crown of Egbert. I cannot even imagine what the coins themselves would bring if they were sold separately," states William Brett.

William Brett gets up from his chair and thinks for a moment before he says, "Captain Mcbaine, Lieutenant, I've always wanted to see the Americas and now I have my chance. Captain, sign me up as a crew member."

The words from the Port Major have taken the Captain by surprise. The astonished Captain glances at the Lieutenant.

"What do you think, Lieutenant? Is the Sara Rose in need of another crew member?" asks the Captain.

"Oh, I am not sure what to say. I believe it is your decision Captain,"

"Mr. Brett, do you have any close personal ties to Stornoway, such as a wife and children?" asks the Captain.

"No, I do not. I want to join the ship on this voyage. I feel I am responsible for the artifacts, especially with the Hardie Jenkins situation. And Sir, I am well-trained in the use of firearms and cannon."

"Go get your belongings. Be quick about it. We sail at first light," orders the Captain. "Lieutenant, go wake Thomas Quinn. He can help the Port Major with his belongings."

The Port Major salutes his Corporal, who stands guard on the dock. William Brett and the Corporal walk a few steps from the others for a moment of discussion between themselves. They salute each other. The Port Major and Thomas Quinn walk into the dimly lit town.

Matthew stands alone on the deck overlooking the dock and notices William Brett and Thomas walking into the sleeping town. The damp air settles into his clothes, and a chill has found him, while he patiently waits for Susannah. He shakes himself to ward off the oncoming dampness. He is frustrated with his stubbornness for not listening to his brother sooner.

Quickly he turns and finds his way back to the steerage section of the ship. He crawls into his bunk without removing his damp clothes. Pulling the blanket over himself, he shuffles his makeshift pillow and holds his head as if in pain. He is kept awake by the constant snoring and the occasional unconscious outburst of the sleeping men. The roll of the ship bumping against the dock causes an echo in the hollow depths of the vessel. He is now plagued with thoughts that he may have lost Susannah.

Chapter 31

The sleeping town of Stornoway lay motionless, succumbing to the silence of the night. An advancing dawn descends onto the church steeple and rooftops of the houses, allowing nature's dew to cling to all that she touches.

The cobblestone walkways to Lewis Castle lie naked and serene. The band of stray dogs that control the night streets are quiet and still. Under the sidewalk, sleeps the cat that enjoys the chase.

Hanging limply from above the town hall, the St. Andrew's Cross is motionless, drenched in the morning dew. The emerging sun barely peeks over the distant horizon, slowly chasing away the hiding darkness. A new day has arrived and the sun generously displays the colours of the small town.

* * *

There are no dockworkers present this early morning, but the armed guards remain at their posts. The Captain and Lieutenant both had a sleepless night. They begin the morning roll call.

The high riggers climb the tall masts of the ship, and brave the slippery spars, stepping over the metal hoops that hold the sails. They cling like the dew, swinging from sail to sail. The foremast is given priority and the lower sails are pulled into position by the deck crew. The riggers swing to the next spars as if they were performing for a crowd below. The jigger mast is next to receive her blanket of sails.

There is an excitement onboard the ship. Even the newly lifted sails crave the feeling of a morning breeze. Each sail makes a sound of its own as the first winds caress these massive man-made structures.

The popping sounds of the awakening sails bring a cheer of 'Hurrah' from the deck crew, as the Sara Rose has found her freedom. Like a curtain being opened, the harbour is revealed as the sea beckons the ship.

The Union Jack finds its strength in a gust of wind and shakes the morning dew off its colours, whispering across the harbour to awaken the sleeping St. Andrew's Cross. The pride of Scotland surrenders the morning dew into the breeze and waves a goodbye to its friend.

Captain Mcbaine and Timothy Rodgers stand together and look back at Lewis Castle as the morning sun gives the great structure its full credit.

In the distance, the church bells ring this Sunday morning loudly, calling her congregation to prayer. The band of dogs congregates in the centre of town, but their howls do not harmonize with the sounds of the church bells.

Several of the upper class passengers, awakened by the ringing bells, rush to the deck to see Stornoway slip out of view.

The Sara Rose quietly makes her way out of the protected harbour. William Brett approaches the Captain and Lieutenant. Pointing to the hillsides surrounding the harbour he calmly says, "You can understand why the Vikings in their day chose this harbour. It's protected on all sides; even the great northern winds are halted here."

* * *

The Captain calls to Jimmy Brown in the crow's nest, ordering the high riggers to set all the sails, giving the ship the freedom she needs. The ship begins to find her stride and lunges forcefully at the sea waters. The smells of the sea find all onboard. The Captain turns to his Lieutenant, saying, "Sir, it is a good day to be at sea."

Excusing himself, the Captain enters the galley and dips a tin cup into the large pail of boiling tea. As he walks to the port side of the vessel, his concerns for the days to come are soon eased, with the sea calming him.

The Sara Rose glides her large hull over the calm water, causing sea spray to shower into the air. While the ship carves her new path, the morning sun releases its warmth into the clear skies. The Captain sips his tea and breathes the smell of the sea, giving his soul a rejuvenating effect. Rubbing his left hand across his bearded face, the Captain reaches into his pocket for his pipe. He strikes a match on the wooden railing and inhales the relaxing smoke.

The Captain's thoughts take him back to the nameless lad who was murdered on his ship. Bowing his head this Sunday morning, the Captain says a prayer for the lost lad.

* * *

Martin knows he has a task to tend to this morning and waits for Matthew's arrival. The bulging barrels of waste need emptying. The cook suggests Martin get on with the job, for the smells are seeping into the kitchen and dining area. Martin knows he has no choice other than to wake his brother.

The little mouse has been lying on its side as its stomach is in turmoil. Throughout the long night, the rodent has been kicking with its right hind leg to ease the pain. The feeling whiskers of the mouse have drooped to the planked floor, while its tail is still like a piece of wire. The exposed ear of the sick rodent weakly flops. With its nose covered in sweat, the little stowaway rests. Its rhythmic breathing slows and the helpless creature can only be thankful that it made it back to the hole in the wall after its last excursion.

Captain Mcbaine enters his cabin and locks the door behind himself. Setting his cap on the bed, he sits at his desk with his head down, supported by his hands. The church bells have stirred his inner feelings. He sips the last of the cold tea and leans back in his chair. Thoughts of his wife enter his mind, and the consoling memories send him adrift, as he succumbs to his dreams.

Martin pleads with Matthew to get out of bed and help empty the kitchen barrels. "Matthew, the cook is getting mad. I know if we don't get there soon, he will find someone else to replace us. We need every shilling we can muster. Now, let's go!"

"All right Martin. Just give me a minute."

The Sara Rose is sailing with the morning sun on her port side. The crusty coast of Lewis Island is viewed on the starboard side. The crew turns the foremast to allow the warm westerly wind to power the mainsails. The Rose lunges ahead, begging to find her true speed, trekking in a southwest direction in the North Minch waters.

The Lieutenant takes William Brett down a set of stairs to where the crew sleep. Each carries a duffel bag packed with the Port Major's belongings. There is a distinctive smell of body odour and stale air as the two men get closer to the bottom of the stairwell. On both sides of them are bunk beds, with layers of blankets over the boards to serve as mattresses. Most sailors have two duffel bags on their bunks. Both are packed with clothing and supplies; one is often used as a pillow.

A musty, damp odour permeates the air. The two men walk between the bunks, entering a larger room with hammocks tied from the ceiling. Below the hammocks are open storage shelves for extra boots, gloves and heavy outerwear. Across from the hammocks are partitions made up of ragged cloth curtains, creating three small rooms.

The Lieutenant takes the Port Major to the last room, sliding the curtain open and setting the duffel bag on the bed. "Sir, this will be your bunk. Mine is the first room we passed. The room between us is used as a sickbay."

"Thank you, Lieutenant. It was a long night. Do I have your permission to lie down if I am not needed?"

"Yes. I have to get back to the helm. The Captain will call for you when you are needed."

Matthew finally joins Martin on deck. Taking a tin cup, he dips it into the pail of tea. He is drinking his tea quickly while Martin stands with a nervous look on his face. Matthew puts down his cup and helps Martin roll the big barrel to the stern of the ship. They tilt the barrel up, then proceed with the other barrel.

Martin takes the top off the first barrel, releasing a stench that drives both of them back a few steps. "You start first," chuckles Martin. Matthew grimaces and reaches into the barrel of slop, pulling out chunks of meat and bone that have been stewing in the barrel for days. With a swing of his arm, he throws the waste to the sea. There are corn husks, beet leaves and chunks of bread that have turned mouldy green.

Far back from the odour, one of their friends from steerage shouts, "Barrel Boys, what's for lunch?"

Martin waves his fist jokingly at their friend and reaches in the barrel with both hands, scooping up the smelly slop to drop overboard. Suddenly he stops and moves closer to the stern, grabbing the railing tightly in both hands. Matthew stops to see why Martin has stopped working.

In an instant, Martin belches and discharges his last meal into the sea waters. Matthew bends forward, laughing and quickly comments, "I see you were well brought up, brother."

Martin regains control of himself and wipes his mouth with his bare hand while Matthew laughs at him. "Martin, I wish our brother and sisters were here to see this."

The Captain wakes from the short nap in his chair, rubs his eyes, and reaches for his tea. He consumes the few drops in the tin before placing his cap on his head and leaving the cabin. There is a smell of fresh tea in the air, and the Captain finds himself walking in the direction of the galley.

The Rose has found her stride, and the warmth of the day has the upper class on deck. A few passengers are reading books in lounge chairs. Others are sipping tea with a touch of rum added, to prevent the fever.

Children are running up and down the deck playing a game of hide-and-seek. In the distance, the Captain can see Mr. Rodgers coming in his direction. "Lieutenant, how are you holding up?"

"Captain, I am having a hard time of it, but the fresh air is keeping me awake."

"Did you manage to get William Brett settled in? Did you find a place for his belongings?" asks the Captain.

"Yes, the Port Major has a room near mine. His luggage is there also. He asked permission to lie down for a while. I told him to do so."

"Very good Lieutenant. Now, you get some sleep. We may not get much in the way of rest with Hardie aboard the ship. So, take advantage of the moment," says the Captain. "Lieutenant, sleep with an eye open."

Chapter 32

The entrancing view has beckoned Donald and Aggie to leave their deck chairs and stand on the starboard side. The rugged coastline has many inlets cutting into it that seem to run inland for a mile. Steep banks of rocks extend upwards for hundreds of feet on both sides. Coniferous spruce trees protrude from the rocks and tower upward. Autumn shows off its colours as the hardwood trees still wear their coats of red and yellow leaves. A pair of eagles soar high above the tree tops and look down on this scene. This untamed forest of dreams supports small herds of red deer grazing the native grasses.

Rocky sides of the inlets spew water in several locations. These falls of freshwater cause a swirling turbulence when the water plummets into the waiting sea. The massive blue-grey rocks that withstood time pose as guardians of the island and shine in the sun as droplets of water sprinkle over them. Receiving a constant cleansing, these custodians deliver a sublime view.

On each side of these intimidating rock walls is a band of sour green moss growing between the layered rocks. One can only assume that the Creator of this masterpiece had a blueprint on which to build and that no man would ever be tempted to destroy this oasis of true splendour.

"Oh, this is where the two of you are," says Susannah.

"Susannah, you missed the view of the inlet. It was breathtaking! Your father said that, if he could come back in another lifetime, he would choose to be a Viking, and this is where we will find him," smiles Aggie. She goes on to say, "Donald, I hope you included me in your other lifetime wish?"

"Of course, dear. This is an amazing country with a charm all its own," says Donald, taking a deep breath and smiling at Aggie.

The Captain stands at the helm with Mr. Downing as the two men embrace the sea air. "Mr. Downing, is there any other place you would rather be than here? Look at the sea and hear how she speaks to us. The view we witness will forever be moulded in our minds. I wish Mrs. Mcbaine was here to see this."

"Yes, I agree with you, Captain. This is a day at sea; I shall not soon forget," calmly states Roddy Downing.

Roddy Downing then asks the Captain if he may speak freely. The Captain nods. "Sir, what are we going to do about Hardie? If he is hiding up in the ceiling of the lower decks, we can't get to him without a few of our crew getting killed. We cannot starve him out; he probably provided enough food for himself. No doubt, when night comes, he can sneak out and help himself from the fresh water barrels and storage bins. Hardie knows every inch of this ship."

"Yes. Mr. Downing, you are right. Please keep this to yourself. We believe Hardie took a bribe in Brighton and is controlled by greed. He killed the young stowaway to protect his plot. Hardie may come out of hiding when we are attacked by his pirate friends. In all probability, he was paid to work from the inside. This is a very ingenious scheme, except for Hardie's thirst for rum. Jackal and Randel stated he came into the inn well after they had arrived. He flaunted his shillings around and bought rum all night for all the crew who were present."

"Yes, I believe all the pieces fit into the puzzle concerning Hardie. I hope the promise to kill the Lieutenant was only the rum talking," says the First Mate in a worried manner.

"I believe the Lieutenant is also worried. We must keep an eye on Mr. Rodgers."

"Captain, I've sailed with you for many years. I know you have a plan to catch Hardie!" comments Roddy Downing.

The day's sun leans over the starboard side of the ship and casts its shadow on the deck. The high-spirited Molly is engaged in conversation with Joseph Cunningham. Her rolled cigarette hangs on her bottom lip when she talks. Molly is more interested in Joseph, and surrenders her cigarette butt to the sea while nudging herself closer to the unsuspecting Joseph. The flirtatious Molly places her hand on Joseph's hand, which he does not withdraw. The view of the passing island is no longer on Joseph's mind.

* * *

The coming evening begins to cover the horizon with a filament of darkness. The threat of Hardie Jenkins returns to haunt the crew with the descending sun retreating into the far west. They nervously look over their shoulders, feeling they are constantly being watched. A shout from the crow's nest or the ring of the ship's bell puts them into an internal frenzy. The sound of a loose canvas sail in a sudden gust of wind raises their blood pressure to new heights.

The mouse is in constant pain and struggles to turn its weakened body. Feebly, it begins to breathe more evenly. The rodent has no desire to roam the decks this night. It realizes it missed the chance to escape from the ship and is now held captive.

The dinner bell has rung, the upper class passengers are enjoying their first evening meal at sea in days. The travellers are impressed that they are dining on fresh beef, a rare treat on the sea.

The second-class passengers enter the dining room and begin serving themselves. The Peters family members are among the dinner guests in line. Peters can see the cigar smoke coming from Jones' table. Jones turns to see Peters looking at him, and nods. Noticing her husband glancing in Jones' direction, Mrs. Peters gives her husband a poke in the ribs, disciplining him. Jones chuckles.

Donald and Aggie Evens have found seats in the lounging area. Susannah strolls to the starboard side of the ship and looks out to sea. Her thoughts are of Matthew. She looks upward into the night sky. Susannah is daydreaming, and the soothing motions of the ship relax her thoughts. She is undecided whether or not to come on deck later tonight and wait for Matthew. She quickly comes out of her reverie when a northern gust sends shivers down her back.

The high riggers have lowered the mainsails for the evening, causing the ship to maintain a speed of six to eight knots during the night. This allows ample time to maneuver, in case of an obstacle ahead. Again, the long poles go out at a forty-five-degree angle with the lanterns tied to them. Every few minutes Parker calls, "All Clear." This assures the crew and the helmsman that the ship is safe for the moment.

The Captain spots the young Thomas Quinn leaning on the mast pole chatting with Angelo. "Hey, lads, is there no work available for the two of you? Thomas, fetch Arthur and tell him to meet me in my cabin. Angelo, I hear you have been leaving your swabbing pail unattended. I distinctly recall telling you about this before. The barrel will be awaiting you if we have this conversation again. Is this understood?"

"Yes. Yes Sir, Captain, the Lieutenant already chewed my ear off about that. I am sorry, Sir," answers Angelo, standing at attention, red-faced and shaking.

Doctor Eden approaches while the Captain is scolding the young apprentice. The Doctor waits several feet away till the lad leaves.

"Oh, Doctor, how are you tonight?" asks the grinning Captain.

"I am feeling fine. Thank you for asking. Sir. I see the boys need a bit of training," chuckles the Doctor.

"Yes, they do. A few lashes over the barrel would do wonders for them. Can I help you with anything tonight, Doctor?"

"I was just curious about our route and next port of call. I have a few sick passengers in steerage and have to ration certain medicines."

"Doctor, I will be discussing the matter with William Brett and the Lieutenant. The ship's safety is our priority.

"All right, Captain. Let me know what you decide, and I will ration supplies as I see fit," states the Doctor. The two men bid each other a good night.

* * *

Martin is in his bunk covered with a blanket. The experience with the barrels of fermenting garbage has left him tired and weak. Matthew has washed and returned to his bunk. Taking his cleanest shirt, he tries to iron the wrinkles out of it by putting the shirt around a small beam and pulling it back and forth tightly. Matthew turns it inside out and repeats the action. He opens the shirt, gives it a quick shake, and puts it on. Martin, with one eye opened, calmly asks Matthew, "Are you going to meet Susannah tonight?"

"Yes, I hope she comes on deck tonight. I am not sure what I will say to her."

"Regardless, Matthew, you have to go tonight and wait for her. Remember what mother always said; a good man will always wait patiently for a lady."

The Captain is at the helm when Arthur approaches. The two men greet each other and walk toward the Captain's cabin. "Arthur, please sit down. We took the same route to Stornoway as the Scarlett did in thirty-nine when you served under Captain Perkins. What route did the Scarlett return on?"

"Well, Captain, once we loaded and unloaded the cargo, we left Stornoway late in the afternoon the next day. I recall that all right. It was cold and windy, the seas were restless, and the grey rolling clouds followed us all that day. The Scarlett saw the tip of Skye two days later. We then sailed around the northern edge of Skye. A day later we could see the Isle of Rum, and then Eigg a day after that. The Scarlett made port at the small village of Mallaig," states Arthur. He becomes curious why the Captain is asking about the route. "Captain, do you think we may be attacked by a pirate ship?"

"I can't be sure Arthur, but a lot of the facts do suggest this. What we speak of remains with us."

"Aye Captain."

"I reckon the Scarlett followed the Scottish coast and advanced southwest to the Isle of Mull. Then the Isle of Coll remained on the starboard side of the Scarlett."

187

"No Captain, the Scarlett turned southeast and took the channel between the mainland and the Isle of Mull. We docked at Oban for cargo. Reckon it was for two nights. Captain, I would not recommend the route through the channel. It is deep but narrow. It would be a perfect place for a pirate ship to trap the Rose."

Chapter 33

The rodent begins vomiting where it lays. The stench brings tears to its eyes. Fear in its mind outweighs the trauma the mouse is going through. Being stowed away on a vessel with Hardie Jenkins, who is ready to pounce on the rodent at any time. The call of home seeps into the stowaway's thoughts and it begins to whimper.

The popping sounds of the awakening sails bring a cheer of 'Hurrah' from the deck crew as the Sara Rose has found her freedom. Like a curtain being opened, the harbour is revealed, and the sea beckons the ship.

The Union Jack finds its strength in a gust of wind and shakes the morning dew off its colours, whispering across the harbour to awaken the sleeping St. Andrew's Cross. The pride of Scotland surrenders the morning dew into the breeze and waves goodbye to its friend.

Matthew dabs on a bit of the cologne that Johnnie lent him, and puts on the woollen jacket that he used for a pillow. He makes his way up the stairwell, placing one hand on the wall to soften his climb upward and prevent the squeak of the worn steps. There are no armed guards on the well-lit top deck as Matthew goes directly to where he last met Susannah. He looks up and down the lengthy deck, but there is no sign of Susannah.

Jimmy Brown calls "All Clear," breaking the silence of the night air. Matthew sees a shadow. His heart races with excitement but the shadow is not in the direction that Susannah would come from. He then quietly moves across the deck and along the lounge wall. A voice from behind suddenly stops him in his tracks. Flashes of Hardie Jenkins instantly swoop into Matthew's terrified mind.

"Good evening, Matthew," says the Captain.

"Oh, Captain! Yes, good evening."

"Did I startle you, Matthew?

"Ahhh, yes, I mean no," replies the red-faced Matthew.

Matthew's face remains flushed and speechless, as it did in his youth when caught at a prank, He now dreads a reprimand from the Captain.

"By the way, Matthew, Mr. Evens is a friend of mine. He tells me you are rather smitten with his daughter." The Captain smiles at the nervous lad.

"Yes. Yes, I am Captain. I have taken quite a liking to Miss Evens."

Captain Mcbaine dips a tin cup into the pail of tea, turning the tin cup slowly in his hand. He pauses briefly, "Well, Matthew, I am not sure what to say, nor do I have a right to say anything. I can tell you I followed my heart, and I am glad I did." The Captain turns and leaves the galley for the helm.

The Lieutenant surfaces on the top deck and approaches the Captain, who is chatting with Third Mate Benjamin Johnson at the helm. The Captain turns, "Lieutenant, the ship is on course. I will meet with you and William Brett tomorrow to discuss our route. I am off to my cabin to catch up on some rest. Goodnight, Mr. Rodgers."

"Enter," calls out Jones, as the door opens partially. "Well, well. Come in, Mr. Peters. What brings you here tonight?"

Peters looks in both directions of the hallway, then quickly enters the cabin before anyone notices him. He removes his hat, holding it with both hands in front of himself. "You did give me the offer to regain my losses, did you not?" says the nervous Peters.

"Yes, I did. Peters, come in and sit down."

The pupils of Jones' beady eyes are dilated, and his heart of stone begins to pump warm blood. His cold face now has a rare smile. Removing the cigar stub from his watering mouth, he drops it to the floor and spits out the tobacco clinging to his lips. He then crushes the smoking cigar butt into the planked floor with his boot. Jones knows he controls the moment as his lips welcome another cigar.

"Peters, get the candle from the nightstand and hold it while I light my cigar." Peters does what is asked of him.

"Well Peters, is it a game of chance you are interested in playing?"

"Yes, Mr. Jones. I surely would like to regain some of my losses. My family and I need the finances, and my wife has not forgiven me for losing our savings."

"Peters, you must feel lucky tonight. What game of chance do you desire?"

"I only have nine shillings on my person. Mrs. Peters tends to hide the savings. I am sure I can find more resources, perhaps for another game at a later date."

The snickering Jones puffs on his cigar then says, "Well, pick your game, Peters."

"All right Mr. Jones. A shilling a hand, five-card draw and the deck of cards remains on the table after shuffling. Is that agreeable with you?"

"It's your game, Peters. Let's play." The two men begin the game of chance; Jones retires another cigar to the ash-covered floor. Peters' eyes enlarge as he keeps pulling the shillings he won closer to him. Jones conceals his excitement, delighted that Peters is stacking up a few shillings.

Peters' hands become moist, causing the cards to stick to his fingers. He begins to speak louder, chanting to the cards in his hand. The excitement of winning and the confidence Peters is enjoying results in him making mistakes; but much to his delight, he wins most of the hands.

* * *

With a burst of inner strength, the suffering mouse manages to stand. The shaky rodent does not know which way to turn. It becomes nauseous and weaves back and forth with the rhythm of the ship. The ship's stowaway falls back to the planked floor and resumes expelling its stomach's contents.

191

Two sailors return from the agonizing duty of guarding the ship's hull. Like everyone else, they are on edge and haunted by the spectre of Hardie Jenkins. They nervously approach the galley and fumble for tin cups.

One of the sailors says, "It's rum we need, not tea after being in that chamber of hell."

"Yes! That damn Hardie. We should have taken care of him a long time ago when we had our chance. Now, look at us!"

Matthew patiently waits in the shadows for the two sailors to leave the deck. In his mind, he relives the moments he shared with Susannah. Every word she has spoken to him is locked in his memory. He closes his eyes as if he were making a wish.

The lonely seconds pass slowly. Darkness retains its hold on the night while Matthew's hopes are fading. He feels his chest tighten, and his thoughts become knotted, twisting and turning in his mind.

Time begins to take its toll on Matthew's mixed emotions. Martin's reminder of what their mother always said, remains ingrained in his mind. "A good man will always wait patiently for a lady."

Now thoughts of his mother and father begin to flood his mind. Memories of the Village of Blackburn in Lancashire County, which he and Martin left behind, add to his frustrations. Matthew sits on the deck with his back to the railing. The soothing motion of the ship calms his built-up anxiety and lulls him to sleep.

* * *

Matthew's dreams become a reality when a warm hand touches his face. He opens his eyes to see Susannah leaning over him. He quickly stands, shaking the cobwebs loose. Matthew searches for words; but he is speechless, remaining transfixed.

The candle Susannah is holding reveals her beauty. Her blonde hair enhances her features and her magnetic blue eyes instantly weaken him. The breeze of the envious night silences and the candle retains its glow.

Susannah speaks. "Matthew, I am sorry for not coming sooner. I wasn't sure if I was going to meet you tonight. My feelings grow so much stronger when I am away from you. Matthew, I missed you."

Susannah's puts her arms around Matthew and passionately kisses him. Holding her closely in his arms, Matthew whispers the words he has only dreamt of saying, "I love you, Susannah. I love you."

The watching moon blushes, turning the colour red. Circling clouds cover the moon's emotional eyes. The night breezes are halted. Susannah softly whispers.

"I love you, Matthew."

Chapter 34

Peters opens the door of Jones' cabin and peers down the hallway, noticing an armed sailor at one end. He nods to Jones as he leaves the cabin. Sneaking through the poorly lit hall, he turns at the stairwell and climbs to the top of the deck.

Peters is elated after beating Jones at his game. He is reluctant to return to his cabin for fear of waking his wife and having to explain where he has been till this late hour. Looking towards the sea, he lights the cigar Jones gave him and inhales the cigar smoke with pleasure. The jingling of coins in his pocket turns his thoughts to the possibility that he could have won more money. He pulls out the coins and counts them again, one guinea and fourteen shillings. His heart races, rolling the coins in his hands.

Peters stuffs the coins into three different pockets, to prevent a bulge in just one pocket of his trousers. He notices a blanket left on a lounging chair and sits, covering himself. He encourages his thoughts, for he now believes his luck has finally changed.

Cool night air has suspended itself over the deck of the ship. The peaceful sky surrenders a blanket of clouds over the moon that cover its glow.

The sailors on guard this evening are warmly dressed, holding their firearms close to themselves. The ship creaks, stretching herself further into the chilled waters of the sea. Parker's calm shout of 'All Clear!' echoes down the lonely planked deck. Third Mate Johnson is holding the wheel of the ship in his hands, occasionally looking at the Union Jack to determine the wind direction.

Angelo, the apprentice, is wrapped in a blanket. Squatting next to the helm wall, he watches every move of the helmsman, for he must act as messenger in the event of an emergency.

The footsteps of the little mouse will not be heard on the planked deck this night.

* * *

The dreams of the passengers are left behind when a new dawn creeps aboard the vessel. The tender rays of orange and yellow appear in the eastern sky.

Newly formed dew covers every part of the ship and acts as nature's blessing for the new day. A morning breeze chisels its way from the north, causing the dew to form crystallized shapes. The new formations glitter and chime with the ship's movement. Crystal images slowly begin melting, forming puddles with the arriving sun.

Mrs. Peters stands over her husband, who is asleep in the lounge chair. She cuffs him roughly. He grumbles to her about the shaking he is receiving. "Where were you all night?" she angrily demands.

Peters, with a foggy look about him, replies, "I couldn't sleep, so I came for a walk on the deck. It was late and I didn't want to wake you."

"The children were asking for you during the night and I didn't know how to answer them," says the extremely upset Mrs. Peters.

"I'm sorry, but I couldn't sleep."

"Hurry, get back to the cabin before the other guests see you," says the suspicious Mrs. Peters as she follows her husband. She can see cigar ashes falling to the floor from his clothes as he walks.

Captain Mcbaine leaves his cabin and looks to the port side of the ship. He notices an outline of land in the distance. The sun is pushing the darkness out of its way, as the ship continues in a southwest direction. He steps quickly to the helm and confronts the helmsman.

"Mr. Quinn, what hour did you come on duty and replace Mr. Johnson?"

"I have been at the helm for an hour, Captain," says Mr. Quinn in a curious manner.

"I take it that is the Isle of Rona in the morning's light."

The Second Mate is puzzled, "Yes Sir, it is, Captain. Mr. Johnson told me we had changed course during the night."

"Yes, we have Mr. Quinn. This route may be a day longer, but we have the advantage. There will not be an iceberg issue on the east side of Skye. Well Sir, I must find a tin of tea and my Lieutenant."

Martin throws a dirty old shirt at Matthew, to wake him. Matthew turns on his side, "Go away. Let me sleep."

"Get up Matthew. Tell me what happened last night?"

"It's not any of your business. Now go away," pleads Matthew pulling the covers over his head.

"The other night, you made it my business. Now tell me what happened last night."

"Yes, Martin. Susannah met me on deck. Now go away!"

* * *

Several of the steerage travellers gather at the stern. The female passengers are wrapped in their blankets, rolling cigarettes that they crave. The men, wearing their flat caps and heavy coats, stay true to their pipes.

 The Captain enters the kitchen. He joins William Brett and the Lieutenant, who are seated at a dining room table waiting for breakfast.

Suddenly, Randel staggers into the room, moaning in pain, holding the back of his head. He sways from side to side as blood runs over his fingers and drips onto the floor. His left hand reaches for the kitchen counter, but he falls to the deck unconscious.

"Steward, go get the Doctor!" yells the Captain. "Lieutenant, come with me! Now!"

197

The Lieutenant and William Brett run behind the Captain. Entering the stairwell, they swiftly descend the steps to the bottom of the first landing.

"Captain, the trail of blood goes this way," says the Lieutenant springing ahead of the men. Drawing his trusted sabre from its sheath, he leads the others down the set of steps to the dark bottom of the ship. They stop; allowing their eyes to become accustomed to the darkness. The only sound heard is the heavy breathing from the three nervous men. Each feel as if his spine is slowly unbuckling. The thumping of their hearts causes a flush of cold sweat to break out on the back of their necks.

The Captain fumbles in his pocket for a match, striking it on a beam. A brief burst of light flashes in front of him. The match extinguishes. The Captain reaches into his pocket again, pulls out two more matches and strikes them on the beam.

Looking downward, the men realize they are standing in a pool of blood. The Captain throws the burnt matches to the floor. The three men back away from the horror they have seen.

The Captain whispers, "Lieutenant, you and William Brett get lanterns and the armed men down here quick. Give me your sabre, Lieutenant!"

Doctor Eden kneels on the floor beside Randel. The cook passes him towels to stem the flow of blood streaming from the gash on the back of Randel's head. Randel remains unconscious, while Doctor Eden continues applying pressure to his wound.

The deck of the ship is a frenzy of activity with the hustle of armed sailors. The Lieutenant runs to the side of the ship for a lantern, while telling men to grab lanterns and follow him.

Two men carrying firearms pass the Captain on the stairwell. Shouting in raised voices gives them the courage to charge into the bowels of the ship. They are quickly silenced, upon entering the cargo area and finding themselves standing in the fresh blood. In the dim light of the lanterns, dust floats off the beams, adding to the eerie sensation.

The exposed cobwebs hang in the flickering light, retaining their secrets. With a sabre in hand, the Captain pushes past the two sailors, then waves them closer, as he needs their lantern's light. Captain Mcbaine looks down to find that he is standing over a body.

The stairwell is a rush of men coming into the cargo hold, carrying firearms, pointing in all directions. The men go to different sections of the ship in search of the murderer. The cautious pursuers slowly move for they are willing to follow, but fear to lead.

The Lieutenant, screams at the men to get on with the task and joins the Captain, "It's Reed, Sir! It's Henry Reed!"

"Yes, Lieutenant. That damned Hardie! We must flush him out soon and put an end to Hardie Jenkins."

The blood slowly seeps from a large open gash across Reed's neck. Blood covers the right side of his face and has saturated his red hair. His mouth is open, while his left eye stares into the unknown. The pooled blood finds its way into the cracks of the joined planks.

The Captain looks around the body. "Lieutenant, the firearms Randel and Reed had are gone. Hardie is collecting all the arms he can."

William Brett returns to the Captain. "No sign of anyone, Sir. We followed the bloody footprints, but they disappeared.

"I expect we will not find Hardie. We need to smoke him out in another way," says the Captain quietly. He turns and speaks loudly, "Arthur, come over here. Get a few men and blankets, to wrap Reed in. Place his body on the port deck."

The Doctor cuts a large patch of hair from Randel's scalp before pouring a sharp smelling liquid over the cut. He takes a long-curved needle and a length of thick thread out of his bag. Doctor Eden stitches the split flesh together, as one would sew ripped trousers. The cooks and crew turn their heads away, while the Doctor performs his art.

The Captain rushes back to the galley, "Doctor, how is Randel? Will he be all right?"

"Yes, Captain, he will be fine. That whack on the head sure put him to sleep. Let's get him below to the sick room. He will need the quiet and I imagine he will have a nasty headache for days."

Two men grab Randel's lanky legs. Two other men struggle with his shoulders while a blanket is slid under him. They pick up the four corners of the blanket and carry Randel down to a waiting bed.

Chapter 35

The Isle of Rona is in view toward the east, with the morning sun rising over the tops of the mountains. The Isle shows off its mountain range to the passing ship and passengers. The rocky domain supports little in the way of natural growth. From the deck, a few red willow shrubs and minimal amounts of grasses can be seen. The barren ground is covered with large rocks. They stand in silence, seemingly to be guarding the Isle.

Captain Mcbaine calls William Brett and the Lieutenant to the privacy of his cabin. "Gentlemen, grab a chair. During the night, I instructed Mr. Johnson to turn the Sara Rose due south. We are proceeding on a new course. You can see on the map that this was the route we took to Stornoway. This is our present location. I decided on this course at the last minute."

William Brett stands to obtain a better look at the map. "I would have thought the open sea might be the safer route."

"I also agree that the open sea may be to our advantage," comments the Lieutenant while peering at the map.

"Yes, I thought you both would agree, and I felt the same way. Arthur also suggested the open sea route, so we are all in agreement. If we are followed by pirate ships, which are looking for us, the ship will head to the open sea."

"I see your logic, Captain," comments the Lieutenant.

"Go ahead, Lieutenant. Tells us what you see."

"Well, Captain, the Isle of Skye has lots of inlets on both the northern and westerly sides. There are many places for ships to lie in wait for the approaching Rose. They would have a view of the seas for miles, and could easily alert one another."

"I am glad you caught that Lieutenant. That is precisely why I had Mr. Johnson turn south. The night crew extinguished all the lanterns when we turned south, under cover of darkness. Right or wrong, this is the course we are on now."

The Captain seats himself, resting his elbows on the arms of the chair. He strokes his greying beard with his left hand. Taking his pipe off the desk, he relights it. The room quiets as the men ponder.

The Captain draws smoke from his pipe and says, "We must be silent about Mr. Reed. We don't want panic aboard the ship at this point. Lieutenant, you and Mr. Brett tell the crew that they are not to repeat anything of Hardie's deeds to the passengers. This is an order! Any betrayal and the barrel will be waiting!"

* * *

Susannah stays late in bed, missing morning breakfast. She sits with her shoulders high on two pillows, twirling her blond hair with her fingers while holding a book in her right hand. The book does not hold her attention and Susannah quickly throws it aside. She closes her eyes and tries to sleep, but her thoughts turn to Matthew, and the words she whispered to him. Susannah's heart is in emotional turmoil and does not fully understand what tugs at her.

Mr. Peters walks with his wife and their three children on the port side of the ship, stopping to look at the Isle of Rona before it disappears from view. From the corner of his eye, Peters can see Jones perched on a deck chair. Without drawing attention to himself, Peters turns and walks his family in another direction.

Donald and Aggie Evens are leaning over the railing of the ship admiring the view of Rona. "Donald, what are we to do with Susannah? I feel for her. She has deep feelings for Matthew. To be honest Donald, I like him very much. By his actions, I can tell he is deeply in love with Susannah."

"Whoa, Aggie, those are strong words, especially in the morning air. Aggie, Matthew has nothing to offer our Susannah. I would bet he has only a few shillings to his name and the clothes on his back."

202

"Donald, tell me what you had when we first met."

"Everything was different then."

"No, it was not, Donald. Susannah has to make up her mind about what she wants. This is something she has to do on her own. I am going to take a cup of tea down to her cabin and talk with her."

Arthur is directing the apprentices who are cleaning up the blood when the Captain returns to the bottom of the ship. "Gentlemen, not one word will be spoken to any passenger of what occurred here this morning. Are you clear on that? From now on, there will be three men on guard here at all times. Arthur, arrange a new schedule."

"Aye Aye, Captain."

It is high noon and Second Mate Quinn is in control of the helm, allowing Mr. Downing to take readings with the sextant. The Isle of Raasay will be in view shortly and the two men adjust the course of the ship.

Aggie Evens knocks on her daughter's cabin door. Susannah opens the door, greeting her mother. Aggie passes her a cup of tea. "How are you feeling, Susannah?"

"I feel fine, but I am so confused."

"I believe I know what you are going through. I went through the same thing when I was your age. There is no easy answer. It's fine to follow your heart. All I know is my heart hurt when I wasn't around your father. That began soon after meeting him. Susannah, I miss your father when we are apart."

* * *

The Captain is returning to his cabin and notices the Lieutenant approaching from the starboard side of the ship. "Well Lieutenant, I guess our shipmate, Henry Reed, will meet the Mistress of the Sea tonight."

"Aye Captain, that he will."

"Reed was a good sailor. He served with the Rose for three years," says the Captain while walking to his cabin. "I hope all the crew understood what you told them?" The Lieutenant nods affirmatively.

William Brett approaches, and the three men enter the Captain's cabin. "Gentlemen, we must flush Hardie Jenkins out. I can't ask the men to guard the hull of the ship much longer, as most are at their wit's end. The three of us will each be taking a turn at guarding the hull. I will go down and replace one of the men when we finish here."

William Brett and the Lieutenant look at each other in surprise. They do not like the Captain's comment. They choose not to respond.

The Captain sternly says, "Mr. Brett, you said, you're experienced in the use of weapons and cannon?"

William Brett nods. "Sir, I want you and any spare men to service the cannon. Remove the protective doors that hide the cannon from the outside. I am not sure how long it will take you to ready them. Do not fire any of the cannons until you have my order. Make sure there are armed guards with you at all times. Hardie can't get into the cannon area from where he is hiding. Hopefully, he will be unaware of what you are doing. But we can't take any chances; please take an armed guard. Is that clear?"

"Are you expecting an attack from pirates soon?" nervously asks the Lieutenant.

"We cannot be caught unprepared. The cannons must be serviced. The Sara Rose carries ample cannons and cannonballs. We have kegs of gunpowder and men who served on warships. Our cannon fire at a nonexistent enemy may draw Hardie Jenkins out into the open. We have to do this soon. The crew can't take much more, nor can I."

"I see your plan, Captain and believe it will work. I may need the help of Lieutenant Rodgers, as the men may not take orders from me," says William Brett.

"That may be true. All right, let's get to it. Remember, we have a service for Reed tonight."

Arthur is at the stern of the ship sipping tea with his friend, Jackal. The two talk quietly about the day's excitement and the tragedy which befell their shipmate, Reed. "Have you seen Randel? How is he?" asks Arthur.

"Yes, I saw him a short time ago. He will have a bump on his head the size of an onion. That Hardie sure gave him a heck of a wallop. It's a good thing Randel is a tough old bird."

Joey and Neil come up to the table where Arthur and Jackal are talking; Arthur quickly changes the subject and says, "We will be approaching the Isle of Raasay on the starboard side of the ship soon. If you lads are around later tonight, I will tell you a story of the Isle that I heard many years ago," says Arthur.

"Oh good, I will tell my friends. We will find you tonight," exclaims Joey.

* * *

Time advances slowly. The sun lazily crosses over the deck of the Sara Rose to warm the starboard side of the ship. From the crow's nest, Jimmy Brown can see the outline of Raasay, and shouts to the helmsman that the Isle is sighted.

Jones has fallen asleep on deck. His cigar stub remains in his mouth, but no smoke rises from it. The jacket he wears remains covered in ashes. His walking stick has fallen to the right side of the lounge chair and rolls back and forth on the deck with the motion of the ship.

Donald and Aggie Evens are in conversation with Floyd and Diane Ogden in the dining area. There are many chuckles and gestures from Donald. He has everyone amused as he relates stories and adventures of their farm life.

Returning from a shift of guard duty, Captain Mcbaine has strengthened the bond which exists among his crew. He ventures into the galley for a late lunch then makes his way between the men's bunks to Randel's bedside. "Doctor, how is Randel?"

"Randel took a very hard blow to the head. He will be fine with some rest and when that nasty headache leaves him."

"Randel, I guess you are not in the mood for talking right now?" asks the Captain.

"No, I'm fine, Captain. I feel bad for Henry Reed. The Doctor told me what happened to him. As I told the Doctor, I never heard a thing."

"You were lucky, Randel. I will tell a steward to bring you hot tea and some stew. You rest now."

"Captain, I would prefer a few rations of rum instead of stew and tea. I am sure it will help me rest easy," says Randel in a sincere voice.

The Captain smiles at Randel, "Rum it shall be."

Chapter 36

With the approaching dusk, the Isle of Raasay is viewed from the starboard side of the ship. Orange and reddish rays of sunset slip through the openings between the peaks of her mountain range. The arresting colours continue to glide downward to the lower hills of the coastline. The wake of the ship can be seen rippling slowly against the rocks at the water's edge. The calming water takes on a lime green colour.

On the port side, three orca whales enthrall the passengers who have crowded to the railings to watch. The whales keep time with each other; gracefully rising out of the sea they expel water through their blowholes. Their massive bodies return to the sea, then they repeat this pre-rehearsed act for the Sara Rose. Finally, they vanish into the horizon, leaving the crew and passengers applauding at what they have witnessed.

* * *

Martin sits on a small barrel in the galley, breathing into his handkerchief, as the newly arriving moist air plays havoc with his lungs. Matthew notices that Martin is having issues breathing and gets him a tin of hot tea. "Here Martin, drink this, it will help. Then go below and get into bed."

"All right Matthew. I feel tired anyway. Are you going to see Susannah tonight?"

"I sure am. I can hardly wait. I should go below and get cleaned up."

Henry Reed is bound in tightly wrapped white cloth. Thin braided ropes are used to hold the white covering against the corpse. His body lies on two flat boards that are fastened together with supports from underneath. In each of the four corners are holes, with short ropes attached for makeshift handles. The sailors call this, 'The Board of Death,' and is only used for burials at sea.

Doctor Eden helps Randel climb the steps to the top deck of the ship. Randel has a white strip of cloth wrapped around his head several times, then tied in a knot. At the back of the cloth, a bloodstain can be seen. The tall, lanky Randel walks slowly supporting his head with one hand. The crew immediately gives him a cheer the moment they see him.

Randel raises his other hand and says, "Be quiet. You all are giving me a headache. The one I have is bad enough." They all laugh at Randel's comment. A fellow crew member quickly finds Randel a small barrel to sit on.

Darkness encases the Sara Rose; cold damp air begins to seep into the clothing of the men. Only two lanterns have been lit for this private service for their shipmate. Captain Mcbaine nods, and four men take the rope handles in their hands. They pick up 'The Board of Death' where Reed lies and turn to the port side of the ship. The two men who have the front of the board set it on the railing, and the other two men hold their end high, but steady.

Captain Mcbaine removes his Bible from his pocket, opening it to a page, reading from **John: Chapter Fourteen.** He reads verses one through six. The Captain closes the Bible. The men remain standing in silence with their heads bowed. Some cross themselves, while a few wipe away a tear.

From the darkness comes the sound of a single violin. Jackal, with his magical hands, guides the bow across the strings to make the violin weep into the evening air. The violin becomes part of him. Jackal plays from his soul for his departed friend Henry Reed, while the sound of '**Rock of Ages**' caresses the night air.

Captain Mcbaine nods to the men holding 'The Board of Death.' They lift the board with the help of fellow crew members. The body of Henry Reed slides down the board into the sea, released into the waiting arms of the 'Mistress of the Sea.'

* * *

There's a knock on the door of Susannah's cabin. She gets up from the comfort of the bed and opens the door. "Mother, come in."

"How are you feeling? Did you get any rest?"

"I don't know how I am feeling. Every time I close my eyes, I see Matthew. There is a constant aching in my chest and it only goes away when I am with him," exclaims Susannah.

"Well Susannah, there is no need to fetch Doctor Eden for you. We both know what is happening. You're in love with Matthew. Susannah, have you given any thought to what kind of life the two of you would have? You know as well as I do, Matthew only has what he carries with him."

"Mother, I have thought about that a lot. None of us knows what waits for us in America. He talks about Martin and him going to a place called Montana in the Americas and becoming cowboys. Mother, what are cowboys? They plan to ride horses and chase cows. Why would they want to chase cows? Do people in America do things like that?" asks Susannah, breaking out in tears.

Aggie Evens embraces her daughter, "Now Susannah, there must be a reason why they chase the cows in the Americas. I will ask your father if he knows anything about a place called Montana and why people would do such things."

Frances Cunningham walks with her two brothers and three young girls up the steps to the stern of the ship. Neil is holding hands with one of the girls, while Joey carries a lantern.

"Hello, Jackal. Hello, Arthur. We did not forget that you promised to tell us a story about the Isle of Raasay."

"Yes, I did lads. I'm sorry, but it's been a long hard day," says Arthur.

"But you promised," says Neil, with a slight whine in his voice.

"All right, I will then. Who are your friends that came with you?" smiles Arthur.

Neil grins and lowers his head, sliding his right foot back and forth on the wooden deck. He twists and turns. Finally, he lets go of the girl's hand and quietly says, "This is Emma. She is a girl. And my friend."

209

Arthur covers his smile with his hand and asks, "And who are these two young ladies?"

"They are just Emma's sisters, Martha and Isabell."

Arthur places his tin cup on the table and puts his ageing hands together. He sits and ponders for a moment, before he begins to speak, "Now, all you children gather around, and be quiet and I will tell you the story. Joey put your lantern on the table and sit here."

Arthur is not sure how to start. He looks at Jackal and the other crew members sitting around the table. They all give him a blank stare.

"Come on, Arthur. We're waiting for another true story of yours," chuckles Hassard, one of the crew members.

"All right children. As Hassard said, this is a true story. I wish there was daylight so you could see the spot I am talking about." Arthur extends his hand to point into the darkness. "See out there! Look into the dark and maybe you will see the spot I'm talking about." All the children stand and stare where Arthur is pointing.

"Yes," says Joey, "I can see something out there."

"I see the spot, too," says Emma. Now, all the children point and agree they can see something. Their fertile, young imaginations are running wild, waiting in suspense for Arthur's story to begin.

"This story was told to me many years ago by a crew whose ship wrecked on the Isle of Raasay. It was told to them by a small colony of prisoners. The prisoners were set adrift near the Isle over a hundred years ago. They had no homeland or family, so they made the Isle their home. They discovered the secrets of this famous Isle that go back a thousand, maybe two thousand years ago.

Yes, before the Vikings ruled the northern seas." Arthur looks up to the sky and points. The children remain silent and stare at Arthur's finger as if it were a magic wand.

"From the sky, many years ago, fell a lost star from the Heavens. It fell faster and faster through the night. There was a flame of fire coming from the falling star. As it fell, it lit up the night skies and turned night into day."

Arthur has the children glued to their seats, as he uses his hands to emphasize the story. "The star was on fire, and it fell straight to the Isle of Raasay. The whole Isle was ablaze that night and for many nights to follow. Did you see it? Did you see when we passed Raasay? Did you see how the mountain has disappeared in the middle of the Raasay?"

"Yes, yes, we did see that," sounds the choir of young voices in agreement.

"Then you saw the steam rising from the centre of Raasay?" The children are quiet, nodding to Arthur. Their eyes widen, remaining locked on him. "The star fell and hit the mountains, making a big, big hole on the Isle of Raasay. The huge hole from the falling star, filled with the water from the snow and rains over many years. Now, Raasay has a large lake where the falling star landed. The prisoners named the large lake, Heaven's Lake."

Mesmerized by Arthur's every word, the children look upward into the night sky and visualize what he is saying. "The heat from the star that lit the sky that night, still keeps the water of Heaven's Lake warm all year long. This is where the Angels gather to quench their thirst and rest when they go to bless the children of the north. Heaven's Lake is where Father Christmas also stops for a rest when he comes with all the gifts for the good children." The children's thoughts spin within their minds and their eyes are bulging. The crew listening to Arthur are quiet and intrigued as well.

Silence is broken by the young Neil Cunningham. "Arthur, Arthur, tell the Captain to turn the ship back."

"Whatever for?" asks Arthur.

"We want to go to Heaven's Lake! Father Christmas might be there!"

The crew chuckle at the youngster's comments. Arthur smiles as the children jump up and down, pleading for him to speak with the Captain and turn the ship around.

Chapter 37

The mouse has regained its lost strength and begins to feel hunger pains. With trembling legs, the mouse stands, hearing no sounds of footsteps or voices.

Bravely, the stowaway slips its head out of the hole in the wall. Inviting odours waft from the dining room, tempting the mouse. The rodent ignores its instincts once again and runs in the direction of the dripping water to drink from the puddle. Searching under the tables for dropped food, the little stowaway happily nibbles on a crust of bread.

Light rain has started to fall in the east, with lightning beginning to dominate the sky. The sea is nervous this night, as the storm approaches.

* * *

Susannah can hear footsteps on the starboard side of the ship. She is nervous and excited as Matthew appears. He walks directly to her without saying a word, embraces her.

The light rain softly wets the deck while grey-black clouds hold the moon hostage this night. The young lovers hold each other tightly. Susannah is the first to speak, "Matthew, I could not get you out of my mind all day."

"Yes, that's how I feel. No matter what I am doing or to whom I talk, you are always in my thoughts. Sometimes my thoughts turn into fears."

The cobwebs holding so many secrets at the bottom of the ship become heavy with the weight of the damp sea air. The Lieutenant and two crewmen go down the steps to relieve the three men guarding the hull of the vessel.

The Sara Rose has put the Isle of Raasay behind her. The suspicious seawaters are agitated by the overhead thunderstorm. Lanterns lighting the ship's deck begin to dim when hit by raindrops, causing the hot glass to send small columns of steam upward. Falling rain increases its intensity, accompanied by flakes of snow, with occasional lightning strikes in the east.

* * *

Lightning from the east has abated, and the thunder which had roared from the Heavens has ceased. The ferocity of the rain and snow has diminished, but some precipitation continues to fall lightly. The northern wind is held at bay this night.

The awakening sun begins to rise in the east as a northern breeze sweeps a chill across the deck. Night crew are drenched to their core from performing their duties in the sleet. The Rose slows with the extra weight of the precipitation on her canvas sails and deck. The Union Jack tries to hide from the dampness and wraps itself around the top of the mast.

Secure in the hole in the wall; the mouse is lying curled up in the corner with its long tail tucked under its body for warmth. The long facial whiskers no longer droop to the floor, and a sheen has returned to its brownish-grey coat. The sleeping rodent occasionally twitches, as if in a bad dream.

Angelo knocks on the Captain's door, "Captain Sir, are you awake? The First Mate wants to see you. We are approaching a small village."

"I will be there soon," says the Captain and begins to dress after another night with little sleep. He steps out from his cabin into the drizzling rain, looks at the sea to get his sense of direction, then walks to the helm. "Angelo, fetch me a tin of tea."

Roddy Downing greets the Captain on the helm. "Sir, Parker called out that there is a small village on our port side. I don't believe it shows on the ship's map."

"Yes, I can see the village, Mr. Downing. There is the channel we must take, on our starboard side," says the Captain pointing into the distance.

From the Sara Rose, it looks like this is a small settlement with a dock large enough for small fishing boats and barges. There are only eight or nine tiny shack-like buildings, with no visible smoke or activity in the village.

The First Mate turns the wheel of the vessel while the crew stabilizes the foremast. The ship turns to starboard. The large sails cast their shadow forward in the channel, leaving the silent village behind in the ship's wake.

On the starboard side, the crew can see the Isle of Skye with the Scottish mainland lying on the port side of the ship. Each side of the channel is vastly different from the other.

William Brett and the Lieutenant are in the galley when the Captain comes in. "Gentlemen, would the two of you come to my cabin with me?"

The two men walk alongside the Captain to his cabin. "Please sit down, gentlemen. Mr. Brett, are all the cannon cleaned and ready for use?"

"Yes, the cannon are in working condition, and there are ample gunpowder and cannonball," says William Brett confidently.

"Good, I'm glad to hear that, Sir."

"Lieutenant, do you think this is an ideal place to test our guns?"

The Lieutenant turns to the Captain with an eager look. "Oh yes, I think we are in the perfect place to test the cannon. We have land on both sides so we can set our range. The sun is at our backs and the rain has left us. Yes, this is an ideal spot, Sir."

The Captain pauses for a moment, "Yes, Lieutenant, I agree with you. This is a good place to get the men accustomed to the cannon. We will be close to the settlement of Mallaig within the next twenty-four hours. We have the day to practise our skills. But the real reason I suggest we fire the cannon is to draw Hardie Jenkins out of hiding."

Captain Mcbaine stands, takes out his pipe and packs it with fresh tobacco. He then sits on the edge of his desk, striking a match across the bottom of his boot. The smoke from his pipe greets the musty air in the cabin. He looks down at the two seated men, waiting for a response. Neither William Brett, nor the Lieutenant says a word while waiting in suspense for the Captain to continue his comments.

"Gentlemen, I think we all agree that Hardie took money and made promises in Brighton. He came into the inn a few hours later than everyone else. He bragged to the men he socialized with that night that he was coming into more money. He provided payment for the drinks most of the night. A few men said they had seen him with a pouch of coins the night the men were on leave from the ship. It all points to Hardie working for pirates, or other sources. I believe he sold his soul, betrayed the ship and the flag we fly. I would like to know your thoughts. Please speak freely, Gentlemen."

* * *

The Harris's and Ogden's sit at a table chatting about the cold, wet weather that came during the night. Diane Ogden mentions that the thunder kept her up most of the night. Ronald Harris stands and says, "Thunder, rain and snow all in the same night. That was the first time I have witnessed such weather. Let's go for a walk on the deck while we have the sun in our favour."

The stewards busily wipe the rain and melted snow off the deck chairs. Jones commands, "Wipe this chair and leave me a few dry towels to sit on. I can't stand here all day. Bring me a cup of rum and add a touch of tea. This damp weather makes my old bones ache," whines Jones.

Donald Evens remains in his cabin intending to have a nap after breakfast, while Aggie is talking with Susannah in her room. They take a few of Susannah's dresses out of the large trucks and place them on the bed. "I like this dress. It looked nice on you the last time I saw you in it. I believe you wore it for your Father's birthday. Oh dear, that was two months ago," says Aggie.

"You're right Mother; I did wear the dress that day. I think I shall wear it tonight when I meet Matthew."

"You are very cheerful this morning. May I ask why you are in such a good mood?"

"Well, you know, Mother, it is Matthew. When I saw him asleep on deck waiting for me, I touched his face with my hand. I knew then, that it is love I felt for Matthew."

* * *

"Hardie's mistake may have been picking a fight with you, Mr. Rodgers. Perhaps it was a stroke of luck. If he is helping whoever is after the artifacts, then we will be attacked at sea. They do not know we are onto Hardie. I am sure they expected the Sara Rose to take the same route from Stornoway that she came on. I bet they watched us from the northern side of the Isle of Skye. I believe I made the right choice in selecting the course we are on now."

"Captain, what plan of attack do you think Hardie has in his mind? We know he has Reed's and Randel's firearms. I hope he has not managed to get a keg of gunpowder," says the Lieutenant.

The Captain relights his pipe and says, "Once we start firing the cannon, Hardie will think his friends are attacking the ship. We will call whoever is guarding the bottom of the ship at the time to help man the cannon. This will draw him out. He will believe his pirate friends are firing cannon at the Rose. Hardie will make his way to the main deck, where he will try and kill as many of us as he can. He would need to gain control of the helm. With the helm in his control, he could slow the ship, thus allowing the pirate ship to come alongside and board the Rose."

William Brett and the Lieutenant look at each other astonished at what the Captain has just said.

Continuing, the Captain says, "The wealth on the Sara Rose is enormous. The two small crates here in my cabin would fetch a King's ransom, and the five crates of artifacts are priceless. Let us not forget the upper class passengers. A lot of these families are very rich and have every shilling they own with them. I can't imagine the slaughter that would take place aboard this ship once pirates are in control. I would

217

also wager that some of the steerage travellers would join the pirates."
The Captain leans back in his chair and relights his pipe.

Chapter 38

Joey and Neil Cunningham run up the stairwell from the steerage section to the deck. Frances is following behind them. "You two, wait for me. You know what father said." The two youths turn and laugh at Frances then continue on their way.

Neil sees Arthur sitting alone at the table and approaches him. "Arthur, that story you told us. Was it a true story?"

"Yes. Yes, of course, it was true," says Arthur with a bit of a grin.

"Martha and Isabell told Emma that you made up the story. Emma cried all night, and now she will not talk to me," says the confused Neil.

Mrs. Peters is schooling her children, reading the Bible to them. She stops from time to time to quiz the children on what she has read.

Mr. Peters is walking on deck, often turning to see if anyone is watching him. He spots Jones slumped in a lounge chair with his cigar protruding from his lips. In the breeze, the ashes from his cigar move back and forth on his trousers. Jones' head is jerking up and down as he snores, causing his top hat to sway back and forth. Peters nudges Jones, but Jones does not respond. Peters looks around before he shakes the sleeping Jones again. Jones awakens and gruffly responds, "What do you want, Peters? Strike a match. My cigar is out."

"I knocked on your cabin door last night, but you never answered," timidly says Peters.

"I don't recall, Peters. I must have been sleeping. Now strike me a match."

Peters strikes a match and holds it till Jones gets his cigar lit. "I'll see if I can get away tonight for a game of chance after the family falls asleep.

"Peters, go away. Send the steward here, now."

*　*　*

It is early afternoon, and the upper class passengers are on the deck, enjoying the sunshine. Children run back and forth playing games. A few are hiding from each other in a game of hide-and-seek. They spring out and scare the other as soon as their seeker gets close to them. A few boys have taken the walking canes from the napping guests, using the canes as swords and pretend they are Captain Kidd and Blackbeard. One boy has a red handkerchief tied on his head. Another boy, pretending to be wounded, has taken a soiled napkin off a dining table and wrapped it around his head. With his boyish chest puffed out, one lad claims to be Captain Morgan. Captain Morgan swings his make-believe sword in a mock skirmish with the other young pirates.

A few of the passengers are entertained watching the boys at play. Some girls have joined the boys in the game of hide-and-seek, while the quieter girls are encouraged by their mothers to stay close. The young girls cling to their mothers' dresses and, at times, shyly put their heads on their mothers' laps.

The passengers on deck are delighted with the view. Mrs. Harris has her easel on deck, trying to capture the moment. From the port side of the ship she is depicting the beauty of Scotland's mainland, where the waters of the channel embrace the distant, stony shore. The many creeks and rivers offer new life, releasing freshwater to the waiting sea. Sea otters thrive on the abundance of clams and small fish that the fresh waters deliver.

Upstream of the creeks and rivers, beavers are busy building their winter dams and can be seen swimming with aspen branches in their mouths. In the distance, a doe is mothering her two offspring. The male, with his proud rack of antlers, keeps watch.

A congregation of sparrows flutters in the aspen trees near the water's edge. They bring the trees to life, grouping together, chattering at the passing Rose. Then, in an instant, the sparrows take to the sky like a ribbon in the wind.

The Captain joins the starboard viewers and remarks to a few how lucky they are to have witnessed this beauty. The starboard view of the Isle of Skye is quite the opposite of the port side view.

Skye's majestic cliffs climb upward above the sea as if being called by the Heavens. The granite walls pillar two hundred feet skyward and at times, touch the clouds. They look down at the Sara Rose as she floats by, like a mere oak branch in the waters.

One can see ledges that time has carved into the granite walls. They have become nesting areas for gulls, and in places, their droppings have painted the granite white and grey.

As the vessel passes, her wake gently caresses the shore of Skye. The afternoon sun has cast its departing shadows and leaves a coldness behind.

Captain Mcbaine asks all the passengers on the starboard side of the ship to go to their cabins, telling them to stay there as a safety precaution until the routine testing of the cannon is complete. He then tips his hat to the passengers and walks to the port side, where he repeats the same message.

"Is this common procedure for a passenger and cargo ship?" asks Mr. Harris.

"Yes indeed, the seas are never safe from pirates or unfriendly ports of call," comments the Captain.

"Can we stay on deck and watch? What harm would it do for us to watch?"

"I'm sorry, Mr. Harris, but the crew needs the deck for spotting and shot calling. I do not think you or your wife would appreciate the smell of the gunpowder soaking into your clothing, nor the deafening sounds."

The Lieutenant is at the stern of the ship directing the steerage passengers to go below. Captain Mcbaine orders the doors to the stairwell of the first and second-class passengers be closed and locked.

He walks hurriedly to the Lieutenant and orders the steerage doors to be closed and locked as well.

The Sara Rose is at full sail, proudly displaying herself when a robust breeze fills her sails, moving the vessel swiftly. The overhead clouds gracefully follow the ship through the picturesque channel.

The Captain stands at the helm of the ship and takes his pipe from his pocket. He strikes a match and inhales the smoke deep inside his lungs. Knowing it is time to act, his blood shivers, and his thoughts focus on all that could go wrong. Once again, he draws smoke from his pipe. Then turns to his crew that have gathered. Captain Mcbaine salutes his men, perhaps for the last time.

The Lieutenant and William Brett approach Captain Mcbaine and all three men look down at the planked floor momentarily. The Captain breaks the brief silence, "Gentlemen, we have our plan in place. Let us carry it out now, while we have daylight. Lieutenant, this is an order. You stay in the background. Hardie will be coming for you. Is that understood, Mr. Rodgers? All right then, let's get to the task at hand. Good luck, Gentlemen."

The ships stowaway overhears the conversation and scurries to the safety of its hole in the wall.

Below deck, the sailors await orders to commence firing of the cannon. On deck, crewmen remain silent, nervously holding their firearms. Every man reaches into his soul for strength. Captain Mcbaine suddenly shouts, "Fire at will men."

The deafening sound of six cannon echo in the channel and the smell of gunpowder drifts to the starboard deck. The ship lists to the port side. The men firing the cannon make their way quickly through the narrow corridors across to the port side, leaving a few men behind to reload the cannon.

Now,the six cannon from the port side now roar. The Rose lists to the starboard side, with smoke from the cannon rising to the deck. Half the men return through the corridor to the waiting cannon on the starboard side. Now both sides of the ship are firing cannonball at random.

222

The barrage of gunfire and the loud voices of the crew create the effect that the Sara Rose is under attack. The repeating blasts of the cannon fill the channel with intense fear. The nervous wildlife instinctively flees deep into the forests. The birds frantically dissolve their chain of flight and individually disappear into the horizon. The granite cliffs of Skye tremble, causing the sea waters to ripple outward to the centre of the channel.

Captain Mcbaine sends Arthur below to call the three men who guard the bottom of the ship. All the crew members know of the Captain's plot to bring Hardie Jenkins out in the open. Arthur makes his way as fast as he can, down the steps of the stairwell to the bottom of the ship. "Mates, Mates come quickly. We are under attack! Bring your firearms. Be quick Mates," Arthur shouts. The three men run up the stairs, leaving Arthur behind. He quickly turns and follows the men to the top deck, where he swiftly makes his way to the helm to protect Third Mate Johnson.

The sound of cannon blasting continues from the ship. Sailors on deck shoot their firearms into the air for added effect. The men yell back and forth as if they truly are under attack.

The suspense of the event is unsettling the crew. As the nauseating smell of gunpowder permeates the air, smoke from the barrage floats above the deck like fog. The crew's ears ring with the pounding sounds of cannon fire.

The Union Jack is silently awaiting the outcome. Shadows cast from the cliffs of Skye generate a coldness across the deck.

A nightmare-like trance grips the men's thoughts and they stand as if frozen in time. Cold sweat runs off their blank faces and down into their well-worn shirts. Fear of the unknown has become their greatest concern. Emotions peak as time stands still.

Chapter 39

Shrouded within the smoke of the cannon fire, the ghostly appearance of Hardie Jenkins becomes visible. Hardie stands menacingly on the deck of vessel. His teeth clenched tightly; he displays the bloodthirsty eyes of a killer.

Angelo immediately locks the stairwell door behind Hardie from the inside. Hardie is trapped on deck. He looks in all directions, but there is no other ship or any of his pirate friends to be seen.

There is no one on the deck. Hardie stands with a sword and a knife hanging from his belt. He carries two firearms, one in each hand. The look of evil on his face would cause the Devil himself to surrender.

Captain Mcbaine steps on to the deck with a sword gripped in his hand. "Hardie Jenkins, I order you to drop your weapons," shouts Captain Mcbaine.

Hardie is confused as to what has just happened. The Captain repeats, "Hardie, you have no way out. Drop your weapons. Now, Hardie."

One by one, the crew members appear from their hiding spots. Hardie runs to the stairwell door. He pushes the door but to no avail, for it is locked. Hardie turns and sees all his shipmates pointing firearms directly at him. In a group, the men slowly walk toward Hardie. "Arrr Matey! I'm your shipmate. Don't do this to me. We are mates!"

The men shiver in their boots while stepping closer. The cannon continue firing. The smoke weaves a blanket over the deck. The noise echoes within the minds of all and the tension on the ship climbs to new heights.

Hardie makes his stand. Raising his firearm, he aims in the direction of the Lieutenant. Smoke flares from his gun. He drops the firearm, raises his second gun and aims at the Captain. Hardie fires. Immediately, Captain Mcbaine is knocked to the floor.

The men are motionless. Hardie throws the spent firearm at a crew member. With his right hand, he draws the sword from his belt. His left hand pulls out a knife. He wildly begins swinging his sword.

In an instant, blood spews from the neck of Jimmy Brown, who falls to the deck. The men rush Hardie, whose sword has found the stomach of Harmond. Pulling the sword out of his shipmate's stomach, Hardie cries out, "Arrr Matey! I told you I would get my revenge."

Randel jumps back, avoiding the wrath of Hardie's knife. Startled, Randel aims his firearm at Hardie. The weapon misfires. In desperation, Randel swings his long handle firearm at Hardie's head. A loud thump sounds in the tense air as Hardie falls to the planked deck. Randel grins, "Arrr! I got my revenge, Matey!"

The Captain struggles to his feet. He regains his balance and slowly steps to where Hardie lies. He looks down at the unconscious Hardie and shakes his head. "Doctor Eden, get over here quick! Arthur, get below and tell them to stop firing the cannon. Be quick."

Jimmy Brown is dead. The blood is pooling around him and soaking into his clothing.

The Doctor kneels beside Harmond and rips his shirt open. Harmond's intestines are protruding through his wound. Doctor Eden begins applying pressure to the wound with his bare hands. He tells a member of the crew to reach into his medical bag to take out a bottle and pour its contents over the wound. Harmond screams in horror as his body begins to shake uncontrollably.

Another sailor kneels and holds Harmond's head up. Blood continues to gush from the wound, covering the Doctor's hands. The knees of the Doctor's trousers and the sleeves of his jacket are saturated with blood. Harmond gasps for air, trying to spit out the blood filling his mouth. His legs jerk and his arms flail. His screams echo along the deck. The men feel their shipmate's pain and their bodies' shudder, as they are helpless.

Time loses all meaning. Now, time has stopped for Harmond. One by one, they take their caps off. The Captain crosses himself, and the crew follows his action.

The channel becomes quiet — the cannon silences. Smoke continues to find its way to the deck. The air remains filled with the pungent odour of gunpowder.

"Get Hardie out of my sight, clap him in irons. Drag and chain him to the anchor." shouts the Captain.

In the confusion, everyone has lost track of one another. The Captain notices a crew member lying on the deck and rushes over. "Lieutenant, you're wounded! Doctor, get over here!"

The Captain drops to his knees. The Lieutenant is curled up on the deck holding his left shoulder with his right hand. Blood has soaked through his uniform and runs onto his shirt. "Lieutenant, you took the musket ball meant for me. Why, Lieutenant? Why?"

"Get his jacket off and lay him flat. Jackal hold his arms down," orders the Doctor excitedly. He cuts the Lieutenant's shirt open and places a knife handle in the Lieutenant's mouth. "Bite down on this," says the Doctor as he pours a liquid over the wound. The Lieutenant bites down hard on the knife handle. He closes his eyes; every muscle in his body tightens and squirms. The Lieutenant's heart races, thumping in his chest, and his blue eyes open to see only red as he succumbs to the pain and lies unconscious.

"Doctor, what can we do for the Lieutenant?" asks the Captain

"Get a table from the dining room out here, quickly. I need to get the musket ball out of his shoulder before he wakes. Let's be quick men," says the Doctor gruffly.

There is a pounding on the locked doors of the stairwell. "Is it safe for me to open the doors yet?" calls Angelo in a terrified voice.

"Yes, open the door and come out," says one of the crewmen. Angelo opens the doors. He stares in disbelief at the two bloodied bodies lying on the deck. Angelo's hand immediately covers his mouth and his body buckles forward slightly. The smell of the smoke and the pooling blood has no mercy on the youth's stomach.

He runs, holding his hand over his mouth to the railing on the port side of the ship. With his hands gripping the railing, Angelo discharges his stomach contents into the channel. He holds his head down in embarrassment. His biggest fear becomes true. Now, what will the crew think of him?

* * *

The afternoon sun tries to hide from what it has witnessed and begins its descent, vanishing into the western horizon.

Captain Mcbaine is pacing the deck. He walks a few feet, turns, and comes back. With the Lieutenant on the dining table, the Doctor cleans the wound before looking for the slug in the Lieutenant's shoulder. The blood continues to seep from the wound and now drips off the table onto the floor.

"Captain, get over here and wipe the blood from the wound. I can't see what I am doing," orders Doctor Eden loudly.

The Doctor has his finger in the flesh of the Lieutenant's shoulder. His eyes are closed, trying to feel where the musket ball lodged. With each probe of his fingers, blood streams out of the wound. The Doctor's trousers become soaked as blood trickles down his pant legs and onto his shoes.

"Captain, I can feel the musket ball. Slide my instrument bag closer and keep drawing the blood from the wound." Sweat from the Doctor's forehead runs down his face as his index finger holds the musket ball. With his free arm, he wipes his forehead with his jacket sleeve. Fumbling through his instruments, he grabs the forceps and slides them into the wound. Blood from the Lieutenant's shoulder squirts in fine pulses over the Doctor's hands. Doctor Eden clenches his teeth. Again, he closes his eyes.

"I have it, Captain. I have the musket ball." The Doctor is holding the musket ball with the forceps.

"Good job, Doctor. Will the Lieutenant be all right now?" apprehensively asks the Captain.

"Only time can answer that. The Lieutenant has lost a lot of blood. His youth is on his side. I will stitch his wound the best I can and wrap a bandage around his shoulder. We will get him moved to his bed before he wakes."

The events of the past few hours have taken their toll on the Captain. Exhibiting calmness, he walks toward the two dead sailors whose motionless bodies lay covered with blankets.

"We will all miss the voice of Jimmy Brown." sadly comments the Captain. "Old Harmond was a friend to everyone; the sea was his life. Carry the men over by the anchor and prepare them for burial at sea. You men, get the buckets and swab up the blood. We can't have the passengers seeing all this blood on the deck. Angelo, you get below and lay down. You look worse than I feel."

* * *

The upper class passengers have their cabin doors open. They walk back and forth, mingling with each other. Ronald Harris steps into the open doorway of the Even's cabin. "That sounded like quite an impressive display of cannon fire."

"It sure was, Harris. My ears are still ringing. I wonder when we will be allowed back on deck. It would be nice to see the sun before it sets this evening," comments Donald Evens.

"The listing of the ship and the smell of gunpowder, has my stomach upset," says Aggie Evens to Ronald Harris.

"Yes, my wife feels the same. She had to lie down for a while."

In the steerage section of the ship, a violin is heard. It is Joey Cunningham with his new violin. Joseph and Neil sit on Joey's bunk as the youngster stands with his new violin. The proud Joey has a gleam in his eye and a smile that lights up the dark room. He is not playing any particular song, just short excerpts from the many tunes he knows. Joseph and Neil Cunningham cheer on Joey.

Martin is involved in a game of checkers with a fellow passenger. A crowd gathers as the men debate who will take on the winner.

The deafening cannon fire has terrified the little mouse. Its nose is pushed deep into the corner and its tiny body continues to tremble. The cannon fire has brought back scary memories of the swooshing sounds of the corn broom.

The sun stretches itself further and further from the Sara Rose and the air in the channel has begun a cooling trend. The distinctive smell of gunpowder lingers as if it is embedded into the air they breathe and into the wood of the ship. The small port of Mallaig comes into view along the Scottish coast.

The horizon sends a cold wind into the channel as if it wants to distance itself from the events of the day. The Union Jack lowers in honour of Jimmy Brown and Harmond. The blood is gone from the planked deck, but the memory will never fade from the deck of the Sara Rose.

Chapter 40

The first signs of darkness are sent across the deck as the sun fully retreats into the west. The village of Mallaig can be seen from the Sara Rose. Large piles of wood are stacked alongside the shanty style houses, with smoke rising from the chimneys. There is a light in every window of the village. Men have gathered in the centre of the small town, holding lanterns. Barking dogs come running to the dock, forming a protective clan and howl at the passing ship.

"Mr. Johnson, we are now safely out of the channel. Let's run the sea tonight. Tell the crew there must be no lanterns on the deck this night. Get the riggers up the masts and on the spars. Let's be quick."

The Captain makes his way down the stairwell to the sleeping area of his men. He tells them to remain at ease, as he continues to the Lieutenant's quarters.

"Doctor, has the Lieutenant woken yet? Did he move at all?"

"No Captain, the Lieutenant hasn't woken or moved. He has lost a lot of blood and now it is a matter of time."

"All right, Doctor. I will arrange for some food to be brought to you. Is there anything else you would like?"

"Hot food would do nicely. Thank you, Captain."

* * *

The Rose sails on a new course. A northern wind targets the ship, bringing colder temperatures. The moon is playing hide-and-seek with the passing clouds, forcing the stars to retreat closer to the heavens for warmth. Only the Northern Star braves the cold and stays true.

The ship's stowaway has been waiting for the decks to become silent. It scampers directly to the table and chair legs for protection. Running its nose on the planked floor, it finds a crust of bread. It runs towards the dripping water, where the rodent steps directly into the puddle of water and quenches its thirst. The water has given the mouse the relief it needed as gurgling sounds now come from its stomach.

The early morning has left its calling. A new collection of dew slowly drips onto the deck of the ship, and the timid sunlight is slow to share itself. The lazy fog and damp air send shivers through the crew.

The sails of the Sara Rose await the northerly wind to wipe the clinging dew off its canvas structures. Emotionless clouds struggle, passing slowly overhead and the relentless fog retains its grip.

The ship stays her course in the grey morning. The Isle of Rum is on the starboard side, with the Isle of Eigg coming into view on the ship's port side.

Captain Mcbaine exits his cabin wearing a heavy overcoat. He speaks briefly to Second Mate Quinn at the helm. He continues directly from the stairwell to the Lieutenant's room. Doctor Eden is asleep in a chair next to the Lieutenant's bed.

"Captain, I'm happy to see you." comes the weak voice of the Lieutenant.

The Captain replies with a smile, "We were all worried about you. I'm glad to see you're awake. I must thank you, Lieutenant, for your brave actions on the deck yesterday. You took the musket ball meant for me. I am beholding to you, Sir. You get some much needed rest," says the Captain, saluting his Lieutenant.

* * *

The sudden sound of cannonball shrieks across the greying sky. The ship's bell rings, and the Captain calls for his high riggers. Parker is ordered to the crow's nest. The Captain quickly approaches the helm. "Mr. Quinn put the Rose into a zigzag heading. Begin turning the ship to the north."

The high riggers are not concerned about safety this morning. They are up the mast and on the spars in short order. The sails are being pulled

232

up by the deck crew. Another cannonball whistles over the Sara Rose, and drops into the sea.

Parker shouts down to the Captain. "Two ships and they are in chase!" The Captain tells Arthur to lock the doors to the steerage section and the upper class entrance. He orders a group of men to take the bow cannon to the stern. The men pull the massive cannon on rollers across the decks. They are then bolted to the deck on a revolving plate, allowing the cannon in turn to any direction.

"We are full sail, Captain. I believe the Rose is holding her own on the sea," shouts Parker.

Second Mate Quinn keeps the ship in a zigzag heading, thus making it more difficult for the ships in chase to keep their cannon trained on the Sara Rose.

The ship struggles to find her stride in the dull morning. The sounds of cannonball whirling across the deck frighten all, but the crew and high riggers remain at their posts.

William Brett approaches the Captain. "The cannon are secured and await your command."

"All right. Fire at will. Let our cannon find their mark."

The sea waters around the Rose tremble with the first cannonballs being hurled back at the enemy ships. The four cannon at the stern release a continuous volley of cannon fire into a rumbling sky. The sailors cheer the blast but shudder at the returning fire.

The Sara Rose suddenly lists to the port side when the mizzenmast is struck. The outer part of the spar falls to the sea, taking a high rigger with it. The sailor clings desperately to the wooden spar in the cold waters, waving frantically for the ship to stop and rescue him. But the Rose blindly continues to claw her way, leaving the frantic sailor behind.

Parker calls from the crow's nest, "We're gaining sea on the Devil ships." The crew of the ship sound off a loud cheer with Parker's news. The high riggers have begun repairing the damage to the spar. The vessel captures the northern wind in her sails and the ship desperately advances.

Arthur comes to the Captain's side, "Sir, we lost Red Tanner when the spar went down."

"Yes, Arthur, I saw Tanner go into the sea with the spar. The cold sea will extend its hand to Tanner and put him to sleep in quick fashion. Arthur, with the Lieutenant injured, I will depend on you more than ever."

"Aye, Captain. I will do my best. Is there anything that needs attending to?"

"Yes, Arthur. We are in safe waters for the time being. Get the cooks up on deck. Then unlock the entrance doors for the steerage and upper deck passengers.

The Captain walks over to Hardie, who is chained to the anchor and looks at him. Hardie has his back leaning against the anchor. His wrists are chained together, with leg irons clapped around his ankles. Hardie Jenkins looks up at the Captain. He quickly looks away in shame.

Martin and Matthew are called to the kitchen. Martin is sent down to the food locker, while Matthew and Haydn are directed to the dining room to set the tables. The Captain walks among the guests in the lounge area and explains that they were under attack by two pirate ships. He tells them that the Sara Rose's speed has outrun the vessels in pursuit.

Donald Evens stands, "We are grateful to you Captain. Most of us are a bit suspicious of all the secrecy on the ship. Is there more we should know? Will the Sara Rose dock in Ireland as planned?"

Captain Mcbaine hesitates before he says, "I am not sure if we will dock in Ireland. Today's events may have changed our route. My orders call for the ship to dock there, but I am more concerned about our safety. You may be relieved to know that Hardie Jenkins is now our prisoner."

* * *

The afternoon sun takes charge and begins to shine on the northern seas. The brisk air shows the Sara Rose no favouritism. The restless winds generate large white caps, making the massive vessel clumsy in the rough waters. The ship climbs its way to the top of each wave and then lunges downward. This continuous rocking of the ship sends most of the passengers to their cabins.

The rodent, backed into its favourite corner digs its claws into the planked floor. The different choices of its meal last night are beginning to become unsettled with the rocking of the ship.

Chapter 41

The ship carves her way into the North Atlantic waters, nervously stretching out on a new course. The rushing wake of the ship hides the anxious path she leaves behind. The great northern wind is in control, pushing the temperature lower and lower.

Captain Mcbaine and First Mate Downing are at the helm, discussing the day's weather and the ship's course. William Brett and Arthur join them. "Captain, are we to proceed on this northerly course? Won't this heading take us directly to Iceland?" inquires the First Mate.

"You are correct, Mr. Downing. The course we are on now will take the ship to Iceland. Arthur, gather a few men and meet me at the stern," orders the Captain.

A cold chill from the sea seeps on board, slowly creeping to all sections of the ship. The upper deck passengers have eaten their evening meal in haste. They depart quickly to their cabins without the usual stroll on the deck, leaving the lounge area vacant.

Martin is in his bunk, covered with a blanket. His cough has returned, creating the need to breathe through a handkerchief. Matthew covers Martin with his blanket in hopes his brother will rest easier.

"Arthur, you and Angelo light all the lanterns that are on deck. Tell Parker to light the lanterns in the crow's nest, then get the two jolly boats on the deck. Fetch a few of the long poles we use at night to hold the lanterns. Haydn, get a spool of rope from the storage bunk. Young Quinn, follow Haydn and bring up some old torn canvas sails."

"All right men, we will put a few ships of our own to sea." The puzzled crew looks at the Captain, but all refrain from commenting. They gather around the jolly boats and wait for the Captain to continue.

"We will create two ships of our own for the pirates to follow. With the long poles, we will make masts on the jolly boats, tying them securely. Then we will put together a makeshift sail on both jolly boats."

The Captain walks back and forth between the two jolly boats. He packs his pipe with tobacco, Arthur approaches the Captain. "I see what you are thinking, Captain. It is a grand idea."

"I am sure this will help confuse the pirates for a few days, Arthur. Hopefully, the current will take the jolly boats westerly. Good work, men! Now tie a row of lit lanterns across the jolly boat and let's lower it to the sea," says Captain Mcbaine while lighting his pipe.

The Sara Rose finds her strength, pounding her way northwest on the untamed waters. The day's light stretches itself and the greying colours of evening blend into the northern air. The dropping temperatures have eased and the cold winds have found their contentment, allowing the clouds to hover in groups in the night sky.

* * *

"How are you feeling Lieutenant, or should I even ask that question?" asks the Doctor.

"The pain in my shoulder is unbearable. There is a constant throbbing. I can feel every heartbeat and hear every footstep down the hallway. Each sound echoes in my head."

"Here, Lieutenant. I brought you a few rum rations. This will help to dull the pain."

The crew looks at the jolly boat they have released to the sea. Light from the lanterns is still visible. The men continue getting the second boat ready. Arthur jokes to Randel, "Matey, we should put Hardie Jenkins in this boat."

"All right, men. Get those lanterns lit." The Captain watches as the second jolly boat is lowered to the water.

"Now men, put out all the lanterns on the Rose. We will become a ghost ship tonight."

238

The Captain walks to the helm. "Mr. Downing, let us escape these northern waters. Turn the Sara Rose due south and set a course for Ireland."

"Aye Aye, Sir!" smiles the First Mate while turning the wheel of the ship into the night. "Captain, I believe the dropping of the jolly boats will keep our pirate friends busy."

"The jolly boats will keep them confused as they follow the lanterns. I do not believe they will send one ship to Iceland and one to Ireland. They need the support of each other. I will speak with the Port Major of Galway when we arrive at port in Ireland. Perhaps they have a warship to deal with the scoundrels. Excuse me, Mr. Downing, I must find Arthur. We have two shipmates to ready for the Mistress of the sea."

The ship's little mouse anxiously waits for the footsteps to distance themselves — constant dripping of freshwater calls. The thirsty rodent disregards all caution and begins its trek, hiding along the chair and table legs. It ignores the crumbs of bread on the floor, for its thirst is greater than its hunger. The mouse wiggles its nose in the air and feeling safe makes a run for the pooled water. It quickly laps water from the puddle. Returning footsteps cause the mouse to run to the nearby cupboard and hide. The surprised mouse has climbed into the flour bin and begins to sneeze while rolling in the flour. The experience has the mouse excited and it enjoys this new playground.

No lanterns are lit on the deck, leaving the pale moon as the only source of light. Matthew is on the starboard side of the ship leaning against the railing, when Susannah appears. He quickly steps in her direction and takes her in his arms. Before she can speak, he kisses her.

Matthew impulsively kisses her again, while his fingers rise upward to fondle her hair. Her shawl falls to the floor. Matthew kisses her eyes. Susannah backs against the wall, and opens Matthew's jacket. He presses himself against her, and she pulls him closer. The silent night backs away without a sound and the clouds quickly cover the moon's stare.

* * *

The crew gathers around their Captain. Captain Mcbaine takes his cap off, tucking it under his arm and bows his head. The crew follows his lead. He takes his Bible from his pocket and opens it to a marked page.

"Men, this is a sad time for all of us. The Sara Rose was fortunate to have these men serve on her deck, and we are very fortunate to have known these great men. I am proud to call them friends.

My heart went out to Red Tanner when a cannonball splintered the ship's spar, and he fell to the sea's mercy. Red knew the ship could not stop and return for him. Jimmy Brown's voice will always echo to us from the crow's nest. There was no finer man than Harmond. We will all miss his stories. The sea has called these men home."

"I believe the three men would appreciate these words." The Captain opens the Bible and begins to read **Revelation 21:14. 'He will wipe every tear from their eyes, and death shall be no more, neither shall there be mourning, nor crying, nor pain anymore, for the former things have passed away.'**

The Captain pauses. He closes his Bible. The men stand in silence. The Captain nods and four men approach the body of Jimmy Brown. His body is wrapped in white cloth, secured with thin ropes. They slide his body onto the 'Board.' The men then pick up the 'Board of Death' and place one end on the railing. The crew members cross themselves. Jackal begins to play his violin in honour of his lost shipmates. The sound of **'Amazing Grace'** brings a tear to all when Jimmy Brown's body is given to the sea.

The men then place the 'Board of Death' by the body of Harmond and repeat the same procedure. Jackal again gives life to his violin. The calling sea receives Harmond's body. Crew members bow their heads, and stand quietly, as their thoughts focus on their lost shipmates who have gone to meet 'The Mistress of the Sea.'

On the unlit deck, the crew have a sense of emptiness, for they have lost far more than their shipmates. Gone is the close unity and friendship they shared. The sea has taken three of their shipmates to their final resting place.

The Sara Rose struggles southward into the night. Restless northern winds calm. The moon hides behind the clouds, and the stars dim this night to share their grief.

Doctor Eden walks down the stairwell through the narrow corridor of empty bunks to the Lieutenant's room. He can see the bloody area on the bandages has increased in size. The rum has done its job, for the Lieutenant is fast asleep. The Doctor picks up a pen which had fallen alongside the sleeping Lieutenant and takes the sheet of paper from his hand. He sets the pen and paper next to the ink bottle on the chair. The Doctor rejoins the men on deck. They are releasing their sorrow by reminiscing about their lost shipmates.

The Captain interrupts their conversations, "Men, I know a lot of you have been wondering what we should do with Hardie. I believe this is a matter for all of you to decide as a crew. You have three options. One is to hand Hardie over to the authorities in Ireland. The second thing we can do is return Hardie to England for trial after we have completed our Caribbean route. The third option, well, gentlemen, you all know what that is."

Captain Mcbaine takes a few steps and picks up a corn broom. He takes out his knife and cuts off a handful of straws from the broom. The men form a circle around the Captain. He hands each man a corn straw of the same length. "All right, men. You will decide the fate of Hardie Jenkins. I will abstain from casting a straw. I will only voice my opinion in the event of a tie. Throw your straw into the bucket, and we will all count the straws together. If the straw is in full-length, we give Hardie to the authorities in Ireland. If the straw is bent in half, Hardie continues on the Sara Rose with us back to England to stand trial. Gentlemen, if the straw is broken in two, it's the plank for Hardie Jenkins. Are we clear about what I just said?"

The men are all silent. They put their heads down and step away from the Captain. Their emotions have changed, now that the decision must come from their souls. They separate from each other but still glance at one another in the hope of an answer. No sailor has moved. Each holds a straw. No one has dropped his straw into the bucket.

Chapter 42

Captain Mcbaine breaks the silence, "Men, I am going below deck to talk to the Lieutenant. I will give him a straw and explain our situation. He should have the same say in determining Hardie's fate."

Entering the Lieutenant's room, he moves the Lieutenant's writing material to the counter then seats himself. Captain Mcbaine removes his hat, pausing for a moment before placing his hand on the Lieutenant's right shoulder and shaking him gently. When the Lieutenant does not respond, the Captain leaves the room.

* * *

Susannah quietly walks down the hallway to her cabin. She is undecided as to whether or not she should speak to her mother tonight. Hesitating, she decides not to.

In her room, Susannah sits on the edge of her bed with her shawl over her shoulders. Memories of the evening replay continuously in her mind. She spreads her arms out wide and allows herself to fall backward onto the bed. Staring at the ceiling, she can only see Matthew in her thoughts.

Peters leaves his cabin and cautiously sneaks down the hallway, looking back to see if Mrs. Peters may be following him. He goes up the stairwell to the next deck, turns to his left and walks the corridor to Jones' door. Knocking quietly on the door, Peters stands back, waiting for an answer. He looks in both directions, then knocks louder.

The little mouse is white, covered with flour. Its hiding spot in the flour bin causes it to sneeze continually. The mouse sprints for a few feet on the deck and stops to shake itself. A small cloud of flour rises upward from the rodent's coat. Confused, it runs in a circle trying to catch its white tail. The more it runs; the more flour falls off its coat. The mouse stops to sneeze again.

* * *

With the rise of the morning sun on the eastern horizon, the Sara Rose advances southward. The dew has been wiped away with the sun taking command of the skies. The night clouds have been driven from sight. The moderate northwest winds bless the canvas sails, allowing the ship to maintain eighteen knots while slicing through the waters. The smell of breakfast is teasing the morning air.

Frances and her two brothers leave the steerage section and make their way to the stern. Joey and Neil notice Arthur and Jackal sitting at their usual table and run ahead to greet them. The two lads immediately ask Jackal when they can play their instruments with him. Jackal does not have a chance to answer, when Frances asks, "Arthur, I have not seen Lieutenant Rodgers for a few days. Is he all right?"

Arthur is unsure how to answer the question. He looks at Jackal, who lowers his head.

"Is the Lieutenant sick? Is he hurt?" asks Frances wiping her eyes.

"Miss Frances, the Lieutenant is not feeling well. The Doctor has confined him to his bed," says Arthur quietly.

"Can I see him?" Frances asks anxiously.

"No passengers are allowed in the crew's sleeping area," replies Arthur.

"Tell me, Arthur. What is wrong with the Lieutenant? Tell me, please."

"I am sorry, Miss Frances. I am not at liberty to discuss this matter."

Leaving the dining area with his wife, Mr. Harris tips his hat to Mr. Peters, who is still having breakfast with his family. Mrs. Peters tells the children to go and play in the lounge area. "Well, I see you went for a walk last night," says Mrs. Peters sharply.

"Yes, I did. I needed some air for a headache that was coming on. I was only gone for a short while."

"Mrs. Ogden told me she saw you walking in the upper deck hallway last night. I thought you said you were going for fresh air?"

"Yes dear, I did go for fresh air. I just turned the wrong way at the stairwell. The ship was poorly lit last night." The red-faced Mr. Peters puts his head down and carves into the last piece of pork on his plate.

Martin's coughing has eased, Matthew suggests he remain in his bunk today. He repeats his request to Martin, telling him he will bring a tin of hot tea for him. Matthew enters the dining area, where Haydn is sweeping the floor. Haydn points to the floor. Matthew looks to see a trail of white powder on the planked deck.

"Matthew, I think I found where your mouse lives."

"My mouse?"

"Yes, your mouse. The mouse that jumped on the Lieutenant's lap causing the tea to spill on Miss Evens. The mouse that helped you win over Miss Evens."

"All right, Haydn. I know what you mean now," laughs Matthew. "Yes, I do owe that mouse a debt of gratitude. Let's keep this our secret."

* * *

An endless display of blue can be seen with the horizon gently touching the sea. The Sara Rose reaches new speeds and the friendly winds guide the ship on her course.

The Captain makes his way down the steps to the crew's quarters. Reaching the bottom of the steps, he turns down the narrow corridor between the bunks. He makes his way to the Lieutenant's room and looks in. Doctor Eden is sitting with the Lieutenant. Captain Mcbaine salutes his Lieutenant. "Mr. Rodger, I see you're awake. How are you feeling?"

"I'm feeling much better, Sir. My shoulder still aches and throbs, but my head is clearing."

Doctor Eden stands, "You get some rest. I'll check on you later, Lieutenant."

The Captain seats himself and begins by speaking of the service they had the night before for their shipmates. The Lieutenant attentively listens. Captain Mcbaine elaborates on the details regarding Hardie's capture. He continues, relating the various options for dealing with Hardie. Handing the Lieutenant a straw, the Captain stands, "I will send someone down later to retrieve the straw from you."

"Sir, this would have been an easy decision a few days ago, but now I am uncertain how I feel. I know several men are dead because of Hardie."

The Captain salutes the Lieutenant and begins to leave the room. "Captain, please give this letter to Frances Cunningham. She is in the steerage section."

Captain Mcbaine smiles at Mr. Rodgers, then tucks the rolled-up letter into his pocket and leaves the room.

Donald and Aggie Evens are comfortably seated in lounge chairs. Staring quietly at the sea, Donald is mesmerized by the slow rocking of the ship and soon succumbs to his dreams. Aggie looks over and sees him sound asleep in the chair. Setting the novel 'Redemption' down, she removes the blanket from her lap and covers Donald.

Aggie goes in search of her daughter, finding Susannah in her room. "Susannah, are you still lying in bed? You never came for breakfast with us and now you have missed lunch. Are you feeling all right?"

"Mother, it's Matthew! I can't stop thinking about him. I know I love him and want to spend my life with him. He is in my thoughts constantly and is in all my dreams. Every time I see him, my feelings for him grow stronger. When I am away from him, I feel empty."

"I know what you're saying, Susannah. What are you writing?"

"Mother, it may sound silly, but I'm writing Matthew a letter about how I feel."

"Oh, Susannah, do you think that's wise? When your father was courting me, I waited for him to write me words of romance and love. My, my, how times have changed. Get dressed, and let's enjoy the sunshine."

* * *

Captain Mcbaine makes his way down the stairwell to the steerage section. At the bottom of the stairs, he is assaulted by the rank odours and dampness of the steerage section. He waits while his eyes adapt to the hazy conditions, but his sense of smell does not adjust.

The Captain looks into the open area of the men's sleeping quarters, then continues to where the women are lodged. Stepping into the open room, he noticed the room becomes quiet. Walking among the women and small children, the Captain smiles and tips his hat. He asks a woman, who is holding her child, where Frances Cunningham can be found. The nervous woman points across the room to Frances.

Frances's heart races, seeing the Captain approaching in her direction. Her mind races with thoughts of what she might have done wrong and closes the book she was reading.

Captain Mcbaine stops at her bunk. Feeling absolutely overwhelmed, Frances looks up at the Captain in fear. He introduces himself to her and smiles, "The Lieutenant asked me to give you this letter," says the Captain as he hands Frances the note.

Frances is puzzled and quickly asks, "Where is the Lieutenant? I have not seen him in days?"

The Captain hesitates before he explains, "Lieutenant Rodgers was injured while on duty. He is resting quite comfortably. We expect to see him back at his duties soon."

Her hand comes up to her lips, and she lowers her eyes as if she is in pain. Frances looks at the Captain while wiping the tears from her cheek. "I must see the Lieutenant."

Captain Mcbaine is touched by Frances's feelings for the Lieutenant. He strokes his beard with his left hand and stumbles for the words to console

247

Frances. "Let us give the Lieutenant a few days to rest and then we will see." The Captain tips his hat to Frances and makes his way back to the deck of the ship.

Frances sits on her bunk holding the rolled-up letter in her hand. It is tied with a blue ribbon, and she can smell the fresh ink. Her left hand continually wipes her tears away, as panic sets in regarding the contents of the note.

Molly rushes over to Frances. "What did the Captain have to say? Did your brothers get into trouble again? Was it about the Lieutenant?"

"Molly, the Lieutenant was injured. The Captain said he is recovering and will be all right in a few days."

"What are you crying about then?" asks Molly.

"I am not sure," sobs Frances. "The Lieutenant wrote me a letter and I am afraid to read it."

When Frances gains control of her tears, her emotions begin to settle. She squeezes the letter tighter in her hand and tells Molly she wants to be alone. She begins to make her way up the stairs. Anticipating bad news in the message, Molly follows Frances to the deck but remains at a distance.

The evening sun greets Frances while she walks to the railing of the ship. Looking down at the wake the vessel leaves in its passing, she takes one end of the blue ribbon and unties the bow. She weaves the ribbon around her fingers. Her trembling fingers unroll the letter. Frances begins crying as she reads. She looks at the sea to hide her tears.

Molly comes running to console Frances. She puts her arms around her as if Frances were her own daughter. "It's all right, Frances. It will be all right."

The red-eyed Frances turns; tears flood onto her cheeks. Her hands tremble holding the note. She whispers, "He loves me. The Lieutenant loves me. Look what he wrote to me."

I Adore You.

Tis only you that makes my day seem so right,

And only you, I want in my morning light.

Oh, how I adore you.

Now I dream of the coming night,

Tis only you, that cause the blushing moon to lose its sight.

Oh, how my thoughts adore you.

Only you, can ask the stars to shine so bright.

Tis only you, I want to hold this night.

Oh, how in my dreams, I adore you.

Timothy Rodgers

"Look, Molly, the Lieutenant even signed his name at the bottom. He wrote this just for me. I told you the Lieutenant loves me."

Molly breaks out in tears and hugs Frances. "Oh, that Lieutenant! That rascal! I am beginning to love him too. You're a lucky young lady. Oh, yes. Yes, you are Frances."

"Molly, I can hardly breathe."

Chapter 43

The western sky takes charge and begins to retract the light along with the warmth of the sun. The soft blues of the horizon vanish, replaced with a subtle grey.

The Sara Rose gracefully parts the sea. The easterly wind hints to the crew of the possibility of rain. A blanket of clouds fills the greying sky and the moon reluctantly begins to tip, quickly recalling her tides. The sea awaits its role with the grey turning to an inevitable ebony.

* * *

Leaning on the stern's railing, Frances gazes blindly at the sea. Her thoughts are far away. Her emotions now tug at her. Frances holds the blue ribbon in her hand and presses the Lieutenant's note tightly to her chest with her other hand.

A group of male passengers are enjoying a game of chance in the lounge this evening. Floyd Ogden chuckles as he wins another hand of cards. He pulls the money to himself and stacks it on the table. Ronald Harris shakes his head. "Sir, you beat us again. This is your night, Ogden." Jones watches in silence, while the greed in his eyes burns into the money that is on the table. His devious mind memorizes every card played. The smoke he exhales from his cigar hovers in the air around him. Ashes continually fall off his pants, forming a pile under his chair.

The crew gathers on deck, talking among themselves. The men are undecided as to how to cast their straws. They know Hardie must pay for his crimes, yet the haunting thought of putting a former crew member to death does not sit well with them. Hardie was never a friend to any crew member but the bond of true shipmates remains strong.

"Mr. Quinn, how are you this evening?" asks the Captain tapping his pipe on the railing to remove the old tobacco.

"Just fine, Captain. I take it we are to decide Hardie's fate tonight?"

"Yes, Mr. Quinn. I will send Mr. Johnson to relieve you when we call for your decision."

A brisk wind sweeps its way across the deck. A chilling eeriness assumes control of the night air. The men feel agitated and edgy. The Captain approaches his men, who are nervously discussing the issue of Hardie. "If we are to decide the fate of Hardie Jenkins, then in all fairness, he should be present. Arthur take three men and get Hardie. Chain him to the foremast so he can witness these proceedings. Doctor, fetch the Lieutenant's straw. You three apprentices, are excused."

Hardie Jenkins shuffles one foot in front of the other. His hands are shackled in front of him and leg irons clamped to the ankles of his bootless feet. There is dried blood on both the leg irons. A chain from his hands leads down to the chain that connects to each leg iron.

Hardie's hair is matted and hangs below his ears. His scruffy, bearded face has not been washed in weeks. One can see where tears may have run from his eyes. The worn, black jacket he wears extends down to his knees and is caked with dirt. Bloodstains are visible on the sleeves. The jacket is open, exposing the once white shirt that is soiled and encrusted on his chest. His brown trousers are torn at the knees. The stench of Hardie and his clothing keeps his guards at a distance.

Hardie's head is down. His shipmates are silent as he nears. The men who guard Hardie order him to back against the mast, where two men wrap a chain around him. He stands propped to the mast pole. Arthur walks behind Hardie and puts a lock on the chain. The Captain instructs that the table is placed closer, so that Hardie may watch the straws being placed on the table.

The Captain raises his eyes and looks at the sad image of Hardie. He pulls a document from his jacket pocket and begins to read:

"Hardie Jenkins, you are accused of murder in the death of the nameless stowaway, and in the death of Red Tanner, Harmond and Jimmy Brown. These vicious acts were committed on the Sara Rose, on or about September twenty-seventh to October ninth, Eighteen Hundred and Fifty-Three. Sir, you are also accused of attempted murder."

Hardie lifts his head and shouts at the Captain, "Who did I attempt to kill? I killed all I wanted to. Now I see more that need killing!"

"Sir, you attempted to kill Lieutenant Rodgers!"

"I did kill the Lieutenant. I saw him fall with a musket ball in him. I told you all I would get my revenge, Arrr!"

Captain Mcbaine looks at his crew. He then looks back at Hardie and begins to read again.

"You are also accused of betrayal to the Sara Rose and to the sailors who serve on this ship. Hardie Jenkins, what is your plea?"

The gusting winds pause; a cold silence is felt on deck, as the sea simmers into a quiet hush. The stars brighten the deck, awaiting an answer. The waiting moon forces the gathering clouds away in the hope of a better view.

The Captain repeats the question, "Hardie Jenkins, what is your plea?"

Hardie does not comply with the Captain's request.

"All right, men, line up along the table and put your straws down." The men look at each other, but no one moves. The Captain nods to Jackal, who walks to the table. Jackal stares at Hardie and throws down his straw. The straw is broken in half. Arthur follows, looking at Hardie until Hardie looks at him. Arthur casts down a straw that is broken in two. Randel approaches the table but cannot look at Hardie. He also puts down a straw broken in two. One by one the men come to the table; each lays down a straw broken in half.

The Captain sees all the straws in one pile. He nods to acknowledge his crew. He then looks at Hardie, "Sir, it is unanimous. You will meet the ship's plank tonight. May God have mercy on your soul."

The suspicious night air darkens, to cover the guilt on the faces of the crew. The chilling gusts of wind find their way into Hardie's open jacket. His spine begins to come unhinged, as does his mind. He awaits his fate. The chains that bind him clang against each other as he trembles.

Hell's fury is tormenting his soul. His heart pounds, exceeding its normal rate. Hardie's throat is parched, and his knees are too weak to support him. Were it not for the chain holding him to the mast, he would fall to the deck. Although his mind is begging for forgiveness, Hardie can only look at the planked floor in disgrace.

"Captain, Captain, wait!"

Hardie recognizes the voice and turns his head. He is shocked as his piercing eyes search the darkened vessel. From the shadows, the Doctor can be seen assisting the Lieutenant. The crew lift their hats and cheer the approaching Lieutenant. The Lieutenant is wearing his cap; his trusted sabre strapped to his side. Inside the belt, which holds his sabre, a pair of white gloves is visible. His jacket has a large hole in the shoulder area where the musket ball entered. His tattered shirt hangs on him like a rag. A large bandage across his chest shows a circle of dried blood.

The Lieutenant appears to be very weak, yet he forces himself onward. His wounded left shoulder is motionless. The Doctor continues to support the Lieutenant until they come to a stop in front of the Captain. Doctor Eden leaves his side and Lieutenant Rodgers salutes his Captain.

Captain Mcbaine returns the salute with a generous smile. "Welcome back to the deck of the ship, Mr. Rodgers."

The Lieutenant turns and salutes the crew who warmly respond by returning the salute. The Lieutenant retains his balance and turns slowly to Hardie. He struggles closer. Hardie tries to back away, but he is chained to the mast. The Lieutenant stops within a foot of Hardie and stares into the steel eyes of the man who wanted him dead.

Beads of sweat appear across Hardie's forehead. Embarrassed by his deeds, he lowers his head in shame. The Lieutenant averts his eyes and steps back. He is thoroughly repulsed by the sight of his former enemy, now a broken man. Equally repulsive is the foul odour emanating from Hardie's body.

Standing silent, the Captain and crew await the Lieutenant's motive. The Lieutenant steps forward. With his right arm, he removes the white leather gloves held by his belt.

The silence suddenly breaks, as the sobering sound of leather whipped across Hardie's face. Hardie lifts his head in shock. Beads of sweat from his forehead drop onto the planked floor. Foam drools from his mouth and his upper lip begins to bleed. Hardie swallows the mixture of blood and saliva, along with his pride.

"Revenge, you want? Revenge, you shall have!" shouts the Lieutenant. "One week from today. I demand retribution. A sword of your choosing Mr. Jenkins."

Chapter 44

Susannah runs into Matthew's waiting arms. They embrace each other, and their lips meet — an instinctive craving yearns. Their lips become moist. They can feel each other's breath inside of them. The more they kiss, the deeper the wanting breath enters. They are magnetized to each other. Desires intensify, and their breathing becomes heavier. Susannah wraps her arms around Matthew's neck. He lifts her feet off the deck, turns and braces himself against the wall.

The mouse sneaks into the kitchen and scurries across the greasy floor. The irritating smells of the floor send the ship's little stowaway into the dining area. Ignoring a piece of pork, it stops at an apple core. It begins to nibble on the apple but quickly spits it from its mouth. The sour taste of apple does not agree with the rodent.

The curious mouse attempts to climb onto the apple core but rolls on the floor. Finally, it manages to get its front feet on top of the core, which begins to roll with the mouse walking on its back feet. The excited rodent is enjoying this new-found ability. It stops and slides its front feet to the floor, then circles the apple core. Hesitating briefly, the mouse scampers to a crust of bread.

The night sky opens and begins to deliver a light rain. Hardie is taken to the bow of the ship and chained to the anchor. He does not speak to his handlers. Arthur shows compassion and throws a torn piece of canvas over Hardie to keep him dry. The sharp crack of thunder in the eastern skies causes the ship to tremble, while the dimming stars scatter for the night, and the clouds rule the sky.

The eastern winds have delivered their promise of rain. The volume of thunder increases, with visible streaks of lightning filling the southern sky.

Jones grumpily rises from his bed to answer the quiet knock at his cabin door. Peters is standing nervously in the hallway, looking in both directions to see if anyone is watching. He wiggles past Jones at the door and enters the cabin. Jones is smiling to himself; he knows he has Peters where he wants him. "Peters, I presume you are interested in a game of chance tonight? You must want to win the rest of my money," sneers Jones.

* * *

The Sara Rose continues on her journey with the night gravitating toward morning. The rain begins to ease. Thunder finds comfort and fades into the eastern skies. The pre-dawn smells of the sea radiate across the deck of the ship.

First Mate Downing sees the first lights of Ireland and tells the apprentice to wake the Captain.

"Good morning Mr. Downing. I hope it was an uneventful shift for you, and the ship performed well. I presume those are the portlights of Galway?"

"Yes, Captain. The vessel stayed her course, and I believe we were only on the edge of the storm."

"Let's not anchor at sea. We will just slowly proceed to the dock. The morning sun will be with us soon. We will get Mr. Johnson to signal the port when we have first light," says the Captain.

"Aye Aye, Captain. That will save us a great deal of time if the port takes us without anchoring."

Mrs. Peters tosses and turns in bed. She sits up, wondering where her husband is. She touches his cold pillow. Her mind fills with a clutter of thoughts as she slips out from under the covers. She opens the door of the cabin and looks down the hallway. Mr. Peters is nowhere to be seen. Mrs. Peters closes the door and sits on the bed, agitated.

The mouse is resting after a meal of honey it found on the crusts of bread. The curious mind of the mouse is thinking of its new friend, the apple core, which it explored earlier. The mouse pokes its nose out the hole in the wall. No footsteps can be heard and the little rodent circles the apple core several times before stopping. Then without hesitation, it places its two front feet over the apple core. Excitedly, the mouse begins pushing with its back feet, and the core begins to move. Bravely the rodent walks the core across the dining room to the approaching wall. It stops abruptly, with most of its weight on top of the core. The momentum projects the mouse over the apple, which then passes over the surprised rodent. The ship's little stowaway stands and shakes its bewildered head.

* * *

The morning sun reveals the first signs of light and the night's rain drips off the ropes and sails onto the deck. The high riggers lower the ship's topsails, and the idle morning winds lie calm. The harbour of Galway is now completely visible.

Third Mate Johnson meets the Captain at the bow of the ship. "Mr. Johnson, alert the port with the signal flags that the Sara Rose encountered pirates at sea. Request permission to enter the port and dock immediately."

Lieutenant Rodgers makes his way up the stairs to the dining area, with the aid of the Doctor. The two men seat themselves at a table, Haydn rushes over with tins of hot tea for Mr. Rodgers and the Doctor.

Mrs. Peters leaves her children sleeping in their cabin. Walking down the hallway slowly, she briefly listens at every door for her husband's voice. She walks up the stairs to the next deck and proceeds to do the same, before making her way to the main deck of the ship. No passengers are about this morning as she makes her way through the port and starboard sides of the ship. She enters the dining room, where the Doctor and Lieutenant are seated.

Embarrassed, Mrs. Peters walks directly to the table where the two men are enjoying their tea. "Sorry to interrupt you, have you seen Mr. Peters, my husband? I woke in the middle of the night, and he was gone. I am deeply worried about him."

"No, we have not seen him. But I will let the Captain know. We will all keep an eye out for him. Perhaps he fell asleep on one of the deck chairs," replies the Doctor.

The Third Mate calls to the Captain, "Captain, the port is allowing us to proceed directly to the dock. They are sending a small boat to guide us in."

The Sara Rose is guided to its berth. Ropes are thrown over the starboard side of the ship for the dock crew, who begin tying the vessel to the large bollards. The Captain orders the number three hatch opened, handing a sailor the clipboard listing the articles to be unloaded. The Captain asks for the gangway to be lowered and informs Mr. Quinn that no one is allowed on or off the ship. He quickly makes his way down the walkway and finds the dockworker in charge. He hands him a list of supplies the vessels needs.

Captain Mcbaine is directed to the Port Major's office, where the two men greet each other with a salute. The Captain explains the episode they experienced with the pirates at sea.

"I see your predicament, Captain. We have no naval ships in the area. Sir, I will send couriers from Galway to the outlying ports to alert the navy. We have extra men to help load the ship. This will help get you back to sea as soon as possible," says the Port Major of Galway.

The Captain salutes the Port Major, "Thank you, Sir."

"Godspeed Captain."

Chapter 45

The noise coming from the dock awakens Susannah. She sits on the edge of her bed with a blanket over her shoulders. The pillow she dreamt on; she places on her lap. The dreams that took her away, she recalls. The smile she fell asleep with, she retains.

The Lieutenant asks to be excused and gets up slowly from the table. Doctor Eden reminds him to be careful, so as not to reopen his wound. Mr. Rodgers begins to make his way toward the stern of the ship in hopes of seeing Frances, when Randel stops to talk with the Lieutenant. Arthur joins them, and in a few minutes most of the crew encircle the Lieutenant. They praise the Lieutenant for his deeds and question him as to how he is feeling. "Get back to work men!" hollers Third Mate Johnson.

Captain Mcbaine makes his way back to his ship; he tips his hat to the new passengers who are beginning to line up on the wharf. Mr. Johnson lowers the gangway for him.

"Johnson, how is the loading of the cargo going?"

"Sir, all the unloading and loading is completed. The new passengers may board when you are ready."

The Doctor sees the Captain board the ship and walks over to him, telling him what Mrs. Peters has told him.

"Doctor, seek out Mrs. Peters. Perhaps she found her husband. If not, gather a few free men and do a search. Get back to me on the matter. I have passengers boarding who will need my assistance."

"All right, Mr. Johnson, let's get the new passengers aboard. I saw only four first-class passengers when I came aboard."

"Captain, I am Jonathon O'Reilly, and this is my wife, Catherine." The Captain shakes Mr. O'Reilly's hand, then tips his hat to Catherine. She smiles and says, "Captain, when do you expect the Sara Rose to dock in Norfolk?"

"I am not certain Mrs. O'Reilly. I can assure you; we are on schedule and the weather is in our favour," smiles the Captain.

Jonathan takes Catherine by the hand and proudly says to the Captain, "Catherine and I are excited to be on this voyage. Our daughter and her husband sailed on the Weaver to Virginia, three years ago. They opened a dry goods store in Richmond. We are anxious to see our new granddaughter."

The Captain smiles at the O'Reilly's. He then instructs Arthur to show the new guests to their cabin.

The Captain turns to greet two jovial, middle-aged ladies. The shorter one is approximately five feet two, has dark black hair and is quite plain looking. She is wearing a long-sleeved forest green dress with black trimming at the neckline. Her bonnet matches her dress. Captain Mcbaine approaches her and welcomes her aboard. She extends her hand to him. "My name is Sadie. This is my dear friend and travelling companion, Olivia."

Olivia is taller than her friend Sadie. Olivia is about five feet eight and appears to be slightly overweight. A light blue dress enhances her ample bosom and shapely hips. An abundance of reddish-orange hair escapes from under her matching bonnet.

Olivia's open white umbrella rests on her shoulder, shading her alluring green eyes. Her front teeth protrude slightly, giving her a unique appearance. Her freckled face and wider than average lips intrigue the Captain, and he is rather taken with Olivia. She flutters her eyelashes at him when he takes her hand. She squeezes the Captain's hand suggestively. He does not shake her hand but puts his free hand over hers.

Mr. Johnson quickly interrupts, "Sir, I will get Haydn to take these two ladies to their rooms."

"No, we are staying together in the same cabin." Sadie blushes as she speaks. The Third Mate looks at the Captain in surprise.

The Captain immediately releases Olivia's hand and steps back from her. He puts his hand on his beard and thinks for a moment. "Haydn, these two ladies will be sharing the same cabin. Please take their luggage and show them to their cabin."

"Mr. Johnson, I think you have something to say," smirks the Captain.

With a reddened face, the Third Mate turns to the Captain and quietly says, "Sir, I think this will be an interesting voyage with those two ladies aboard."

Captain Mcbaine smiles, then speaks softly to Mr. Johnson, "I believe you are right. They are a rather friendly pair. I hope they do not disrupt our other passengers or crew. Let us get the steerage passengers aboard."

Captain Mcbaine and Third Mate Johnson look over the railing of the ship to the wharf. "Mr. Johnson, I see they are a lively bunch. I better go down to the dock and set them right before they are allowed on the ship."

The Captain steps onto the wharf. "All right, gather around. I am Captain Mcbaine. It is a privilege for you to sail on this vessel. I demand your complete respect for this ship and her crew. Any fighting, stealing or mischievous activity will be dealt with swiftly. If anyone objects to these rules, please step out of the line now. Am I understood?"

The Captain walks toward Doctor Eden, who is waiting for him near the walkway. "Doctor, did Mrs. Peters find her husband?"

"No, Captain, we looked everywhere possible on the ship. We asked all onboard. No one has seen Mr. Peters since yesterday."

Captain Mcbaine is puzzled and says, "Doctor, come with me." The two men walk together, down two sets of stairs. They proceed along the hallway. Captain Mcbaine looks at the names on each door they pass. He stops and points to a door with a name on it. The Doctor looks surprised. The Captain knocks. A gruff voice from within replies, "Enter."

The Captain swings the door open but remains in the hallway. "Jones, come out here."

The room reeks with the unpleasant smells of cigar smoke and stale perspiration. In a corner of his cabin, next to the bed, is a pile of soiled clothes. His cabin chair has a faded shirt on it. The shirt, which may have been white at one time, is thrown over the crest rail. Two pairs of suspenders hang over the top of the chair. The seat is littered with cigar butts and spent matches. Jones has utilized the large ashtray as a spittoon. Lingering smoke in the room drifts into the hallway. The Captain and the Doctor step back. Jones sits up in his bed, swings his feet to the floor, stiffly stands and steps toward the open door. "What is it, Captain?"

"Were you and Peters involved in a game of chance late last night?"

"What concern is it of yours, Captain? My cabin is paid for, and what goes on in here is private."

"It is my concern, Jones. Peters is missing, and no one has seen him since yesterday. Was Peters in your room last night?"

"Yes, Captain, we played cards late into the night. Peters lost every cent he had. He never said a word when I took his last shilling. He turned as white as a ghost and began to tremble. He started to sob, then got up without saying a word and walked out. I saw that look before on men who lost everything, Captain. Losing was his inevitable fate, so do not judge me."

"Jones, I thank you for being truthful with me. I will be calling on you again."

"There you have it, Doctor. I believe we both know what happened to Mr. Peters. Such a shame! The power of a game of chance and how it can control one's soul. The turn of a card and everything is lost. Now to break the news to Mrs. Peters, but first I have to get the ship back to sea."

The Rose slowly eases her way from the pier, followed by the customary waving of the crew to the dockworkers. The Port Major of Galway stands on the dock and salutes the Captain, who, in turn, returns the salute.

"Mr. Downing, you're in control of the helm. Take us out to the sea and set a course for the eastern shores of North America."

Pausing at a cabin door, the Captain takes a deep breath before knocking. Mrs. Peters opens the door in tears, holding her youngest child in her arms. She lays the child on the bed and wipes her tears. The other two children are rolling marbles against the wall, unaware of what has happened to their father. The Captain removes his cap, wipes his lips with his other hand and bows his head. Trying to keep his emotions under control, the Captain searches for the words to say to Mrs. Peters.

"Children go play on deck. I will join you shortly. Captain, please sit down," says Mrs. Peters.

"Mrs. Peters, thank you, but I prefer to stand. I am not sure how to tell you, but Mr. Peters was involved in a game of chance with Mr. Jones. Jones said your husband lost every cent he had. He went on to say your husband walked out of the room without saying a word. I believe the guilt of his folly led him to jump off the ship during the night, taking his life. I am truly sorry, Mrs. Peters."

Chapter 46

The westerly wind wipes away the morning mist, and the Union Jack surrenders the morning dew, allowing its colours to meet the new day. An endless blue horizon romances the seductive waters, while sea spray at the bow of the ship showers the deck in a constant cycle.

The relaxed sea allows the Sara Rose to split the waters with her newly-found speed. A quiet humming of the tightened mast ropes releases a gentle melody. The morning air on deck mingles with the aroma of the fresh brewing tea. The scent of baked biscuits taunts the memories of the crew as if they are being called home.

* * *

The Lieutenant comments to Second Mate Quinn, "It's a good day to be at sea."

Mr. Quinn smiles back at the Lieutenant, "Yes, Lieutenant, it is a good day to be at sea. We are into our fourth day since we last saw the coast of Ireland and the trade winds have favoured us."

The afternoon sun retains its warmth as passengers stroll the deck and gaze at an endless sea. Captain Mcbaine walks among the upper class guests. Sadie and Olivia, the two women who boarded in Galway, are attracting attention from the male travellers. The Captain stops to chat with Mr. and Mrs. Ogden. Donald Evens approaches the Captain, "Captain, may I have a moment of your time?"

"Yes, Mr. Evens. What can I do for you, Sir?"

"It's a personal matter. May I see you in private?"

"Yes, I am heading to my cabin. We can talk there."

Lieutenant Rodgers makes his way to the stern of the ship. He walks among the steerage passengers with extreme caution, avoiding being bumped. Frances smiles at the Lieutenant as he approaches, reaches for his hand. She kisses him on the cheek. Timothy whispers to Frances, "I missed you, even though it was only an hour since I last felt your touch."

"Timothy, I love you, and I missed you too."

* * *

Captain Mcbaine takes out his pipe and packs it with fresh tobacco as they enter his cabin. "What can I do for you, Mr. Evens?"

"As you know, Captain, my daughter, Susannah, has become very fond of Matthew. Mrs. Evens and I like Matthew and his brother, Martin." The Captain leans back in his chair, lights his pipe, and listens.

"The Doctor tells me Martin is not well. The steerage conditions are less than desirable. If it were possible to move the two brothers to a second-class cabin, would this not greatly improve Martin's condition? Captain, I would gladly pay for their new accommodations."

"That is a very generous offer, Mr. Evens. Unfortunately, this would be looked upon as an act of favouritism. The crew would lose their respect for Martin and Matthew. The upper class passengers would not accept them. Their steerage friends would reject the two brothers and would pick fights with them. I believe we would be doing more harm than good."

"Captain, do you think the passengers would react to an act of kindness in this way?"

"Yes, Mr. Evens, they would."

Easterly winds unexpectedly swoop downward, overpowering the content westerly breeze, forcing it back. Rolling, grey clouds enter the skies and quickly cover the orange sun.

The high riggers go into action, climbing the masts to lower the topsails. The Captain calls for the foremast and jiggermast to be turned.

Matthew and Martin join the crew on the deck. Parker frantically retreats from the crow's nest.

The easterly winds unleash the fury of 'Hell' toward the Sara Rose. The westerly wind cowardly allows itself to be chased back and quietly disappears. Grey clouds in turmoil are forced into an ebony sky. Lanterns swing recklessly on the sides of the ship. Hardie's pleas to be taken under cover go unanswered.

Ropes securing the masts vibrate, stretching to their limits. An incessant roar of thunder causes the sea to tremble, shaking every board loose on the ship. The crew frantically retightens every rope. Some tie a rope to themselves and secure the ropes to the mast poles, for fear of being washed overboard.

The southern skies light up when lightning attacks the awakening sea. Pieces of the spar are launched downward and bounce across the deck. The relentless wind rips a sail, tossing it upward to the sky, like a kite with an endless supply of string. Seawaters splash over the port side of the ship. Massive waves hold the ship in its grip. The Captain and First Mate Downing struggle to hold the wheel of the vessel. The driving rain sweeps the deck clean and extinguishes the lanterns. Sailors cling desperately to anything they can.

The foremast snaps and plummets towards the deck, narrowly missing the Captain and his First Mate. Ropes holding the foremast whip violently as if the ship is receiving lashes from an unexplained force. Splinters from the foremast and the spars cover the helm and bow area.

The Sara Rose is at the mercy of the sea. Every sailor reaches into his soul and prays for this night to end.

A terrified scream is heard as Hardie's prayers are answered. He lies motionless, pinned against the anchor. A three-foot piece of splintered spar protrudes from his chest. His steel grey eyes stare into the unknown. His last breaths fade. The excruciating pain has paralyzed his legs. Body fluids run uncontrollably within his soiled pants. Blood oozes from his wound and soaks into his clothing. Sanguinary foam rolls from his mouth and over his sun-cracked lips.

Every weakening breath is a struggle, and blood in his mouth begins choking him. His chained hands desperately claw at the planked deck, breaking his fingernails, causing his fingers to bleed into the pooled blood surrounding him.

The Devil himself is patiently waiting for this moment to seize the soul of Hardie Jenkins.

Chapter 47

The morning light reveals a horrific scene. Arthur is the first to find the body of Hardie Jenkins. He rushes to the Captain.

"How fitting that the Sara Rose found her revenge. Arthur get a few men and put Hardie's body to the sea. The 'Mistress of the Sea' has been waiting for him. There will be no service for Hardie," says Captain Mcbaine.

"Men, let us get this ship in order! All right, riggers, we have daylight. Get to work. Get that broken spar replaced. Deck crew, clean this mess up."

Second Mate Quinn controls the helm and eases the ship toward calmer waters. Dawn's first light shows the devastation aboard the ship. Frayed ropes are dangling from the masts. Sections of sails are ripped and hang from the broken spars. The foremast lies shattered and splintered at the bow.

There is little movement among the steerage passengers. Everyone has been awake through the night, huddling together and praying for safety.

Matthew and Martin's wet clothing hangs over the wooden beams. Martin has the covers over his head, trying to conceal his cough. Matthew knows his brother's condition is deteriorating daily.

The stress of the night storm has left everyone in need of sleep. Susannah leaves the comfort of her parents' room. Her thoughts control her emotions, and the constant tug at her heart leaves her empty.

* * *

With repairs to Sara Rose completed, the ship regains her confidence. The Union Jack shows its colours to a ship in the distance. Parker looks into his telescope and calls out, "It's the 'Christiania.' She is an eastern European emigrant ship en route to America."

Captain Mcbaine puts down his tin of tea, lights his pipe and pushes his chair back. He puffs on his pipe, slowly blowing smoke rings in the air. The rings of smoke disperse, much like the Captain's thoughts that keep calling him home. He puts his pipe in his pocket and leaves his cabin.

The Captain strolls to the port side of the ship. He sees the two ladies, Sadie and Olivia standing by Jones. Jones is seated in a lounge chair, chatting with the ladies and does not have the customary cigar in his mouth. Olivia is blushing, slowly twisting her body back and forth flirtatiously towards Jones. Jones reacts with a rare smile. Sadie is using her charm, batting her eyelashes at Jones, seeking his attention.

"Captain, Captain."

"Miss Olivia, what can I do for you?" smiles the Captain. The scent of her perfume tickles his mind.

"Captain, perhaps it's something we can do together. I would like for you to give me a tour of the ship," suggests Olivia.

Her smile charms the Captain. Removing his cap, traces of lust enter his thoughts. He nervously holds his cap with both hands. He is about to speak when Donald Evens and Ronald Harris pass and tip their hats to Olivia. She flirtatiously smiles at the two men, who smile back at her.

Olivia turns towards the Captain, "Well, Captain, shall we go for a walk? You can give me a tour of the ship, and perhaps your cabin."

Captain Mcbaine is flustered and blushes. "I'm sorry, Miss Olivia, perhaps another time. I must attend to my duties." The Captain puts his cap on and leaves.

Darkness blends into the night air. Crisp crystals of hoarfrost gather in clusters and form on the canvas sails. An occasional northern gust surprises the unsuspecting sails and shakes a cluster of crystals onto the deck. The graceful moon gently rolls in the sky, tipping the tides back to the eastern shores. The Northern Star conducts an unrehearsed showing of the Northern Lights.

Matthew holds Susannah in his arms under the illuminated sky. The sea waters mellow, and the night breeze fades to a hush as Matthew whispers, "Susannah, will you marry me?"

Susannah instantly answers, "Yes, Matthew. Yes, I will marry you." She wraps her arms around his neck and draws him close. Matthew holds her tightly in his arms and feels her tears of joy on his neck.

* * *

The Sara Rose continues on her southwesterly trek. The painted layers of frost cling to the ship and await the expressions of the morning sun. Greying dawn gives way to the first signs of light. The ship comes alive with the smell of fresh tea blending into the air.

The ship's little mouse has returned from its nightly raid of the dining room and now finds sleep. Its dreams take the stowaway back to the streets of St-Nazaire, France, and the family the mouse left behind.

Aggie and Donald Evens wake to the sound of Susannah's excited voice at their cabin door. Aggie quickly opens the door, and Susannah rushes in. "Mother, Mother, guess what? Mother, guess what? Matthew asked me to marry him!"

"He did! Susannah, I am so happy for you!" Aggie quickly embraces her daughter with a hug.

In a loud, stern voice, Donald asks, "And what did you say?"

"Oh, Father, I said yes. I will marry him."

The news spreads quickly on the deck of the Sara Rose, with the announcement of Susannah Evens giving her hand in marriage to Matthew. The rumours rapidly circulate that Matthew, a steerage passenger and his brother, barely had the funds for the voyage to the Americas. Quiet snickers and whispers among the first-class passengers turn to laughter at the thought of the marriage of a rich girl to a poor lad. The gossip of the possibility of a wedding ceremony on the ship's deck reaches the steerage section.

Martin is the first to shake his brother's hand to congratulate him. Matthew's fellow passengers take turns in offering warm wishes. Many shake his hand and ruffle his hair, extending their greetings. Molly hears the news and rushes toward Matthew, giving him a motherly hug.

Donald and Aggie leave their cabin and make their way to the dining room. They are thoroughly surprised when everyone in the room remains silent with their entrance. Then, the entire dining room stands and applauds Donald and Aggie. A line of well-wishers approaches the Evens to shake their hands and congratulate them. Aggie weeps tears of joy, as hugs from the female passengers smother her.

Wrapped in her favourite blanket with her pillow behind her back, Susannah remains in her cabin. She has pushed herself into the corner with her knees bent up to act as a table. Her fingertips tightly grip the book she holds. Captivated by what she is reading, her eyes are wide open, reading the breathtaking words of an unknown author.

The book, 'The Unforgiven,' tastefully sends her hidden emotions spiralling upward. Susannah's thoughts cannot be contained and soon run away with her. Her daydreams beg to slip into nightdreams.

Chapter 48

The western horizon calls the sun homeward. Darkness begins to smother the dim light of the day.

Frances smiles at the Lieutenant who is approaching. They embrace each other with a hug and move to an unlit area of the stern. The Lieutenant anxiously takes Frances in his arms. Their kiss becomes intense. His hands slide the shawl from her hair, allowing his warm fingertips to caress her neck. Leaning forward, he kisses her again. Frances's arms wrap tightly around the Lieutenant's neck. Their craving lips are locked. A sigh is softly released.

Their eyes are captivated by each other. Unexplained sensations tremble within their bodies. The slow rocking of the ship enhances the moment. Quiet expressions of love continue in the darkened area.

A new day slowly begins. Matthew makes his way to the kitchen area where Haydn greets him with a pat on the back. "I heard the good news Matthew, and I am happy for you."

"There you are Matthew," says the cook. "I was wondering if I was going to see you again on this side of the galley. Matey, I saved the barrels for you, so you and Haydn get to them."

Captain Mcbaine walks to the table where a group of fellow male passengers surrounds Donald Evens. The Captain extends his hand to Donald, "I hear congratulations are in order. Matthew is a fine lad, and I know he and Susannah will be very happy together."

Mr. Evens excuses himself and walks towards the galley, asking a steward of Matthew's whereabouts. The steward points in the direction of the stern. Donald Evens makes his way to the back of the ship, tipping his hat to a few of the steerage passengers he passes into the stern area.

Two crew members are casting fishing lines into the sea, while Matthew and Haydn empty the waste barrels. Matthew notices Mr. Evens and stops his work abruptly. He is embarrassed about the clinging, rank smell of waste. His thinking becomes erratic, and now he fears the worst. Donald approaches him with an extended hand. Nervously Matthew takes Mr. Evens hand and shakes it. Donald withdraws his hand from Matthew's and chuckles.

"Lad, I hope you have something I can wipe my hand with?"

Matthew stands puzzled. Haydn smirks, passing Donald a rag to wipe his hand. "Well, Matthew, Mrs. Evens and I were most surprised when Susannah told us the news. I respect my daughter's wishes, and in turn, I expect you to respect my daughter."

"Yes, yes, of course, Mr. Evens," says Matthew, looking down at the planked deck in search of words. Haydn stares at Matthew, trying to contain his laughter.

"Matthew, can you come and meet with us tonight in our cabin? Let's say after dinner when your duties have been completed. Susannah will be anxious to see you, as well as Mrs. Evens. I will let the Captain know that you will be coming to our cabin."

* * *

The midday sun, shinning gently downward, watches the Sara Rose gracefully split the calm waters. The prisms of the sea overwhelm the onlookers, and the calming moment is gracefully captured in their minds. The sea spray gains its lift from the bow and can be heard recycling back to the waters, like a subtle piano tune in the distance.

A breeze entertains the Union Jack, seeking out a view from beyond the endless horizon. The distant clouds hanging in the southern skies appear to have the image of smoke rings. The smell of the sea enters the lungs of all. This scene will romance everyone's soul for a lifetime.

Lieutenant Rodgers approaches the Captain's cabin and knocks. "Give me a moment," gruffly responds the Captain.

"Lieutenant, come in. You caught me having a nap."

"Sorry to disturb you, Sir."

"That's quite all right. What can I do for you, Lieutenant?" asks the Captain while buttoning up his jacket.

"Well, Sir, I don't know how to begin, but I have been doing a lot of thinking the past few weeks," says the Lieutenant. He pauses and ponders for his next words.

"Go on Lieutenant, continue."

"Sir, uh, uh, as I said, I've had weeks to do a lot of thinking as I lay helplessly in bed from Hardie's musket wound. To be honest with you, Sir, I am not sure the sea is my calling in life. My father's dream has always been for me to be in command of a vessel and follow in his footsteps. But now I am confused about the path I want to take and where my heart lies."

"Yes, I can understand that, Lieutenant. You've been through more than what should have been asked of you. Your shipmates and I hold you in very high regard. You have served the Sara Rose beyond the call of duty. When we return to England, your deeds shall be noted."

"Thank you, Sir. I do not look for notoriety, but rather seek what is calling me. I believe I have found this in my feelings for Frances Cunningham," abruptly blurts out the red-faced Lieutenant.

The astonished Captain sits back in his chair and gently rubs his bearded chin. The momentary silence is broken when a match strikes the desk. The Captain lights his pipe. The relaxing aroma of the pipe tobacco circulates in the room. The two men remain quiet, each looking in different directions. The Captain takes the pipe in his hand and looks directly at the Lieutenant, now seeing him as a friend.

"Mr. Rodgers, the only advice I can offer you is that you must follow your heart. But remember, there are two hearts involved now. You and Miss Frances have a lot to discuss."

The Lieutenant searches for words. Shuffling nervously in his chair, he grasps his sabre for inner strength.

"Lieutenant, I have been married to Mrs. Mcbaine for more years than I can remember. She always knew that the sea was in my veins and that it calls me as I believe it calls you. Mrs. Mcbaine and I have found something sacred in each other. I am a fortunate man."

"Thank you, Captain. Thank you for your time." The Lieutenant stands, saluting his Captain.

Matthew is frantically cleaning the dining room tables. He carries the dishes and silverware to the kitchen for washing. Taking Haydn aside and asks him to cover for him. Matthew quickly leaves the galley and goes directly to his bunk, shuffling through his clothes. He changes into a cleaner pair of trousers. Discarding his shirt on the bed, he proceeds to the washing area.

When Matthew returns from washing himself, Martin is sitting up in his bunk. "Hey, what's going on, you seem to be in a big rush?" asks Martin.

"Mr. Evens found me on deck and asked me to come to their cabin this evening. They want to talk to me, but I'm afraid to go. Martin, I know what you're going to say."

"Yes, you do, Matthew. So just put on your cleanest old shirt and get to it. Find that mirror you were using when you shaved; you missed a spot," teases Martin. Another coughing spell begins to erupt, and Martin lies down.

Feeling extremely panicked, Matthew slowly makes his way to the upper deck of the ship. His mind is smothered with constant thoughts of Susannah and reasons why Donald and Aggie Evens would not allow him to marry their only daughter. He looks over the rail of the ship, where his desire for Susannah first began. His eyes focus on the moonlit night. An image of Susannah inspires his inner strength. Matthew turns from the railing. With new-found confidence, he proceeds to the Evens cabin.

The main deck is quiet this evening as the ship continuously navigates the smooth waters in a southwesterly direction. Lieutenant Rodgers walks to the stern of the ship where Frances waits. The soft moonlight sparkles in her eyes and the moon's rays enhance her dark hair, showing off her tantalizing features. Frances turns. Her smile creates a wanting lust inside Timothy Rodgers's mind.

Timothy sweeps Frances into his arms and kisses her with an intense passion, which could almost stop time. The surprised steerage passengers hush, witnessing the signs of a new romance. Timothy and Frances unlock their feverish lips. The warm rush of uncontrolled desires circulates within their yearning bodies. With their eyes, the young lovers seduce each other's thoughts and their wanting minds lust.

In the watching moonlight, Timothy drops to one knee, "Miss Frances, I would be honoured to have your hand in marriage. Will you marry me?"

A loud cheer comes from the steerage passengers who are caught up in the moment. Joey and Neil are with a group of their friends. They jump up and down with joy for their sister. Joseph Cunningham is embarrassed and steps back. The excited Molly shouts, "Your dreams have come true, Frances."

Overwhelmed by the excitement, Frances's hands rise to cover her face and mouth. Her breathing sharply intensifies — Frances's breath funnels between her fingers. The enthusiasm of Timothy's proposal leaves her speechless, and only murmurs of joyful sounds trickle from her.

Frances becomes energized, gazing down at her Lieutenant, who holds his sabre while he kneels. She squirms back and forth, twisting and turning in all directions, but remains in the same spot. Frances's hands remain covering her face. The flutter of emotions blinds her racing mind. Three unrehearsed words burst from her, "Yes, Timothy. Yes."

Chapter 49

The fresh October morning greets the Sara Rose. A cloudless eastern horizon delivers an offering of sunshine. Trade winds effortlessly melt the night's frosty dew, allowing puddles to pool on the deck.

Timeless tides give into their calling and mellow within the sea. An orchestrated humming of the mast and sail ropes sings a quiet harmony to the ship. The Sara Rose responds with speed and grace; the bow divides the awakening sea waters.

Susannah tosses and turns as vivid dreams unfold. Her desires are begging to be released. Erotic thoughts soak her nightgown, wakening her. She holds her pillow against her chest. Unsatiated desires whirl endlessly in her mind. Susannah's thoughts replay each word, each touch and each kiss. The soothing pillow holds her secrets, taking her back to find her dreams.

* * *

"Good morning, Lieutenant. I take it the ship performed to her expected abilities during the night?"

"Yes, Captain, it was a pleasant evening," smiles the Lieutenant, saluting.

"Is there something I should know, Mr. Rodgers?"

"Captain, I asked Frances for her hand last night, and to my surprise, she said yes. She said, yes, Captain." The smile on the Lieutenant's face widens.

Completely taken by surprise, the Captain stares at his Lieutenant. Removing his cap, he extends a hand to Mr. Rodgers. The Lieutenant shakes Captain Mcbaine's hand vigorously.

"My sincere congratulations, Lieutenant. I am most astounded at this unexpected announcement."

"Thank you, Captain. It came about so quickly. I took your advice and followed my heart. Sir, we want to be married aboard the Sara Rose. Mr. Cunningham gave us his good wishes and blessings."

All welcome the afternoon sun. Even the ship's little mouse has its nose protruding from the hole in the wall, enjoying the warmth.

The appeal of the sunshine attracts many passengers to the deck, including the sour Jones. He can be seen puffing on his cigar in the company of Sadie and Olive.

Arthur is in the crow's nest with Angelo, guiding the high riggers along the spars to the canvas sails in need of repairs. Matthew and Haydn can be seen rolling the empty waste barrels to the galley. Arthur gives Angelo a nudge in the ribs, "None of that, lad. What if the spitball aimed at Haydn caught the wind and hit a passenger? The Captain would have you put over the barrel before the next sunset. Laddie, that salt I would rub into your wounds burns something fierce," chuckles Arthur. Angelo's smirk quickly disappears. The thought of the barrel makes him shudder.

William Brett and Doctor Eden are in the dining room when Captain Mcbaine enters. "Gentlemen, how are you this day?" he asks.

"It's a grand day, Sir," replies the Doctor.

"Yes, the weather has been cooperating, and the trade winds have shown us favour. Mr. Brett, we have not seen any sign of the pirate ships that were in chase. Perhaps the Irish naval guns have put an end to them. Just in case, are the men prepared for battle, if need be?"

"Yes Captain, they are. We are constantly doing maintenance on the cannon, and every man knows his position," says William Brett, confidently.

"That's what I want to hear. We are within a day of the shores of Newfoundland and will be turning due south late tonight. It is possible that the pirates sail at full speed during the night to find our lantern lights, then retreat before sunrise to stay hidden. If attacked, it would certainly be late tomorrow evening when we approach the sands of the

Sable Islands. That would be an ideal place to run us aground and board the Rose. Mr. Brett, all crew members will be on full alert starting tonight."

"Doctor, what is the condition of the steerage passengers?" asks the Captain, lighting his pipe.

"Sir, as you have seen, many have an on-going cough with runny noses, but for the most part, they are healthy," calmly states the Doctor.

"What about Martin?"

"Well Captain, he stays in his bunk most of the time and eats very little. No medicine will cure him. It only eases the pain of the infected lungs." Doctor Eden pauses and looks down at the floor. "Captain. Time is short for Martin; he will not walk the shores of the Americas."

* * *

The first signs of the new day are welcomed. From the crow's nest, Parker stares into the telescope and scans the horizon for trailing ships. The upper decks are alive with passengers enjoying the late afternoon sun. Many of the children form small groups and play games. The young men are always trying to impress the single girls onboard. Smiles are freely given, and harmless flirtations ensue.

Floyd Ogden, sitting in a lounge chair next to Ronald Harris says guardedly, "You know, Harris. I could have sworn I saw old Jones come out of the Irish girls' room this morning."

Harris smirks, gathers his thoughts and says, "Perhaps Jones prefers the occasional scent of women over the lust for money. We all have a weak spot, Mr. Ogden. I certainly have mine."

"I believe he is not the only visitor the ladies get knocking on their door!" jealously responds Ogden. He points to Sadie and Olive, who can be seen walking in their direction.

The evening dinner bell sounds. Captain Mcbaine is there to greet the guests and to shake hands with everyone entering the dining room. He asks the Evens family to join him at his table for dinner. The Captain remains standing while the guests take their seats.

"May I have everyone's attention please?" The passengers refrain from further conversation and sit up in their chairs attentively. Captain Mcbaine continues, "We have been sailing in a southern direction since last night. We will keep our distance from the coast of Canada until we navigate the Sable Island chain."

The Captain's remarks bring cheers and applause from the happy guests. He raises his hand to silence the room. "Please, we are still in danger of being attacked. I want you to be aware of this. The Sara Rose has a great asset, her speed on the seas. God willing, we will dock at Norfolk, Virginia, in five days." The passengers erupt in applause and stand in appreciation of their Captain.

The Captain takes his seat and the stewards begin to serve the evening meal. Captain Mcbaine enjoys light conversation with the Evens. Their talk soon turns to the upcoming marriage. "Well, Susannah, have you and Matthew set a date?"

"We want to get married on the Sara Rose, before we reach America. Captain, will you marry us?" asks Susannah blushing. Aggie places her hand on Susannah's.

"Yes, of course, I would be honoured to marry you and Matthew."

"I wish Matthew was here tonight and could join us," says Susannah. Donald and Aggie look at each other and refrain from commenting.

"If I marry you and Matthew aboard the Rose, your marriage will be recorded under British law. When you step foot on American soil, you and Matthew are still British subjects and will need to apply for American citizenship. America is in need of settlers. British subjects are allowed to apply for one hundred and sixty acres of free land if they choose."

"What about Montana? Can we get free land there? Matthew and Martin talked about starting something called a ranch. They seemed to be excited about chasing cows and becoming cowboys. What the Dickens are cowboys?"

* * *

The lonely October moon follows the Sara Rose with curiosity throughout the night. A shadowy sprinkling of moonlight keeps its distance behind the ship, while the vessel skims across the waters. Motionless clouds tightly hug the dimming stars, snuggly wrapping themselves around their warmth. The southern trade winds circle in the night, delivering a constant breeze with soundless expressions.

The little mouse desperately scurries across the planked deck, for the call of the dripping water barrel entices the thirsty rodent. Finding relief in lapping up the freshwater, the mouse innocently releases little burps. With new energy, the mouse seeks out its playmate, the apple core. The search for its friend is in vain. The rodent feels rejected, saddened and now, alone. A sense of belonging soon erodes.

An inviting aroma soon tempts the dejected mouse. The smell of drops of rum on the wooden floor has the curious mouse delighted. It pushes its facial whiskers into the drops of pooled rum and inhales the sweet smell.

The ship's little stowaway cannot resist the temptation and tastes the alluring liquid. It laps at the beaded rum drops frantically and cannot control the urge for more. Thoughts of its old friend dissipate, and its new friend dispels all inhibitions. Natural instincts are lost. The mouse sways back and forth. The addicting intoxication of the rum spurs the inner cravings of the rodent. It begins to gnaw at the wooden floor on which the drops of rum lay. Its mind has become blurred, and it loses all fear. The seduction of the rum and the rotation of the room cause the mouse to fall suddenly and lie whimpering on the planked floor.

Chapter 50

The weary night slowly gives way to the first signs of a new dawn, as Mother Nature paints a fresh coating of dew across the Sara Rose. Like clockwork, the rising sun begins its task and draws up the beaded dew, giving the ship a serene and fresh look.

Captain Mcbaine leaves the comfort of his cabin and makes his way to the helm. "Mr. Rodgers, with Sable Island behind us, I am sure this will be a good day to be at sea. Lieutenant, you get some rest. I will see you later this evening."

The late afternoon sunshine begins its mellow descent to the waiting western horizon. The approaching breeze from the mainland stirs the sea waters. The sails breathe the new air, and the ship slows in the passive sea as the eastern continents recall their tides.

* * *

'All Clear' sounds from the crow's nest. The deck of the Sara Rose is abuzz with passengers. The cooks are at full staff and the galley bustles with activity. Stewards are aligning tables on the deck, while helpful passengers place white linen tablecloths and silverware.

Two of the crew carry a table from the steerage section and place it next to the helm deck. Third Mate Johnson has a keg of rum on his shoulder. He is grinning broadly as he sets it on the table. Arthur is busy directing traffic on deck and arranging the placement of chairs for the guests and musicians.

The Captain steps out of his cabin dressed in his full-dress naval uniform. His three-quarter length jacket extends almost to his knees. The two rows of brass buttons reach downward on the coat and glitter with every step. The Captain's medals and ribbons are proudly worn on the lapel of the jacket. The golden metals of a Captain are displayed on the shoulders and sleeves. His cap has a narrow golden ribbon matching the markings on his jacket.

Removing the Bible from his pocket, he sets it on the table near the keg of rum. He walks to the entrance of the steerage section and proceeds to the bottom of the stairwell. The lively steerage passengers quickly become quiet; only whispers are heard. The Captain stands, waiting for their attention.

"You have all been invited to the upper deck of the ship for supper and an evening of celebration. In exchange for this invitation, I demand your complete trust and absolute respect for the ship and all passengers. Any misbehaving will be dealt with swiftly and firmly. Is this clear to all?"

The last trailing rays of glimmering sunshine reflect off the sea and illuminate the ship's flag. The Sara Rose is coming alive. Every lantern and candle aboard the ship is lit, thus pushing aside the inevitable night.

The ship's little stowaway is nervously hiding in its hole in the wall. The throbbing of the rodent's head keeps pace with its pulse. It is terrified by any movements. The mind of the mouse begins to play tricks. The rodent wonders what happened during the previous night and what caused this intense pain.

From all sections of the ship, guests arrive on the main deck of the Sara Rose. Members of the crew are placed at entrances to keep passengers from wandering into forbidden areas. The guests mingle, but first-class passengers try to keep to themselves, for a division between the classes exists. The female upper class passengers guard their purses as if they are holding a child, while the men keep checking for their thick wallets and pocket watches.

The Captain raises his hand and walks into the centre of the crowd. All eyes focus on him, and the only sound heard is the sea. "Ladies and gentlemen, I want to thank you all for attending this celebration. Dinner will be served after the ceremony. Shall we begin?"

Captain Mcbaine calls Matthew and Susannah, urging them to come forward, with a wave of his hand. A loud cheer erupts from the crowd when Matthew, with a warm smile, steps toward the Captain. Matthew is wearing a jacket and a white shirt with a black bow tie.

Aggie Evens gives her daughter a hug. Susannah leaves the comfort of her family to join Matthew. The crowd is awed by Susannah's stunning appearance. Her white gown skims along the floor. It is gathered at the waist with a full skirt billowing over the crinoline. The lace at the hem of the long sleeves matches the lace at the neckline. A delicate gold bracelet over her white glove caresses Susannah's left wrist. The plain white bonnet tied with a white satin ribbon frames her face and enhances her blondish hair.

The Captain removes his cap, smiles at the young couple and begins to read from the Bible. He then asks them to place their right hands on the closed Bible. "Now that your hands are joined on this Holy Bible, you have entered into a union of marriage. Matthew, you may kiss your bride. Congratulations."

Many cheers and whistles erupt on the deck of the ship as everyone raises a glass to the new couple. The blushing newlyweds stare at each other, scarcely believing they are married, till Martin gives Matthew a nudge. Matthew timidly turns to Mr. Evens as if he were asking permission to kiss his daughter.

Without hesitation, Susannah slips her arms around Matthew's neck and locks one hand over her wrist. A tear of love slips from the corner of her eye, settling on her cheek. Their lips meet. Time ceases to exist. The kiss joins them as one.

Well-wishers begin to surround Matthew and Susannah, congratulating the new couple. The Captain raises his hand and calls out, "Please! We are not finished here!"

Whispers rapidly circulate among the guests when Lieutenant Rodgers and Frances Cunningham begin to walk toward the Captain. Frances's dark hair escapes from under the white knitted shawl Molly made for her. Her blue cotton dress has a simple rounded white collar, with a white belt at the waist. She wears her mother's gold locket around her neck.

Whispers soon fade. A hush of anticipation falls over the crowd. The Captain puts on his cap and salutes his Lieutenant. The Lieutenant, wearing his full-dress uniform, returns the salute.

Captain Mcbaine smiles at Frances while removing his cap. He is holding the Bible in his right hand. Frances places her trembling hand on the Bible and soon feels the warmth of Timothy's hand on hers. The two strive to control their emotions and focus on the Captain's words as he asks them to proclaim their vows to each other. The Captain then repeats a short prayer from the Bible before saying, "Your hands are now joined as one in marriage. Timothy, you may kiss your bride."

Timothy turns to the waiting Frances and bashfully kisses her on the cheek. A tear of emotion rolls from the corner of her eye and down her cheek. She has been kissed, but without passion.

Her sinking heart finds her inner love for Timothy. Frances wraps her arms around Timothy's neck and impulsively kisses him; like he has never been kissed before.

The guests rush closer with cheers and applause for the two young couples. Martin gives Susannah a hug. He reaches for his brother's hand and warmly shakes it.

"I am so happy for you and Susannah. I wish mother and father were here to see the joy in your eyes. Matthew, I am going to go and lay down for a while. It has been an exhausting day. I will return after I have rested." The two brothers embrace each other and Martin excuses himself. Martin takes a few steps toward the steerage entrance and stops. He turns to Matthew.

"What is it, Martin?"

"It's all right, Matthew. I will tell you when I see you again," says Martin with a warm smile.

* * *

Captain Mcbaine congratulates the Lieutenant and Frances with a handshake. He presents them with a key that bears the number seventeen on it. "Lieutenant, my gift to you and Frances."

"Thank you, Captain, but what is the key for?"

"You and Frances are now travelling in first-class."

Frances runs into the waiting arms of her father and hugs him until her tears subside. She turns to her two younger brothers, Joey and Neil, and gives them both a kiss on the cheek. The two are delighted when the Lieutenant walks over and shakes their hands.

Joseph Cunningham reaches into his pocket. "Frances, I know your mother would want you to wear her ring."

Joseph hands the ring to Timothy. Timothy takes the treasured ring and slides it tenderly on Frances's finger. Frances stares at the ring that once was worn by her mother. Molly rushes in and holds her like a daughter.

* * *

The guests take their assigned seats. Captain Mcbaine stands, bows his head and begins to speak:

"Our Heavenly Father, kind and good.

We thank Thee for our daily food.

We thank Thee for Thy love and care.

Be with us Lord, and hear our prayer."

There is silence among the guests while they keep their heads bowed. "Let us all raise our glasses to Susannah and Matthew, also Frances and Timothy. We wish these two young couples all the joys that life has to offer them," says the Captain, taking a sip of wine from his glass.

The stewards begin to serve the meal. The guests enjoy the feast with friendly and jovial conversation. The keg of rum is replaced for a second time during the evening.

Joey and Neil are excited as they take a place next to Jackal and Arthur, to play their instruments for the crowd. Molly stands and shouts, "Play the Wedding Ballad." Jackal begins the tune, delicately stroking his violin as the band follows his lead.

Everyone starts to clap their hands, encouraging the young couples to get up from the table and begin their first dance. Their families and friends quickly join in. Timothy holds Frances tightly while gliding her across the floor. The two are in perfect unison. Their graceful movements and shadows unite. The guests step back from the dance floor and watch this performance. When the tune comes to an end, the crowd applauds the newlyweds who are lost in the moment.

Holding his sabre at his side, Timothy bows to Frances and kisses her right hand. Frances blushes. She covers her happy smile with her left hand. Timothy then kisses her neck and whispers into her ear, causing her body to quiver. The two join hands and vanish from sight.

Matthew and Susannah are quickly separated by Aggie, rushing in to hug her daughter. Matthew looks anxiously around the room in hopes Martin has returned. The band begins a new tune, and the dance floor soon fills with couples enjoying the evening. The lively music entertains all. The evening, like the candles, linger into the night.

Matthew and Susannah manage to evade everyone and make their way to her cabin. Their anticipation builds with the closing of the door. Susannah's bonnet drops to the floor, releasing her golden hair. Her eyes are glazed and sparkle in the light of the jealous candle. Susannah wraps her arms around Matthew's neck; her inviting lips crave to be kissed. The candle is quickly extinguished, and its envious view is lost.

Chapter 51

Matthew and Susannah are thoroughly intoxicated with each other. They hold hands while making their way up the steps to the deck as husband and wife, with the morning sun greeting them.

The Captain and Doctor Eden meet the newlyweds. The two men stand together in silence, holding their caps; their faces are devoid of expression. Their sombre appearance causes Matthew to stop. His contented smile vanishes as he steps back.

"Is Martin alright?"

"Matthew. Martin has passed away while he slept," replies the Doctor, gripping his cap in his hands. "There was nothing anyone could have done for him. I am truly sorry."

Susannah puts her arms around Matthew and holds him. "Oh, Matthew, I am so very sorry." He feels Susannah's tears on his neck. This time, they are tears of sorrow.

* * *

The new day sends down its hollow light as Doctor Eden wraps Martin's body tightly in white linen cloth, binding the fabric with thin ropes. The body lies on the wooden table, which held the keg of rum just the night before. A Bible and a folded Union Jack lie next to Martin's body.

Darkness begins to compose the evening script. Night forces the last daylight away. The Sara Rose becomes eerie, like a ghost ship, for the only sound heard is the creaking of the wooden deck. Passengers and crew carry candles as they gather around Martin's body. The Captain takes the Bible from the table and hands it to Matthew. Captain Mcbaine unfolds the flag and drapes it over Martin's body.

Diane Ogden kneels by Martin's body and places her hand on the Union Jack that covers him. Floyd Ogden wipes a lone tear from his eye and then places his hand on Diane's shoulder, consoling her.

Diane's silent prayer goes unanswered. Crossing herself, she slowly stands. Taking off her bonnet, she removes the dried purple decorative flowers from the band which surrounds her hat. Her tears fall like soft rain, bringing life to the bouquet she places on Martin's body. She turns to Floyd and smothers her emotions in her husband's arms.

Matthew grips the Bible tightly. His tears flow freely and leave stains on the Bible. Susannah places her hands over Matthew's hands. Their wedding bands touch. Matthew takes a deep breath, then he looks upward to the Heavens, searching for words.

"Martin, you were so much more than a brother; you were my friend. It was always just the two of us. I feel I am lost, a stranger as I stand here. I will always carry you in my thoughts and prayers."

The eyes of God begin to weep. The purple sky can no longer retain its sadness, sending its tears down as soft rain while Martin's body is lowered into the sea. From the darkened shadows on the ship, a lone violinist begins to play 'Amazing Grace.' The weeping violin whispers to the souls of all. The notes carve their way into the silent night, causing all to release their tears, as the haunting sound echoes along the deck of the Sara Rose.

Chapter 52

It has been three long days and nights at sea since Martin's body was put to rest. The passengers have become withdrawn and anxious.

Another cool October day greets the Sara Rose when the ship finds her berth in the Norfolk harbour. The Virginian waters meet the anchor of the ship for the first time. The thick ropes are thrown onto the docks and the workers tie the ship to the large bollards. An armed guard of twelve men marches onto the dock to await the precious cargo the Sara Rose is about to deliver.

Captain Mcbaine looks over the railing of the ship. Two armed guards are placed at the lowered walkway, preventing anyone from entering the vessel. The anxious passengers lean over the rail waving to onlookers. Their waves are returned, for some have relatives and business acquaintances waiting.

The steerage passengers have begun gathering with their meagre luggage, waiting for their turn to leave the ship. The large cranes swing to the ship from the dock, moving cargo and luggage to the wharf. Captain Mcbaine takes his place at the entrance of the ship. Upper deck passengers line up, preparing to leave.

Lieutenant Rodgers quickly walks towards the Captain. The Lieutenant salutes the Captain, who returns the salute and teasingly says, "Welcome, Lieutenant. This is the first I have seen you since your wedding night." The Lieutenant blushes and remains silent. "Lieutenant, you are not required to be here."

"Yes, Captain, but I feel I must."

Most of the female passengers collect tears in their handkerchiefs as they hug the Lieutenant. Some kiss his cheek and wish him and Frances happiness. Most of the first-class passengers have accepted the Lieutenant as family. The Captain bows politely to the departing females, who curtsey to him. The male passengers briskly shake hands with the Captain and the Lieutenant.

Matthew and Susannah extend their hands and express good wishes to the Lieutenant. Timothy responds with his desire that they will encounter only good fortune. The Captain displays his feelings by hugging Susannah. She cannot control her emotions and wipes her eyes with her handkerchief. Spontaneously, she kisses the Captain on the cheek. Matthew's internal feelings dread this moment. Captain Mcbaine has been like a father to him and thoughts of leaving the ship instill new fears. Matthew looks into the face of the man they have called 'Captain.' A fierce emptiness engulfs him. He extends his hand. Captain Mcbaine grips Matthew's hand, as one would grasp life.

"Before the two of you leave the Sara Rose, here is my gift to you." The Captain holds the bottle of champagne, which was presented to him by the Port Major of St-Nazaire, France. "I would be honoured if you and Susannah would accept this gift. I know if Mrs. Mcbaine were here, she would insist."

* * *

Aggie and Donald Evens stand with Matthew and Susannah on the dock, looking up at the ship. The Harris's, along with the Ogden's, are on the ship's walkway, followed by Mrs. Peters and her children. Donald nudges Aggie and points to old Jones. They can see Jones, with a smug smile on his face and the usual cigar in his mouth, confidently standing on the dock. Sadie and Olivia are on either side of him and have their arms locked through his.

The steerage passengers have descended to the dock. Molly is at Joseph Cunningham's side, along with Joey and Neil. Molly takes Joseph's hand as they wave goodbye to Frances. Joey and Neil run back to the ship for their sister, but the two guards stop the youths from going up the gangway. They begin to cry and call out to Frances. Frances looks down at her two brothers, who are begging her not to leave them. Breaking down, she begins to weep.

Feeling their pain, she desperately pushes her way to the walkway in hopes of rejoining her family. Timothy, in desperation, sweeps Frances into his arms and consoles her. Joseph runs to the gangway to retrieve his two sons. He lovingly embraces Neil and Joey. Molly falls to her knees, sobbing. The watching crowd retain their silence.

Matthew has a lump in his throat. Memories rush through his mind, and a sense of loneliness enters him. His soul feels adrift as if he were leaving someone behind.

The Captain lights his pipe and gazes down at Matthew and Susannah. They do not wave to each other, but the meaningful stares are etched firmly in their minds.

Matthew and Susannah turn and walk into the October sun holding hands. They are unaware that the ship's little stowaway is making a new home in Susannah's luggage.

Epilogue

Some forty plus years have come and gone, and time has taken Susannah. The Montana skies, coloured in purples and blues, send down their prayers in the form of rain, giving life to her flower beds.

The morning sun shines on her granite stone, calling her back to her homeland. The great oak, on which we carved our initials that forty plus years ago, stretches over her resting spot, shading her from the afternoon sun. Evening sounds of a whippoorwill, singing from a branch high in the great oak, comforts her.

* * *

Memories of the four sea winds that blew in our faces. The blushing moon that covered its eyes when we kissed and the northern lights that showered over our love are forever etched in our souls.

The haunting that is calling me grows. I must go back, back to the sea and be set free. Like the soft whispering sound of the weeping violin that bled its notes along the deck of the Sara Rose, in the year of eighteen hundred and fifty-three.

Manufactured by Amazon.ca
Bolton, ON